THE
FACE
STONE

A JACK SANGSTER MYSTERY

THE
FACE
STONE

A JACK SANGSTER MYSTERY

LEWIS HINTON

The Book Guild Ltd

First published in Great Britain in 2022 by
The Book Guild Ltd
Unit E2 Airfield Business Park,
Harrison Road, Market Harborough,
Leicestershire. LE16 7UL
Tel: 0116 2792299
www.bookguild.co.uk
Email: info@bookguild.co.uk
Twitter: @bookguild

Typeset in 11pt Adobe Jenson Pro

Printed and bound by CPI Group (UK) Ltd, Croydon, CR0 4YY

ISBN 978 1914471 926

British Library Cataloguing in Publication Data.
A catalogue record for this book is available from the British Library.

For everyone who helped bring *The Face Stone* to life – thank you

SPRING 1969

HOLY TUESDAY
2PM

I t had begun as an afternoon like any other.

Squinting in bright sunshine, I mounted the steep steps that led to the main entrance of the Manor Free. I'd been warned the place had a reputation for considering itself special, and looking around, immediately started to understand why, with the very buildings giving a sense of being different. Some were made from the local red sandstone and clearly dated back hundreds of years, whilst others, like the concrete and iron staircase I had just climbed, and the multi-storey blocks either side and in front of me, with their smoked glass windows and marble cladding, were very recent and built in the most modern style.

The school also had a look of being part of the hill on which it had stood for so long, with a profile that matched the contours of the land, ancient buildings higher up, modern ones lower down, old and new juxtaposed to make a statement that this was the Manor Free, here before me and here after me.

Pausing for a moment to take in the view beyond the car park and playing fields below, I saw steeply sloping heathland that in turn led to the shoreline, no more than a mile distant. Looking on from there across the wide, tidal expanse of the Dee estuary, with the Welsh hills beyond the far shore framing the horizon, I felt the word 'special' to be about right.

I then turned and, taking a deep breath, reached towards one of the large double glass doors in front of me, almost falling forward when the nearest opened before I could touch the handle.

"Mr Sangster, is it?" came a sharp voice through the door, its owner a middle-aged woman wearing horn-rimmed glasses, her mouth painted with the reddest of lipstick, her lacquered black hair piled into a 'beehive' that I fancied would cut any finger that touched it. A brown tailored jacket and pencil skirt twin set, along with matching high-heeled shoes, evoked 1949 more than '69, and my immediate thought was that she suited the atmosphere of the school almost as much as the buildings did.

"Yes, Mrs—"

"Miss," she corrected me. "Eunice Lyons, school secretary. You're from the department of education?"

"The Granville Institute, actually, but yes, I work with the department."

"Then the headmaster's expecting you, so come with me, please."

I followed as she clicked along corridors and stairs, high heels sounding to me like woodpeckers, narrow skirt forcing the tiniest of steps. This had the unfortunate effect, given Miss Lyons was seemingly in a constant hurry, of making her look likely to topple over at any time, so that more than once I felt myself preparing to catch her.

"Wait here," she said, as we arrived outside a row of three doors. "This is the headmaster's study," she added, pointing to the middle door, which bore a brass plate, stating:

'Reverend Thomas W Benton-Wilkins
(MA Oxon), Headmaster'.

"And he will see you shortly." She gestured to a chair, then clicked off down the corridor.

I duly sat, waiting for a traffic-light sign above the door to change colour ('Red Wait, Amber Knock, Green Enter') and feeling for all the world as if I was still at school myself. After staring at the wall opposite for a time, I thought back to my conversation in the department of education offices that morning, when Director Johnson passed me a sheaf of assignment notes. The introduction told of a twelve-year-old boy who had been absent from school for about six weeks, although the department had only just been informed.

"Never mind reading the notes now," said Johnson as I leafed through the file. "This school, Sangster, the Manor Free, d'you know it?"

"Er… I know there are grammar schools in that area. Is it one of those?"

"No, the 'MF', as it's usually known, isn't a grammar school at all. It's all boys and has a bit of a reputation in the department as thinking itself special. Founded in the fifteenth century."

"Special?"

"Yes, and in a way, I suppose the MF is, but it's certainly not 'free', despite the name. Exorbitant fees, and for a few high-achieving boys, there's a privately endowed scholarship."

"But your department only deals with state schools?"

"Well, technically the MF qualifies as a state school as it somehow manages to get some government funding as well. Being so old, I think the place must have fallen through the cracks when the system was being set up. By the way," he said, covering his mouth and seeming to consider for a moment, "they take some boarders."

"Nothing too special in that, Johnson."

"No…" He paused again, this time to dunk a biscuit into his tea. "But… ah…" he continued in a lower voice. "There've been whispers the boarding conditions are not good, boys sick and so on. Plenty of modern buildings as well, mind you, but the school still has a whiff of centuries past about it, you'll see…. um… anyway, Sangster, I could imagine the staff closing ranks if they felt threatened."

3

"I'm an investigator, not a school inspector," I said, wondering why I was being asked to suddenly focus all my energy on such an elite place when the department was already overwhelmed with cases for really troubled children, many in very tangible danger, with no privilege and nobody else to turn to. "But," I then added, keeping my thoughts to myself, "I'll let you know about anything untoward, and you can follow up from there."

"And there have been two cases of missing children around the same age as this boy in the area recently, so people are likely to be sensitive."

"Well, this lad's just a truant, not missing, and this Manor Free just a school, even if it has some history."

"Perhaps, but nevertheless, they don't properly answer to us at the education authority."

"Neither do I."

"That's one reason I picked you. Thought you might be useful. The local officer gets nowhere when she tries to deal with that school, especially its headmaster. Eccentric, been there for twenty or more years."

"Ah, useful, eh?" I laughed. "Now we're getting to it." I held up my visiting card. "Useful because I'm a special investigator for the Granville Institute, a…" I turned the card over and read the tiny script on the back out loud. "*Non-profit organisation for the assistance of troubled children, licensed to operate independently and with the Dept of Education at HM Government discretion.*"

"I know what it says on that card of yours, however small the print may be, and yes, your independence is part of the reason," Johnson said slowly. "But mostly, and don't go getting a big head here, but—"

"You'll make sure I don't." I laughed again.

"As I was saying, mostly because this is an odd case and you have a rep around the department as a bit of a sleuth."

"Anything else?"

"Well," he sighed. "There's nobody else available."

*

4

After what had seemed an eternity, the traffic-light sign turned from red to amber to green, and the door opened, breaking my thoughts, as out tramped a line of four rather dejected-looking boys. The quartet walked silently along the corridor until out of sight of the headmaster's study (although I could still see them), then groaned and held their backsides simultaneously. It was easy enough to guess what had happened behind the study door while I was waiting.

"Come in, come in, Mr Sangster, or should I say Commander Sangster," came a high-pitched, almost whining voice.

"Just plain Mister, thank you. And you are Reverend Wilkins?"

"Quite so," said my host, a slim man of about sixty with grey hair, a wayward lock of which fell over his forehead to one side in a V shape. He wore a light-coloured suit with a clerical collar under a threadbare black gown that was liberally sprinkled with chalk marks. "Did Miss Lyons offer you tea?"

"No, and thanks, but I am fine."

"Good, good," he continued, ushering me into his study, a surprisingly modern and spartan room, with a desk, his own leather and chrome swivel chair, several guest chairs, a small bookshelf, and a locking cupboard. His numerous academic and ecclesiastical certificates hung in frames on the wall, along with a wide-angle photo of the entire school posing on tiered benches. But there were no other pictures, not even photographs of family. "I see you are appraising my wall hangings, Sangster."

"Very impressive," I said, seeing Wilkin's eyes open wide, eager for acknowledgement. "That one," I added, pointing to a document in an ornate gilt frame with a blue velvet surround, the words 'Diocese of Oxford' embossed in gold lettering at the top. "Looks like—"

"Ah, yes, my ordination certificate, and as I think you observe, I am also a confirmed bachelor. The school is my wife, no time to be unfaithful to her. Now, sit down, if you please."

"That lot who came out of your office seemed well chastised." I wriggled as I tried to settle into a chair that seemed designed to be anything but comfortable.

"You mean the 'Bomb Squad', as they are affectionately known."

"Bomb Squad?"

"Indeed. The caretaker caught them letting off a pipe bomb behind the cricket pavilion the other day. Blew a four-foot hole in the back wall. Terrible bang."

"How could boys make a bomb?" I asked with more than a little incredulity. "At school?"

"Oh, the ingredients were all there, in the potting shed, science lab, metalwork shop and so on. MF boys are taught to be resourceful, Mr Sangster." He paused to smile, almost proudly, I thought. "A little matter of building a pipe bomb wouldn't daunt them. And one of those boys' fathers owns a demolition company."

"Very useful for the lad."

"Oh, very," said Wilkins, oblivious to my intended irony. "In fact, the same firm detonated charges close by the school a few weeks ago, to make safe some unstable cliffs, I believe, at a disused quarry."

"Bangs, eh?"

"Oh yes, terrific set of bangs, heard the noise here in my study. Must run in the family."

"Yes, but think of the danger, man."

"Oh, there was no danger, Mr Sangster, professional firm, knew what they were doing, I—"

"The boys," I sighed.

"Ah yes, I did point out the danger to those boys just now. Had to give the henchmen three strokes and the leader six."

"Leader?"

"There's always a leader and henchmen, in any group of boys, Sangster, and we encourage leadership here, so I didn't want to be too harsh." Wilkins grimaced, gesturing to a hooked bamboo cane hanging off one of the shelves. "I do so abhor corporal punishment, don't you?" he then added, with a look that to my eyes said quite the opposite. I didn't reply and we fell silent for a moment. "Anyway, to business," Wilkins finally said. "Did the education department tell you why we called?"

"You have a first-year boy, a Michael Le Conte, long-term truant, I believe."

"Yes, we do, Mr Sangster, yes, we do. It's almost Easter and the lad's only been here two days since half-term in February." I expected more explanation, but Wilkins just sat and shook his head.

"When?"

"I'm sorry?"

"When were the two days this boy did attend school?"

"Oh, er… I see, when." He looked down at a page of notes then leaned back in the manner of the long-sighted. "Hmmm… once on the first day back, so seventeenth of February, and once last Thursday."

"Why didn't you call the education department earlier, or take some other action?"

"Cheeky boy phoned in sick, pretended to be his mother. Then when he did come back, said he'd lost his doctor's note. It was only when the lad didn't show up Friday that we called the parents and found out the truth."

"Friday?"

"Indeed, first thing in the morning. And the parents promised to send him to school yesterday, but of course, the boy didn't show up again, hence I contacted your director." So, I thought angrily, Wilkins had circumvented the local officer (who Johnson had warned me found the school hard to penetrate) and called straight to head office.

"Then why," I said in a raised voice, unable to disguise my frustration, "if I may ask, was I called in if Mrs Hart, who I believe is your local truant officer, hadn't had a go at the case first?"

"Local woman's sick, I'm afraid, and we felt there was no time to lose," Wilkins answered, looking to one side in a way I judged as slightly uncomfortable.

"I see," I said, thinking for a moment there might be something Wilkins was hiding. "But six weeks, I mean, what on Earth could a boy be doing away from school and home every day for all that time?"

"That's something we'd like you to try and find out, Sangster. The education department recommended the Granville Institute and you in particular, so will you help us?"

"Yes, if I can."

"And, of course, discreetly. Wouldn't do the school's reputation much good if people thought we let our pupils truant for weeks on end without taking any action. Not much good at all."

"Of course, discreetly," I repeated, watching him relax as I spoke, whilst telling myself that I'd probably dropped my other casework and driven all this way for what was likely a run-of-the-mill matter of 'sagging off'.

"Then let me see what else I can tell you about this boy." Wilkins lifted up the sheet of notes and placed a pair of rimless 'pince-nez' reading glasses on his nose. "Ahem… he came from a good local prep school, Saint Hildeburgh's, down in the town." He ran his finger down the page and muttered to himself. "Er… been in trouble for fighting a few times, other than that kept his nose clean. And his family seems to be stable."

"Stable?"

"Yes, the Le Contes are more than comfortably off if the home address is anything to go by. Big house, just over the hill."

"Alright," I said, wondering why 'comfortably off' equalled 'stable' in Wilkins' mind. "I'd like to start by talking to some of the other boys, classmates or friends, then the prep school you mentioned."

"You won't visit the parents or interview the boy first?"

"If he's truanting today and still thinks his parents are fooled, he's not likely to come home until the time he would be expected. I'll go later on."

"Ah, a very good observation," said Wilkins. "We could save you some trouble and organise an interview with the boy tomorrow at school."

"You haven't done too well getting him to come to school so far." I laughed. "And anyway, he's more likely to open up to me at home." Wilkins shrugged at this, and I looked him in the eye, wondering whether there was some ulterior motive for wanting me to see the boy on school premises.

"I understand," the headmaster then said, pressing an intercom button on his desk. "Miss Lyons, could you telephone the Le Contes' house and let them know Mr Sangster wishes to call this evening, at about, ah, what time?"

"Seven thirty should work."

"Seven thirty," he repeated down the intercom, then turned back to me. "And, Sangster, all the school's resources are at your disposal. We have a fine library, for example. Now," he said, taking a deep breath and standing very erect, "I may be blowing my own trumpet." You are, I thought, loud and clear. "But we have perhaps the finest range of reference books on the immediate locale to be found anywhere. I gifted the collection to the school, you know. Very valuable, I dare say."

"I'm sure it is, Mr Wilkins, but my immediate interest is background on the boy. You said earlier he came to school on the first day of term?"

"Indeed."

"Then once more, five days ago?"

"Indeed."

"And what did he do?"

"Do?"

"Yes do, during that second day."

"Well, as I understand it, Sangster, he spent most of the day in the library. Didn't attend a single class, according to our registers. Very strange, and a note here says his form teacher also saw him going into the, oh…" He tensed for a moment, loosely folding his arms and rapidly rubbing left and right elbow pads simultaneously, then seemed to regain his composure. "The cellar under the boarding house, with some of those Bomb Squad boys you saw earlier. Out of bounds to day boys."

"Hmmm, is it now?" I wondered why that should disquiet Wilkins. "Do you have any more information on the boy I can take away?"

"Certainly, most certainly," the garrulous reverend replied, pressing his intercom button again. "Miss Lyons, please bring in the full file on Le Conte." A moment later the secretary entered with a brown foolscap-sized cardboard folder.

"Here we are, Headmaster. This has all the boy's details, school reports, disciplinary notes and so on."

"Thank you, Miss Lyons. Mr Sangster will need to borrow this for a while. Please ensure he signs it out."

"Of course." She offered me a piece of paper. "Just sign here and here, please. And Mr Sangster?"

"Yes?" I answered whilst scribbling.

"I'll make you an appointment with the parents, and seven thirty this evening was the time I think you said you wanted?" I nodded. "The address is in the file."

"Thank you."

"Oh, and Sangster," said Wilkins as I grasped the file and stood up to leave. "The MF is a much sought-after school. Places are scarce. If the Le Conte boy doesn't want his place, I won't hesitate to expel him and give it to a boy who does. I intend to recommend a boarding school I know in Shropshire to his parents. In fact—" He was interrupted by the phone on his desk, which Miss Lyons leaned over and answered.

"For you, Headmaster." She passed him the receiver.

"Yes, Wilkins here... yes, Michael Le Conte... just discussing the boy, with the education department... what's happened?" I watched as he reddened then raised his voice. "Missing, you say... yes, of course, we'll help in any way we can... thank you, goodbye... yes... five or ten minutes."

"The Le Conte boy's missing," he said, slamming down the phone. "That was the police. They're organising a search, treating it as a possible kidnapping, wealthy family, ransom and all that. It's like something from a film." He stood up and began pacing the room, then sat again and placed his head in his hands. "They'll be here in a few minutes apparently, and they want to interview me!"

My diaphragm tensed at the words 'missing' and 'kidnapping'. And whether it was just the shock of learning the boy had disappeared,

10

along with some almost subliminal cue from Wilkins' and Miss Lyons' words or body language, or for some other reason entirely, I sensed for the first time that something about this case was far from normal.

"How long's he been gone?" I eventually asked, my voice now breathless.

"Since Sunday. I... I... I fail to understand why the police didn't contact the school then. Surely, we're one of the first places they'd check, it doesn't seem—"

"Oh," said Miss Lyons, her face turning scarlet, eyes watering beneath her glasses.

"Oh what?" shouted Wilkins.

"They did call, Headmaster, yesterday morning. I thought when they said missing... well, I just thought, you know, they meant absent without permission. Truanting. Not 'missing' missing."

At this Wilkins jumped to his feet, wagged his finger and loomed over the secretary, who cowered backwards. He opened his mouth several times to speak but seemed lost for words, pacing all the while and muttering mostly unintelligible whispers (although I fancied hearing a word that sounded like 'accounts' more than once).

"So we knew," he managed to say out loud after a series of grunts. "We knew, and yet we called in Sangster here when the boy had already been reported missing, and we didn't follow up with the police. Didn't two local boys also go missing last week?"

"Yes, Headmaster," said Miss Lyons, tears running down her cheeks.

"Well, that makes us look even worse. What about our reputation, and what will the governors think?" Wilkins began to pace and mutter again, then held his hand up, lifting one finger. "I have it. We'll say Sangster here was called in to help. That's what we've been doing since yesterday." He stood up very straight then leaned forwards and looked at me, intending to be authoritative, I felt sure, but in reality just coming over as imploring. "You could, er... do that, couldn't you, Sangster?"

"I won't lie," I answered, feeling disgust at his focus on the school's reputation rather than the boy's wellbeing. "But if they don't ask me outright then I won't mention the mistake, providing..."

"Yes?" Wilkins and Miss Lyons asked in unison.

"You don't hide anything else, from me or the police."

"Of course, Sangster."

"Very well. Now for the time being, let me get out of your way," I said, walking towards the door. Wilkins shook his head vigorously.

"No, Sangster, please stay, I—" He was interrupted by a high-pitched ringing followed by what, to me, sounded like the distant roaring of a waterfall but was in fact the entire school, hundreds of boys, all moving between classes, filling corridors, the school yard and other outside spaces as they went. "Oh no, the two-twenty bell. The first afternoon period must have finished already."

"And the police are here too," sniffed Miss Lyons. "I'll go and let them in."

I looked out of the window to see a police car pull up, and two figures, one uniformed, one plain clothed, climb out, just as boys flooded into the car park from every direction. The uniformed officer stood waiting by the car whilst the other seemed to almost wade through the torrent of pupils before reaching the relative calm of the concrete steps (Miss Lyons later informed me that the boys were forbidden to use parts of the school, like the main entrance or the corridor that led to the headmaster's study).

"This is Detective Inspector Cooper." Miss Lyons knocked on the already open study door, then entered with the plain-clothed officer, a tall, gaunt-looking man of about forty with high cheekbones and a nose almost beak-like in its profile.

"Reverend Wilkins," the headmaster then said, holding out his hand. "We've brought all the resources to bear that we can to help the police in this most unfortunate matter. And this is Mr Sangster from the Granville Institute. Sangster's working on the Le Conte boy's case, you know." I also extended my hand, whilst gritting my teeth at Wilkins' disingenuity.

"The Granville has a case open on the boy?" asked the inspector, ignoring my gesture. "This is a police matter, and although we've already had two other youngsters go missing in the locality last week, we're still treating this one as a likely ransom attempt. Either way, no time for civil interference."

"Oh no, we, er…" stumbled Wilkins. "Not a case like that, Inspector. A missing person case is for you chaps to handle." As he spoke, I felt at least some relief that the headmaster had decided not to lie outright and say I had been specially called in because the boy was missing.

"Then what?"

"Long-term truanting," I answered before Wilkins could say any more. "Boy's been absenting himself from school for many weeks now. I've been asked by the Chester department of education to investigate. Might be pertinent to your enquiries," I added, trying to use what I thought sounded like police jargon. Cooper clearly wasn't impressed.

"Liverpool, last summer."

"I'm sorry."

"That was your lot," said the inspector, pointing his finger at me.

"What was our lot?"

"Young bucks systematically stealing from the docks. Operation took weeks to set up and your lot ended up tipping the lads off. Meddling do-gooders who get in the way, that's the Granville's rep within the force."

"Shame you feel like that, Inspector Cooper." I shrugged. "And last summer was before my time with the Institute."

"That's as may be, but it's a little crowded in this office, so if you wouldn't mind, I'd like to talk to the headmaster alone. And I'd like to talk to the boy's form master if I may." I left the room as requested, along with Miss Lyons, who hurried off down the corridor, heels now clicking on the floor faster than ever. After a time she returned with a young man looking barely above school age himself and whom I watched enter the headmaster's study with the anxious demeanour of a boy about to receive six of the best. Five minutes later the inspector and the nervous teacher came back out of the door, the inspector turning to me as he walked past.

"I hear from that headmaster your organisation has a formal mandate to work on this boy's case, so I can't stop you, but Sangster?"

"Yes."

"I've been assigned to this case by the chief constable himself," he said, tapping the side of his long nose. "So don't step on my toes and leave this to the professionals."

*

"This is terrible," said Wilkins, peering out of his office door to make sure the inspector was well out of earshot. "Oh, the scandal."

"The scandal, Headmaster," echoed Miss Lyons. "It might result in the authorities, well…" Here she looked at Wilkins with a knowing look. "Poking their noses into the school's affairs."

"And now that detective's gone to interview all the boy's classmates." Wilkins acknowledged her look with the faintest of nods. "This will get back to the parents in no time."

"I think it will anyway, Wilkins," I said. "You can't keep a disappearance like this secret for long. May already have been on TV and radio."

"But what will people say?" he moaned. "Sangster, you came highly recommended."

"Not for finding missing children."

"But can't you do something, man?" he asked, his voice now a high-pitched wail.

"Well…"

"Yes, Sangster?"

"You mentioned Michael Le Conte was friendly with those boys who blew up the pavilion."

"The Bomb Squad?"

"How old are they?"

"Oh, fifteen, rising sixteen."

"Seems odd to me. I mean, is that normal?"

"Um, yes," said Wilkins. "That's the age we normally admit into the fifth form."

"No, I meant a pupil of Michael's age being friendly with boys that old. He's only twelve, after all."

"Ah, I see what you're getting at, Sangster."

"And is Inspector Cooper interviewing them? The Bomb Squad, I mean."

"No," said Miss Lyons. "So far he just asked to speak with the boys in Michael's class."

"Then let's get one of the Bomb Squad lads in. Perhaps the one you described as the ringleader, Wilkins?"

"We can bring them all, Sangster," said the headmaster. "Miss Lyons, could you please fetch Rylance and his friends? Not sure which class he's in but—"

"That's PG Rylance, and he's in Five C," the secretary replied. "They all are, and the class will be in the physics lab right now."

"Woman's a treasure," said Wilkins, his composure apparently now fully regained, his eyes following Miss Lyons (with the main focus on her pencil skirt, I noticed) as she left the office. "Anyone could have made that mistake with the police yesterday."

"Oh yes, anyone," I said with a shrug.

"Eunice, I mean…" He faltered. "Miss Lyons, is an absolute treasure, Sangster."

*

"Now then, gentlemen," Wilkins said to a rather worried-looking Bomb Squad, who were all standing to attention in front of the headmaster's desk. "This is Mr Sangster and he'd like to ask you a few questions." The boys were silent for a number of seconds, then the ringleader, who was taller and a generally more impressive physical specimen than his friends, spoke up.

"We were only messing about, sir," he said. "Just thought it would be a laugh, you know."

"No, I don't know, Rylance," Wilkins snapped back. "But this isn't about the explosion behind the cricket pavilion."

"Sir?"

"Michael Le Conte," I said, as calmly as I could. "I understand he was friendly with you all."

15

At the sound of Michael's name the boys looked at each other, shuffling uncomfortably, due, I presumed, to them having already got wind of Michael's disappearance.

"What, Le Conte from the first year?" Rylance eventually asked.

"Yes."

"Er… yeah, we know who he is," the boy answered slowly, clearly trying to sound as if he didn't care but signalling the opposite emotion by continued shuffling and furtive glances to his fellows.

"This is most serious, gentlemen," said Wilkins. "You noticed the police car outside, I presume." The boys nodded in unison. "Well, Le Conte's gone missing. Since Sunday. Disappeared."

"Disappeared, sir?" Rylance asked with genuine surprise, and also to my surprise given the group's earlier reaction to Michael's name. "From home and everything?"

"Exactly. Now then, you were all seen with Le Conte at lunchtime on, um… now, let me see." Wilkins held his glasses up and looked at his notes sheet. "Yes, on the third of April, last Thursday, in fact. Says here…" He then held the sheet further away from his nose before continuing. "In the quad at morning break, and again going into the cellars underneath the boarding house during lunchtime."

"What do you think of him?" I asked, prompting more furtive looks from the boys.

"Well, Le Conte's not a bad kid," Rylance answered. "We let him hang around with us for a while."

"And you've no idea why Michael might truant for long periods?"

"Or go missing?" added Wilkins.

"No, sir."

"Anything else you can tell us?" I said. "Anything at all about Michael?"

The boys all looked to the ground and then one suddenly blurted out, "Sir, Le Conte thinks it's the end of the world and he's not safe for us to hang around with. He's going to…"

The others turned and looked daggers at their comrade, who stopped talking and resumed his downward gaze.

16

"Going to do what, lad?"

"Er, what Mitchell means, sir," Rylance answered quickly, "is that if Le Conte's been taken then he's not safe."

"Does he now? And the end of the world?"

"Oh, Le Conte just says things like that, sir."

"So there really isn't anything else you can tell us?"

"No, sir."

"And the rest of you?" The other three shook their heads. "Very well," I said, feeling frustrated whilst accepting the conversation had gone as far as it could. "That's enough questions for the time being, thank you." Miss Lyons then went to usher the boys out of the room, only to be stopped by Wilkins.

"Hair's well over the collar, Rylance." The headmaster touched the boy on the shoulder.

"It is worn a little longer these days, sir."

"Not at the Manor Free it isn't," shouted Wilkins, making me smile to myself at his focus on trivia regardless of the circumstances. "Get it cut before the new term starts."

"I'll make a note of that," said Miss Lyons, continuing to shoo the boys out of the room. "And Rylance," she added, looking at the boy's zip-up ankle-length 'winklepickers', "those Chelsea boots are against the school dress code."

"Yes, Miss, of course, Miss," Rylance replied as he left.

*

"Well, Sangster," Wilkins said as the door closed, "I know I asked for help just now, but does this mean that things have changed for you?"

"How do you mean?"

"Well, we've now got a missing persons case, it's all bit outside your brief, eh?"

"I must admit I need to consider carefully whether or not to proceed now the police are involved," I said, doing my best to reply formally and wondering as I spoke why I didn't want to drop the case and leave matters purely in the hands of the law. Certainly not for Wilkins' sake. No, it was that sinking feeling of foreboding I'd experienced a few minutes earlier, something to do with the atmosphere at the school, perhaps, some little hint of the untoward that I'd picked up on but not consciously understood that caused me such a profound emotional response. But whatever the reason, I felt compelled to continue and determined to proceed as I would have done when the case was just about long-term truanting. Given the police involvement, I'd need to call the education director to get clearance, but I felt sure he would agree.

"So no guarantees," I said to Wilkins. "But if I do some more digging, I just might be able to shed some light on it all. Extra pair of eyes and so on."

"You have experience in these things?"

"Yes, in past lives. Naval intelligence, troubleshooting for an oil company."

"Not quite the same, but any help is worth having, I suppose," he sighed. "Resolve this and I'll be eternally grateful. Reputation, you know, don't want the school's dirty laundry hung out to dry for all to see."

"I'm doing it for the parents, Wilkins." I wondered at his indifference to anything but the school's reputation, which in turn hinted that he perhaps had something to hide relating to Michael's disappearance. "It's hard to imagine how those poor people are feeling right now."

"You'll go to their house straight away?"

"No," I answered, thinking grimly to myself that by the evening the situation with Michael Le Conte might have become clearer, one way or another. "I'll stick to my schedule," I then said out loud. "Could someone here call Saint Hildeburgh's School and let them know I'm coming? I can be there about five latest."

"I'll have Miss Lyons let them know, Sangster. And if you have any news, any news at all…"

18

"Yes, Wilkins?"

"Do let me know soonest, before you tell the police or the education department."

*

"Sir, please wait." I turned to my right to see the leader of the Bomb Squad knocking on the car window. Switching off the ignition, I wound the window down.

"Yes, Rylance?"

"Sir, it's Le Conte," he almost shouted. "Well, sir, I didn't tell you everything in the head's study, I—"

"Get in," I said, jerking my head towards the passenger seat then leaning over to open the opposite door. "And tell me, what's your name?"

"Rylance, sir."

"No, your name, lad. You do have a name?"

The boy looked confused for a moment then widened his eyes with understanding. "Paul, sir."

"Close the door." He slammed the door shut, then opened his mouth to speak. "Now, Paul," I said before he could begin to talk. "Slowly, lad. What couldn't you tell me?"

"You won't laugh?" I shook my head. "And you won't tell the head, or the police, or my mum and dad?"

"No promises, but not if I don't have to," I said, shaking my head once again.

"You look like someone I can trust."

"I hope you can, Paul."

"Well, I know Le Conte's just a kid, but he scared us."

"Michael scared you?"

"Yeah. He's got this way of talking to you, it's like…" The boy, now less tongue-tied, then told me what he didn't want to tell Wilkins, albeit with many repetitions and reminders from me to stay on the subject. He began by saying that Michael had, as he put it, 'this way of looking at you so you want to do what he asks'. Paul then explained that he'd first met Michael through the school's Tolkien society the previous September, at the start of the school year ('mostly older lads, sir, no new boys were allowed to join, but Le Conte was different, knew *The Lord of the Rings* front to back'). Michael had then approached Paul and his friends some weeks ago (I remembered Wilkins saying the Le Conte boy had attended school just twice that term, once the previous Friday and once some time in February).

Michael was apparently very interested in the Rylance family business and had specifically asked about the recent explosive work done in the disused quarry. He'd even gone as far as visiting Paul's house one evening to look at papers of his father's that showed where the charges were laid. Michael had also been keen ('a bit weirdly keen, sir', as Paul put it) to understand how pipe bombs could be made and Paul had willingly shown him ('quite simple if you know how, sir'). This all culminated in Paul, Michael and the other three members of the Bomb Squad testing their first pipe bomb together one Saturday at a local refuse tip ('went up like an H bomb, sir, rats running everywhere').

"Did Michael go to see any of your friends at their homes after school?" I then asked, wondering if I should go back and talk to the others.

"No, they're all in Bolshaw, sir."

"I'm sorry?"

"Bolshaw House, sir, for boys who live here at the school." He pointed to a long, squat, two-storey building just visible amongst trees on the far side of a playing field to the left of the car park. "That's where the Bolshaw lads live." I squinted at Bolshaw House, which, I thought, despite the distance, looked somewhat dilapidated. Soot-stained sandstone walls, small leaded windows (those on the upper floor appeared to have bars across them) and a slate roof that had been mended with differently shaded tiles over the years, all spoke of neglect. An ancient-looking belfry sat in the middle of the roof, adding interest to the building's otherwise bland profile, but all in all the place had a feeling of shadow about it despite the sunny day, its gloomy aspect further emphasised by a pall of blue smoke hanging over one gable end, fed by a blackened and multi-potted chimney. Modern heating, it seemed, had yet to arrive in this apparently forgotten corner of the school.

"Is it nice, living there?"

"It's known as Colditz, sir."

"No escape then." I laughed.

"No, sir, it's school dinners three times a day, dorms cold and damp most of the time. Bolshaw lads always come last at games, and they get sick a lot."

"Really, Paul?"

"There's a few down with flu at the moment, sir."

"I see." I remembered the three boarding members of the Bomb Squad looking visibly less healthy than their 'day boy' leader.

"And sir," said Paul, finishing off with a bombshell (almost literally), "it was Le Conte's idea to let the bomb off behind the cricket pavilion."

"Why there?"

"Said he wanted to see what damage it could do, and the place is completely hidden, so we knew we wouldn't be seen by any of the masters or the prefects."

"But you were caught."

"Yes, we didn't realise the caretaker was close by. Only Le Conte managed to get away." He looked down and shook his head. "The rest of us didn't want to do it, sir, and it was a much bigger bomb than we'd made before."

"Then why did you do it?" The boy said nothing, so I pressed further. "Because Michael wanted you to?"

"Yes, sir, Le Conte..." he muttered, going silent for a moment, head hung low, before trying clumsily to explain that Michael had (although Paul didn't explain how) given them no choice and also intimidated them into keeping silent about his involvement when they were caught.

"Anything else you would like to tell me, Paul?" I asked when he finished.

"Well, you know what Mitchell said?"

"Um… oh yes, in the head's study, about the end of the world."

"It's just that, well, sir, all that Tolkien stuff, sorcery and so on?"

"Yes."

"Le Conte thinks it's real and we're in danger from it. I got the feeling he's going to do something."

"What sort of thing?"

"Don't know, sir." The boy shook his head. "Just something that he thinks is important, maybe to do with a bomb. I don't know, sir."

"Very well," I said, the look on Paul's face confirming to me he knew no more. "Then I think we can leave it at that." The boy smiled and stepped out of the car. "And thank you for trusting me, Paul."

"Thank you, sir." He turned to leave. "And that's a nice car. E-Type roadster, 4.2 engine?"

"I can see you love cars, Paul."

"I love Jags." He looked at his watch. "Got to go now, sir, next period in a moment."

"Oh, and Paul," I called after him, "is there a phone box close by?"

"By the Canteen."

"In the school?"

"No, the post office just down the lane, on the right by the edge of the village. Everyone calls it the Canteen, sir. Dunno why."

"Thanks, and by the way, what did the others think of you and your friends hanging around with a first-year?"

"Others, sir?"

"Older boys, fifth-formers and so on."

"Oh, if anyone said anything Le Conte would just give them a look. Then they wouldn't say anything again."

"Just a look?"

"Yes, sir, and Le Conte really does believe all that magical stuff and he really is going to do something bad, sir. This week, I'm sure, he said—" The school bell suddenly rang out and Paul Rylance mouthed something inaudible to me over the noise before walking back to the school building.

3 PM

A few minutes later I parked on the driveway of the 'Canteen', a double-fronted grey-pebbledash building with red-painted window frames. It sat alone and somewhat out of place, two hundred yards or so from a compact red-brick village comprising no more than (as far as I could see) a small church, a village hall and a few residential houses. I went to open the door, looking at a black and white sign above my head.

'Manor Post Office – Proprietors R Jackson, Son, Daughter and Nephew', I read, and looking down again, I saw the faces of two teenage boys staring back at me from a poster fixed to the window. I peered closely at the names, thinking for a moment one might be Michael Le Conte, but neither was. These were the same two Inspector Cooper mentioned, who had disappeared the week before, and the poster was a police notice, asking for the public to come forward with any information on the boys.

I entered the shop, the sound of a rasping bell setting my teeth on edge whilst I took a moment to accustom my eyes to the weak lighting before looking around. As the door closed on its hinge behind me and the bell ceased its noise, the place fell into complete silence.

Apparently deserted, an unoccupied counter guarded shelves filled with cigarettes, rows of glass sweet jars, bottles of every kind of pop imaginable, chocolate bars stacked in piles, bags of potato crisps in boxes and a large cream-coloured fridge of what looked like pre-war vintage, all things that might satisfy the needs of the boys of the MF. The counter was made of dark wood that helped dim the natural light (like much of the decor), and I looked past it to a second room, as dimly lit as the first, where there was a further counter, this time protected by a metal grill (the post office, I assumed). Next to that was a ceiling-high newspaper stand, stacked with every kind of publication, from daily papers, women's weeklies, comics, car and garden journals to a top shelf of 'men's' magazines (I wondered how many of these found their way to the boys of the Manor Free).

At the far end of the room, bookcases with neatly arranged and identically bound volumes made up what looked to be a small lending library, and beyond these (most incongruously of all, to me at least) was a gardening and hardware collection. This stood in a separate annex, untidily stocked with such diverse items as sacks of coal, bundles of firewood, lengths of copper piping, reels of hose, potted plants, a cast-iron stove, hoes, rakes, compost bags and bottles of weedkiller.

"May we help you?"

I jolted, turning to see two men standing behind the counter. Both were short, with white hair and ruddy faces. They were dressed similarly (white shirts, red and green tartan ties with open grey woollen cardigans) and might have been twins, the only discernible difference being that one wore black-rimmed glasses. Thinking it might seem rude to just get change for the phone, I looked around for something to buy, my eye falling on a jar of sweets straight ahead of me.

"Er… four ounces of sherbet lemons, please?"

"Albert," said the bespectacled one. "Could you do the honours?"

"Certainly, Fred," Albert answered, then took a small stepladder, climbed to the top shelf and reached for the appropriate jar.

"Anything else we can do for you?" asked Fred. "Cigarettes, perhaps?"

"No thanks, trying to give up."

"Then a magazine. We have some very interesting new top-shelf issues, and this month's *Parade* is especially suitable for the, er, discerning but discreet gentleman."

I felt in my pocket, but there were no coins. It would have to be a ten-shilling note, and I couldn't ask them to change it up for sixpence worth of sweets. I looked along the shelves as Albert grappled with the sherbet lemons. Toasted teacakes, chocolate dragees, blackjacks, fruit salads, pear drops… the row of jars went on and on. No, I thought, one bag of sweets was enough, so it would have to be something else, and I was guiltily toying with the idea of Fred Jackson's top-shelf magazine offer when I noticed a hand-written sign pinned to the wall behind the counter.

'Tea & Coffee Flasks Filled – 1/-'

"You fill flasks?"

"We do," Fred answered. "One shilling per pint."

"Or part thereof," added Albert from the top of his ladder.

"Well, look, I've a thermos in my car. I'll go and get it if you'll bear with me." I left the shop and just for a moment considered driving off, the atmosphere of the Manor Post Office and its proprietors making me shudder. But of course, I said to myself, I couldn't do that in good conscience, and anyway, I needed the change for the phone, and with an hour to kill, the thought of parking up somewhere with a hot coffee appealed.

"There we are," I said, placing the flask on the counter. "It'll need washing out, I'm afraid."

"Minnie," shouted Albert (now back at ground level), whereupon a woman appeared, almost a mirror image of the two men in both looks and dress, except for a grey skirt as opposed to trousers, and once again, it seemed, materialising out of nowhere. "This gentleman, Minnie, would like a flask of, um…"

"Coffee, please. And," I said, pointing to some bread rolls under a glass dome behind the counter, "those rolls, what's the filling?"

"It's cheese spread," he said, taking two foil-wrapped triangles out of the fridge. "We sell the bun and cheese separately. You unwrap the cheese and put it into the bun yourself. The boys love 'em. Is that alright?"

"Oh, er, yes."

"Milk and sugar?" asked Minnie, as Albert placed the nearest bread roll and the two cheeses into a paper bag and handed them to me.

"Just milk, please."

"Be a couple of minutes." Minnie took my flask, turned and disappeared again. This time I saw how her vanishing act was achieved, the shelves behind the counter being set at a subtle angle, with a doorway in between them and the back wall, invisible to anyone entering the shop. The two men followed my gaze.

"Ah, that's our invisible door," said Albert. "Very useful to, how shall we say, watch the more light-fingered schoolboys."

"I can imagine." I laughed. "Tell me, why do the boys call this place the Canteen?"

"Because the shop once did house a canteen of sorts," answered Fred, pointing to the room beyond the post office counter. "There was a simple eating house over there, in the time of my father, and the name stuck."

"That's my uncle," added Albert. "Old Mr Jackson. He started this place back in 1898, when there were not many houses nearby, just fields, woodlands and the school. We've been catering to the boys' every need since. Now we serve the local community's needs as well, of course."

"First electric refrigerator in the district." Fred pointed to the ancient appliance behind the counter, before leaning over and looking into my eyes. "So what brings you to us?"

"Oh," I answered, instinctively stepping back. "I work with the education department in Chester. Just visiting the school."

"There's another boy gone missing," said Minnie, reappearing with my flask. "We had the police in asking about him. Is that why you're here?"

"In a way, and I see you have a police notice for those other two missing boys, stuck in the window."

"Terrible business," said Fred. "Been gone over a week, disappeared during a big storm, down by the marshes, look, I kept a copy of this." He produced a local newspaper from under the counter and pointed to a picture on the front showing the same portraits of the boys under the headline:

'Police hunt on for missing boys as storm lashes Dee marshes.'

Below that was a photo (which particularly struck me as it showed a place I knew well) of waves crashing over a sea wall, some high enough to spray houses on the landward side of a promenade.

"And now this boy from the school's disappeared as well," Fred added, giving Albert what seemed to me a knowing look. "Police promised us another poster for him, to put in the window."

"Yes, that Le Conte boy," said Albert. "Odd lad."

"Yes, odd lad," repeated Fred. "Talks more like an adult than a boy. Lots of long words. Always paid upfront in cash as well."

"Paid for what?" I asked.

"That'll be half a crown, please." Albert held out his hand, pointedly ignoring my question.

"I've only a ten-shilling note, but could you include a few florins for the phone box in the change, please? If you don't mind."

"That's quite alright. Here's, one, two, three two-bob pieces, a one-bob and two threepenny bits. Seven and six change. But I'm afraid you can't use the phone box."

"Why on Earth not?"

"Vandalised," said Fred. "It usually is."

"Covered in graffiti as well," added Albert. "Most of them seem to be these days."

"Is there another I could—"

"By the Beacon," interrupted Albert, anticipating my question. "Less than a mile away on the main road to the town. Take the village

27

road back the way you came, past the school and then a sharp right at the top of the hill and you can't miss it. Beacon's a big sandstone column, very high, stone globe on top. Marvellous view, all the way to the Isle of Man on a clear day."

"Thanks." I wondered if Albert was avoiding my question about the cash. "But you said just now Michael Le Conte always pays upfront. Pays for what?"

"Gardening materials mostly, buys lots of them. Uses a go-cart to carry the stuff home. For his parents, I imagine, although they've never been in themselves."

"But you say upfront?"

"Oh, just a figure of speech," said Albert quickly, his tone of voice sounding slightly agitated. "What Fred means is that people generally pay on account for that much stuff, you see, but never Michael. The Le Contes always make sure their son has enough cash to pay on the spot. Odd lad, though, as I said, and in fact, with the amount he buys I wonder—"

"Albert," interrupted Fred, pointing to a large wall clock. "Look at the time." The clock showed almost three.

"Oh, I hadn't noticed," cried Albert, running around the end of the counter and over to the front door, which he bolted securely top and bottom before turning and leaning flat against it. "Just in time," he said breathlessly, whilst I felt immediate unease at being locked in the shop.

"Don't worry," said Fred, reading my thoughts. "Albert hasn't gone mad, three o'clock is afternoon break time. The boys will be here any second, listen." He cupped his hand around his ear, and I heard the sound of voices, many voices, first in the distance then closer and louder, a similar cacophony to the one I heard outside the headmaster's study after the school bell rang.

"Why lock them out?" I asked, wondering whether the three shopkeepers had some reason to batten down the hatches against what must surely be a license to print money.

"Oh, just for a minute or two," said Albert. "So the boys can form an orderly queue. We'll let them in soon. They know the rules."

28

"The rules," repeated Fred. "Now then." He looked at me with teeth clenched. "Better brace yourself. Here goes Albert, here goes Minnie." With that, Albert shot the bolts and ran back behind the counter, as boys of all shapes and sizes piled in through the doorway, pressing themselves as close as they could to the counter. I stepped back, waiting for an opportune moment to escape as the 'orderly queue' began to shout out their orders.

"One at a time, one at a time," yelled Fred. "Now, you lad," he said, pointing to a gangling boy whose sharp elbows had propelled him to the front.

"Got any loosies, Fred?"

"How many?"

"Two?"

"Albert, any loose cigarettes left?" called Fred.

"No, hold on a minute, I'll split five Park Drive." I watched as Albert opened a slim blue packet, separated the cigarettes inside and passed them to Fred, who wrapped two of the diminutive Park Drives in a small paper bag. Even unlit, the aroma of the tobacco wafting across the shop from the opened packet made me remember the misery of giving up smoking the year before. I shook myself and, seeing a gap, lunged for the counter.

"Take this." I passed my card to Fred whilst desperately clutching my flask, cheese roll and sherbet lemons. "Call me if you hear anything about the boy, I—" With that I was pushed backwards, and as more boys surged against the counter, Fred held up the card and waved it, as if to say further discussion was futile. I exited the door, managing to squeeze past the main line of boys, which I could see now stretched back towards the school gates, and walked around to the drive where my car was parked. Three boys, all smoking, stood next to it.

"Nice car," one of them said as I opened the door. "British Racing Green?"

"Yes, it is." The boy nodded approvingly, dragged on his cigarette then walked away with his friends. It was at this point the difference between these pupils and those I was used to dealing with really struck home. Most of the Institute's work was with less privileged children, from far less wealthy 'catchment areas', as the education department would say. Children with every reason to be troubled and sullenly reject an authority which had let them down throughout their lives. The Manor Free pupils I had met up to that point were far from sullen and seemed to fall into two basic types, polite or swaggering. And whilst I was sure there would be some exceptions, the underlying rule was privilege. These were boys whose education was either paid for or had been granted through hard work and intellect. Either way, a supportive family life lay in the background, with the school reinforcing a sense of being the chosen elite. So perhaps this wasn't a fair environment for all, but surely it was a place where a boy like Michael should thrive?

I climbed into my car with this thought and was about to close the door when I overheard one of the three boys, who were now standing behind a bush (presumably so they wouldn't be seen smoking) mention Michael's name. They talked loudly, in that uneven register often heard with recently broken voices (sometimes deep baritone, sometimes almost falsetto) and with only a hint of the local accent (another subtle marker for elitism). And whilst I couldn't pick out every word, or tell who said what, and with their liberal Anglo-Saxon punctuation making listening all the more difficult, the gist was clear enough to further reinforce the view I was beginning to form of Michael.

"Heard that Le Conte lad's gone missing. Did you see the cop car earlier?"

"Yeah."

"Know him?"

"Ner… my brother's mate was in Le Conte's class though. Said he hasn't been at school for yonks."

"No, not just sagging off, cops were here because he's missing from home. Probably kidnapped or murdered or something. Just like those two kids who went missing down by the shore last week."

"Saw him Friday."

"Me too."

"Weird lad. Never happy, that's what everyone says."

"Alright, talk behind his back, why don't you?"

"No, it's true. Le Conte's weird. Everyone who knows him says the same. Hangs out with fifth-years and he's, what, eleven, twelve, maybe?"

"Yeah, that is weird."

"They're all shit scared of him."

"Yeah, I saw him get in a few scraps last term. He really hurt that third-year, what was his name?"

"Atkinson."

"Yeah, Atkinson."

"Okay, Le Conte's lanky for a first-year, could maybe fight a second– or third-year, but anyone from fourth year up could take Le Conte."

"Yeah, but they don't. Does what he wants, that lad."

"Yeah, weird," said the three in unison, after which they fell into silence, their vocabulary and will to argue with each other both apparently exhausted.

Who is this boy? I asked myself, opening up the foolscap folder that lay on the passenger seat. Michael's first-term report lay on the top, and I looked over the marks and comments for clues:

English: Extremely well read, excellent creative writing and comprehension. Lazy with homework, prescribed reading and essay subjects.
Maths: Finds this subject simple but shows no real interest.
Art: Our most talented pupil, with great potential, but does not respond to supervision or advice and rarely participates in class projects.
PE, Sports and Pastimes: Shows no interest in team games.
Good cross-country runner, and, I was pleased to discover, a very talented snooker player.

And so the list went on, the teachers' notes against every subject giving roughly the same message. Then came the form teacher's comment, in a separate box at the bottom of the page:

*'Satisfactory academic progress, but well below potential.
Good participation in the school Tolkien club (an exception
where he deigns to join in!) but does not mix well with boys of
his own age or form friendships as one would expect. Le Conte
should be encouraged to socialise more. Overall, I would like to
see him put his undoubted talents to more positive ends next
term. Hard work, teamwork and focus!'*

There was then a signature from the form teacher and a further note
underneath written in the same hand, perhaps as an afterthought.

*'Le Conte must understand that resolving issues through violence
is unacceptable. He must not exert undue influence over other
boys.'*

Another sheet in the folder then caught my eye, a disciplinary report
noting that Michael had received six strokes of the cane for fighting.
MR Le Conte, it said in a neatly typed letter, had hurt his victim
to the point where hospital and X-rays were needed. The fight had
apparently broken out when the other boy, called Atkinson (the name
I'd overheard a few minutes before), had asked Michael, who was
drawing at the time, to clear his desk. Atkinson was one of several older
boys who acted as class monitors for the school art club, responsible
for making sure the room was cleared at the end of the lunch break.
It seemed Michael, after repeatedly being asked to finish, turned on
Atkinson, who had been found bruised and cowering on the floor by
the incoming class.

The report recorded that a letter had been sent to Michael's parents.
A further entry then noted that although Michael was clearly the main
culprit, Atkinson's account had also been questionable, with the boy
saying that Michael had glared at the other monitors and the art teacher
overseeing the club, all of whom had then fled the room, leaving him to
deal with Michael alone. The other boys and the teacher subsequently
denied being aware there had been any trouble with Michael.

I closed the folder then started the car, with more questions in my mind now than before I read the report.

It was only a few hours since I'd first heard Michael Le Conte's name, I thought to myself as I pulled away from the Canteen, and already I had experienced more disquiet than with any other case since joining the Granville Institute. There had been no photo in my briefing notes, and I rebuked myself for making a mental picture of the boy before meeting him, but nevertheless a picture was forming in my mind. Would I ever see Michael in the flesh?

Perhaps, I thought as I drove, rather than 'who is he?', it was more appropriate to ask myself, 'who was he?'

3:30PM

The phone rang three times before the tell-tale pips clicked out of the receiver, signalling me to thrust a florin into the coin slot.

"Hello… yes… Miss Stephens? Sangster here. Yes, if you could, I'll hold." I waited for a moment, then heard the broad Cheshire brogue of Director Johnson.

"Sangster, is that you?"

"Yes, it is. Look, I need to tell—"

"Is everything alright, Sangster?"

"That's a matter of opinion. That boy's case you assigned to me this morning, Michael Le Conte."

"What of him?"

"He's missing."

"That's why we sent you."

"No, missing, as in disappeared. Hasn't been home for two days apparently. It's a matter for the police now, in fact…" I related my day thus far, albeit without some of the odder details I had picked up at the school and in the shop.

"Sounds like a rum business, Sangster," sighed Johnson when I finished. "Wonder why they called us in at all?"

"Bit of a clerical error on the part of Headmaster Wilkins, I think."

"Ha," said Johnson. "And if the police charge him, it'll be a clerical collar."

"Ah, yes, I see." I managed a weak laugh. "No pun intended. Anyway, Wilkins didn't know the boy was missing when he called you this morning, and apparently your department's local woman is sick."

"Sick, my foot, Sangster. If you mean the local truant officer, Janice Hart, I spoke to her just an hour ago."

"Oh," I said after a pause to consider why Wilkins might have lied to me. "So anyway, Johnson, should we proceed or drop it?"

"Hmmm…" I heard Johnson breathe heavily down the phone. "We have a formal mandate for this one, you know, as does the Granville Institute, so unless that mandate's rescinded by a court, nobody can stop us."

"Yes, even the police inspector at the school admitted that. Doesn't think much of the Granville, though."

"I can imagine," said Johnson. "And I think you know that I don't much care for the Manor Free either. It's an anachronism, Sangster."

"Long word for a school, Johnson." I laughed.

"Perhaps, but they're a thorn in my side. Unaccountable…" He paused for a moment. "And now there is a missing boy. What do you think?"

"Well," I answered slowly, wanting to give the impression of considering carefully. "I think, Johnson, on balance we should proceed. Formal mandate and so on, as you say. What I would propose is…" I went on to tell him about my appointments at the prep school and the Le Contes' house.

"Family might not be too keen to see you, Sangster. Imagine the state they'll be in, and you an unqualified outsider."

We were both momentarily lost for words, so I decided to try a different approach.

"Apparently they're wealthy enough to make the police think it might be a ransom job."

"Well," he laughed, "you're not a trained ransom negotiator." I remained silent. "Are you, Sangster?"

35

"No, although we did lose a chap in Nigeria a few years ago, and I was sent with the cash to…" I stopped myself, keen to stay on point. "Anyway, if the Le Contes don't feel up to seeing me, then I can always walk away again, but if I'm going to help at all I must try and meet them."

"Very well, proceed, but take Mrs Hart with you to that boy's house. Gentle touch and all that. Plus you never know when you might need a witness. Understand?"

"Yes."

"Here's her number, and she should be in the office now." I noted the number down and went to say goodbye, but the director continued. "Now, you're good, Sangster, very good, but you're a maverick nonetheless. You go beyond your brief."

"I try and get the job done, if that's what you are saying, by whatever lengths and means are necessary."

"But you do sometimes tend to, you know, jump in where angels fear to tread and all that."

"I hardly think—"

"For heaven's sake, man, remember that case with the boy and the dog last month? You ended up owning a greyhound."

"Only temporarily, and it was for the good of the child."

"Alright, but watch your step, keep me appraised at all times, and, well… just don't make a hash of things. For all our sakes."

"I will."

"Oh, and make sure you clear this one with your people as well, would you?"

*

I then called Mrs Hart, who did indeed seem in the best of health and, after a long explanation, agreed to meet me at the Le Contes' house.

The last call was to my wife, on the off chance she would already be home from work. I heard the pips click and realised I was in luck, but as I was connected, the tone of her voice made me wonder.

"Yes, Sarah, I'll be home late... yes, it's an urgent case... I know you're going away on Thursday... no, this case is only assigned to me, they can't get anyone else... well, if there is a bite of dinner left that would be good, but I can grab something on the way home, fish and... no, of course I'd like you to cook something." And so it went on, as it had so many times since I'd joined the Granville Institute, with Sarah never actually saying out loud she felt neglected and me feeling silently guilty.

*

Phone calls over, I stepped out of the call box and looked at my watch. Four twenty, so still plenty of time for a coffee break before my visit to Saint Hildeburgh's.

Sitting on a bench at this high point of the hill, the sandstone column towering behind me (just as Albert Jackson had described it), I looked over the broad river estuary, sipping my coffee and eating the (surprisingly tasty but awkward to assemble) cheese roll, entranced by the afternoon sun, hanging low as it danced on the water. The scene (which was perhaps even more spectacular than the view from the school), along with the unseasonably warm weather, had a soporific effect, so that with the excitement of the day also taking its toll I soon felt drowsy. Tiredness and lack of need for any immediate activity then blunted those mind filters that keep worry at bay.

Did I do right by Sarah, leaving a well-paid executive job to inflict on her the ups and down of working at the Granville Institute? After all, she was so much younger than me, and it wasn't exactly what she had 'signed up for'. And given the circumstances of my first marriage, with my ex-wife still alive when we met, had it been fair to marry Sarah at all?

I cast my mind back to a winter's day, almost five months ago now, when I had made my decision to change jobs, hoping when I did so that the past could be buried.

*

Was this really going to be the last time I visited the asylum? I'd thought to myself as I walked up to the front door of the Deva hospital.

The doctors had warned me that it might be, with my ex-wife now in the very advanced stages of Huntington's Chorea, the mental wasting disease that gives each generation a fifty-fifty chance.

I would visit Eileen most Sundays, generally staying with her in the hospital common room or taking her in a wheelchair around the gardens on fine days. Her shrunken form, vacant stare and, despite strong medication, occasional fits of what were clearly episodes of internal terror, were difficult to bear and just added to my guilt of having divorced her when perhaps she needed me most. Very occasionally, though, Eileen would experience a patch of what seemed like lucidity and speak.

"It's here. I can see it," she'd suddenly whispered while we sat in the hospital garden arboretum on the day of that final visit. "Another world all around us. Things you wouldn't dream of. Outside of science and reason. Open your eyes, Jack."

It had been sunny when, all of a sudden, and it seemed to me only for a moment, an unexpected darkness fell and the wind blew through the trees, which may have been what stimulated her. I had tried to press Eileen for her meaning, but she quickly faded into vacancy again, and I think that may have been the last time she ever spoke to me.

Eileen passed away a few days later, but by that time I'd already decided to accept the job offered to me by Sir John Granville.

Whether I gave up an executive career to join a philanthropic organisation dedicated to helping troubled youngsters for my own sake or whether to try and make up for the guilt I felt for Eileen, I was never quite sure.

4:40PM

blinked, realising I had fallen asleep with my memories, then drew in a deep breath through the nose and hauled myself up, knees stiff and trembling a little at having been still for so long, the late afternoon sun now insufficient to warm the bench where I sat. I noticed I'd let my coffee spill so shook the droplets off the cup and screwed it back onto the top of the thermos flask, before crumpling the paper bag from the cheese roll into my pocket. Walking back around the base of the Beacon to my car, I suddenly remembered as I passed the phone box that Johnson had asked me to call the Institute. My watch showed twenty to five, so there should still be someone in the office whom I could at least inform, if not get explicit approval from. I went inside the box, pulled out the meagre change left in my pocket and realised it wasn't enough for a call to London.

"Hello, Operator... yes... reverse charges, please... Mayfair 6257701."

"Connecting you now...go ahead, please."

"Hello, is that the Granville Institute? Yes, it's Jack Sangster here... yes, up in Chester... it's a little urgent, so I don't suppose Sir John... he is... oh, that's marvellous... well, yes, right away if you can put me through."

I waited, with a slight knot in my stomach that always came when I was about to talk to Sir John Granville, eccentric millionaire philanthropist, bon viveur of the highest order and, even though I was currently seconded to the Chester Education Department, my ultimate boss.

"Sangster, how the devil are you?" thundered Sir John, so that I had to hold the receiver back from my ear.

"Very well, thank you."

"Good. Now, what can I do for you?"

"I'm calling about…" I gave him the details of the Le Conte case, how it had morphed from truancy to a missing person search involving the police in the space of a few hours and my plans to continue working on the case, subject to the Institute's approval. My explanation then prompted a barrage of questions.

"Alright, Sangster," said Sir John, after satisfying himself with my answers, "you have my blessing to proceed providing you call us here in London with regular reports and contact me directly if there is anything really contentious. And Sangster."

"Yes."

"Tread carefully. After all, in your part of the world the Institute's not top of the police Christmas list. There was that business last year, down by the Liverpool docks. Institute ended up with egg on its face, I don't know if you heard."

"The police inspector at the school did mention it, but anyway, I'm just glad to have got hold of you. I'm keen to see this through, you see, so thanks for your support."

"Take it as a given, Sangster. Ahem…" He then coughed down the phone, causing me to envision a cigar thrust from the corner of his mouth. "Take it as a given," I then heard him repeat, whilst a voice in the background simultaneously whispered that this was a reverse charge call.

"What, you've reversed the charges? D'you know what that kind of a ruddy call costs, Sangster?"

I'd got to know Sir John to the point where hearing the word 'ruddy' was a cue for me to be silent and ride out the storm.

"Do you? During peak hours as well. I mean, you blithering idiot..." I laughed to myself that this was a man who thought nothing of spending something akin to most people's average weekly wage on a single evening's brandy and cigars, whilst holding the receiver even further away from my ear, letting him continue for another (presumably very expensive) minute, before taking my opportunity to interrupt as he finally paused for breath.

"Well, we don't want to run up any more outsized phone bills, Sir John," I said, quickly. "Thanks again for your support, and I'll be getting on to my next appointment now. This really is unfolding into the oddest of cases. Goodbye."

5PM

I rang the doorbell of the imposing and rambling red-brick mansion that was 'Saint Hildeburgh's House Preparatory School, Principals J and EJ Magister' (as stated on a brass wall plaque next to me). The door was opened by a striking grey-haired woman, very tall and slim, dressed entirely in black with a high-necked blouse under a three-quarter-length open cardigan and a narrow, almost floor-length skirt, all of which conveyed an out-of-time, perhaps almost Edwardian air. Even before she spoke, I noticed her piercing eyes, which, despite their sight fading (she had a pair of thick-lensed glasses hanging on a chain round her neck), seemed to look right through me.

"Mrs Magister?"

"Yes."

"I'm Jack Sangster, from the Granville Institute. We work with the Chester education department. My card."

"Oh dear," she said, putting on her spectacles and peering at the card, then making a mock frown. "A special investigator, no less. What have we done?"

"Nothing." I laughed. "Didn't someone call to let you know I was coming?" I wondered if that 'absolute treasure' Miss Lyons had forgotten to make the appointment.

"Perhaps my husband took the call; we run the school together, you see. But anyway, come in." With that she led me to her study, a booklined room with bay windows and an imposing antique wooden desk, along with a large stone chimney breast and cast-iron fireplace, next to which were two armchairs. "Sit please. Cigarette?"

"No thanks."

"Now, how can I help you?" she said, picking up a silver table lighter and reaching to the end of a long cigarette holder, which she kept between her teeth for most of our conversation, able to speak very clearly despite this.

"You don't mind if I take notes?" I asked, getting out my pad and pen.

"Oh no."

"Thank you, Mrs, er…" I looked up to see a certificate hanging on the wall, bearing the crest of the University of Liverpool and stating that 'by resolution of the senate of the faculty of Humanities and Social Science', the degree of Doctor of Philosophy had been conferred upon Edith Josella Magister. "Pardon, Doctor Magister."

"Just plain Missus will do very nicely."

"Sorry, Mrs Magister. I'm investigating a former pupil here, a Michael Le Conte, on behalf of the Manor Free School. I've been called in because he's a repeating truant and I had wondered if you might be kind enough to give me some background on the boy. And you should know—"

"Ah, Michael," she said with a now genuine frown. "I remember him from, er… yes, from last year. He is complex, I—"

"Sorry," I interrupted, "but you should also know that Michael is missing from home, since Sunday."

"Oh my goodness." She rocked back in her chair. "That's the third child to go missing in the district in, what, just over a week?"

"So I believe."

"Are you, um," she gulped, "helping the police with their enquiries, as they say?"

"Not formally, but we're mandated to work on the case by the education department and the school, and my institute has resources at its disposal that just may be of help."

"I understand. In fact, I've actually consulted for the Granville on several occasions myself, for their more, er, challenging cases. I have the time, you see."

"Sorry, I didn't know you'd worked with us." Despite the case having been dropped on me only that morning, and the hectic day, I still felt embarrassment at this oversight in my preparation.

"When did you join them, Mr Sangster?"

"Sorry?"

"The Granville."

"Oh, January this year."

"Ah," she said, shaking her head. "Then I was before your time."

"But you say Michael's complex?"

"I'm a child psychologist, Mr Sangster, as you noticed." She gestured to her certificate and then the bookshelves, which I now saw largely held volumes related to the subject. "And Michael, he…" She covered her eyes and stopped speaking for a moment, sniffing a little. "Oh dear, the boy's missing," she whispered, pulling a handkerchief from her sleeve (also black, I noticed), then dabbing her eyes. "I'm sorry, now, where were we?"

"You were saying you have time to work on challenging cases and that Michael is complex."

"Yes, it's mainly my husband and his staff who are 'hands-on' teachers, as they say. I spend most of my time with research and lecturing. I only focus on interesting subjects now." Emphasising the word 'interesting', she flicked ash, a deft movement given the length of the cigarette holder and one that I subsequently noticed was a mannerism of discomfort.

"Michael was an interesting subject, was he, Mrs Magister?"

"Well, yes, in a way, but he saddens me as well."

"Saddens you?" I asked, noticing she was talking in the present tense about Michael, ostensibly a past pupil.

"Perhaps I wasn't as objective as I should have been with him. I'm not sure, I…" She stopped speaking, seemingly lost in thought for a few seconds, then continued. "Michael was one of my brightest, you see, a good all-rounder and especially promising at art and English. He could focus on a painting or essay for hours, days even."

"Days?" I queried.

"Oh yes. Michael has the capacity for hyper-focus, as some people call it."

"Is that rare?"

"Not common. Anyway, you asked me about Michael."

"Sorry, please go on."

"Well, he was good in the sports department as well, and personable. Rosy cheeks, freckles and a lovely smile. The little girls positively queued up to be his friends." She laughed. "Queued up, they did. I remember joking about young Michael's amours at parents' evening. Lovely people, the Le Contes. Parents and sisters alike. The two Le Conte girls attended Saint Hildeburgh's, as well you know."

"Did you teach him personally?"

"Yes," she said, looking downwards. "I…" Her voice drifted off into thought, so I waited for a quite a few seconds for the silence to break before speaking again.

"Mrs Magister?"

"Er… yes," she whispered, as if waking from a trance. "Yes, I did, Mr Sangster. His creative writing was such that during his last term with us, I gave Michael regular one-to-one lessons. He especially loved anything to do with old myths and legends, and he had, has, I mean, a remarkable talent, well beyond his years."

I was confused. She described a boy who should have everything going for him. Academic, sporting, artistic, popular with the girls even at a young age, from a stable family. And somehow, as I sensed with headmaster Wilkins, there seemed a vague but still present undertone when Mrs Magister talked about Michael. Something that they both knew or perhaps only felt but, for whatever reason, weren't telling me. I decided to be blunt, not least because I was keen to finish quickly and visit the boy's home with Mrs Hart at the appointed time.

"So why, Mrs Magister, are we having this conversation about a boy who on paper has every reason to be happy? You must know more."

"Michael has negative personality traits. He cannot concentrate."

"I thought you said he had this hyper... what was it called?"

"Focus." I nodded. "Yes, if he's interested, but most of the time he just has a distracted stare."

"Must make lessons difficult," I said, remembering the school report.

"Yes, can't sit still for long, and he gets into fights, some quite violent, disrupts the class, leads other children into trouble."

"Lots of boys fit that description, don't they?"

"Of course they do, Mr Sangster," she answered, "but Michael goes too far. Some children were frightened of him but did what he asked of them nevertheless."

"How do you mean?"

"He had an almost Pied Piper-like hold over them."

"Pied Piper?"

"Well... with all my training and experience of the rest of his family, I simply can't explain where that part of Michael's character comes from. Maybe some strange trait from a distant ancestor has been thrown up, who knows?" She shrugged. "So I'm afraid Pied Piper is the best I can do for now, Mr Sangster."

I said nothing, thinking Mrs Magister definitely wasn't as 'objective' about Michael as she could have been.

"One child described Michael's hold on them as a mix of fear and something akin to hypnosis," she then said. "I'm not sure I wasn't a little intimidated by him myself."

"Really?"

"He has a certain way of being, you'll see when you meet him. Oh, perhaps you won't..." She began furiously polishing her glasses with the gothic handkerchief. "And he's a bare-faced liar," she said, now openly crying.

"Is he?"

"I'm sorry." She sniffed, dabbing her eyes once more. "But oh yes, and he knows the truth but chooses to tell complex lies, all without

46

batting an eyelid." She looked thoughtful for a moment. "Might be linked to his creativity, I suppose."

"And you are sure his home life is alright?"

"Well, none of us knows what happens behind closed doors, but that being said, I would choose the Le Contes over most families for stability and kindness. Remember, I taught his two sisters as well, so any home issues would likely have come out by now. No, I believe Michael is simply made the way he is made."

"I'm no expert," I said, looking at the bookshelves again, "but that sounds strange coming from a psychologist. I thought you people all traced mental problems to childhood. Freud and all that."

"I do not hold with Sigmund Freud, Mr Sangster," Mrs Magister replied coldly, for a moment looking every inch the headmistress. "Most mental illness can be ascribed to fatigue, loneliness, perhaps extreme stress like shell shock."

"I can fully understand what you say about shell shock." I nodded. "Sorry, please continue."

"And commonly exacerbated by a bad home life in children and alcohol or perhaps drugs, prescription or otherwise, in adults. But Michael, well..." She reached for a book from the shelf behind her desk, showed me the cover (which read *A Treatise on the Causes of Hyperkinetic Reaction of Childhood*), then carried on talking, now firmly in her stride. "This writer believes children like Michael are born with differences in their minds. Physical differences. He describes cases very similar to Michael's being recorded for almost a hundred years now, but we have few ways to test his theory. You can't vivisect a child's brain."

"Not at all," I solemnly agreed.

"Perhaps in the future we will have the means to, er, shall we say, 'scan' the human brain."

"What, like an X-ray for the mind?"

"You may think me a fanciful old woman," she sighed, "but it's certainly what we need. For now, though, unless we dope the children with sedatives, all we can do is observe them and offer counselling.

And with Michael, you never know when he is telling the truth, so it's even more difficult to help him."

"You believe Michael to be incurable?"

"Perhaps one day we'll have a snappy name, perhaps with just a few letters, to describe his condition, and equally simple drugs. But right now," she whispered, her eyes watering again behind her glasses, "with the tools we currently have at our disposal I'm afraid he is incurable, Mr Sangster."

"And knowing the boy as you do," I asked her. "Can you think of any reason why Michael might be missing? Except for some sort of random accident or abduction, of course."

"As I say, Mr Sangster, Michael has the rare ability to hyper-focus." She flicked her cigarette ash then continued slowly. "So if, and I just say if, he has fixed his mind on something he feels he has to do, then a little matter of disappearing for a day or so and putting his family through trauma and the authorities to enormous trouble wouldn't bother him."

She looked to her left as she spoke, her eyes apparently resting on a large volume lying on its side (*End of Days, Legends and Prophecies of the End Times*, said the spine), then seemed to check herself, almost as if she felt she had said too much.

"Oh, the thought of young Michael being abducted," she whispered, dabbing her eyes again.

"I'm sorry, and I know it's distressing, but do you have any idea what he might have fixed his mind on?"

"None whatsoever," she answered.

7:30PM

The evening shadows of early spring were long by the time I arrived at the Le Contes' house, the last on a leafy cul-de-sac lined with large properties that wound its way up a hill towards the woodlands at the back of the Manor Free school. 'Stapledon Wood', I saw it was called on my ordnance map.

Now, where had I heard that name before?

I tried to recall as my car made a crunching sound on the pebble-covered drive. I parked, next to a sign that said 'No hawkers or canvassers', and surveyed the house. This was certainly a place of privilege, a fine white 'stucco-fronted' mansion boasting the name 'Kingswood House' (as a stone plaque in the boundary wall next to a small lodge stated). Next to this lodge, imposing stone gateposts opened up to a wide drive flanked by neatly tended lawns, one of which was being cut in precise stripes by a man in a black beret astride a sit-down lawn mower. Beyond these lawns were thickets of rhododendrons, under which grew numerous clumps of daffodils, whilst in a far corner a bonfire smouldered, its smell lightly scenting the evening air. And behind the bushes, on all sides but the road, were the trees of Stapledon Wood, the rustling of their leaves in the breeze just audible over the buzz of the mower, the shape of their canopy darkly framing the house in the twilight.

I was so fixed on this scene that I only noticed the police car parked next to me when raised voices caught my attention. I looked towards the house to see three uniformed officers talking to a man and woman by the front door. Two of the officers then turned back to their car, one leaning in through the door and talking quickly into a radio handset. A few moments later, there was a sound of voices and dog barks, as a number of uniformed officers, some with dogs, some carrying poles (to beat the undergrowth, I assumed), came through the front gates. Not long afterwards two police vans arrived, and the officers and dogs climbed aboard. A WPC stayed with the couple by the front door, the two vans and the panda car driving off. The whole operation of loading men and dogs took less than a minute, the sound of the vehicles' engines already fading as I walked over to the front door.

"I'm sorry, no salesmen, and you'll not get your foot in the door by impressing us with that, that..." sobbed the woman, her face stained with mascara and tears. "That vulgar car. Didn't you see the sign?"

"I'm Sangster, with the education department. Sorry to be here at such a difficult moment, but the secretary at the Manor Free said she would let you know I was coming. My card."

"Ah yes, someone did call from the school," said her husband, breathing heavily. "And your colleague is already inside." Mrs Hart, I presumed. "But this is a very difficult time for us, so please, not too long." He held out his hand. "I'm Reg, this is my wife Marcelle."

"Jack Sangster," I said as we shook.

"To be honest, Jack, we are at our wits' end."

"I'll be as brief as possible."

"Come into the house then." He beckoned me over the threshold, the WPC, who didn't introduce herself by name, waiting by the front door. "Please go through to the kitchen, we just need to talk with the officer here." I walked on through the hall as requested, past a fireplace and mantlepiece on which stood a framed photograph, a family scene, the Le Contes standing on some sandstone rocks with the sea in the background, from the previous summer, judging by the weather and their clothing. There were the parents, two girls, one perhaps sixteen, the other perhaps a year younger, and a boy, tall for his age, as far as I could gauge, with blond hair and a broad smile. Michael, I see you now, I thought. But where are you?

I walked on, past a door, slightly ajar, through which a billiard table could be glimpsed, explaining the comment on Michael's report about his talent for snooker. The last door, at the end of the hall, led into the kitchen, where I found a woman with short dark hair sitting at the end of a long refectory table.

"Mr Sangster?"

"Mrs Hart?"

"Janice, please."

"Jack."

"Hello, Jack, this is a super kitchen." She looked admiringly around the room, with its rows of oak cupboards, racks hanging utensils of every shape and size, dressers decked with willow-pattern china, and shelves with pottery and glass storage jars of different sizes, all carefully arranged to look haphazard but to my eye each exactly placed to give the intended rustic 'lived-in' effect. There was even a row of bells hanging over the door to the scullery, each well-polished and with a room name under it ('Morning Room', 'Billiard Room', 'Dining Room', 'Drawing Room', 'East Wing Bedroom One', and so on), presumably a relic from the days when the house ran a large staff, now redundant but preserved, perhaps to remind of times past. This was the kitchen of not only a wealthy family but a deliberate family, one that planned every detail in order to make a comfortable home, a happy home. Not the home of a family that would drive its only son to truancy, or worse.

"Phew, this must be bigger than my lounge and dining room put together." Janice whistled. "And look at that lovely range. I do think an Aga makes a kitchen, don't you?"

"Er, yes, I suppose so," I answered. "But there's a boy missing."

"Of course," she said, reddening. "This is a terrible time, isn't it?"

51

"It most certainly is," I replied as quietly as I could, the distraught voices of Michael's parents and the soothing tones of the WPC resonating through the doorway from the nearby hall, where I could see the three still standing by the front door.

"I am sorry, with dusk drawing in we're going to have to call off the search of the denser woodlands until first light," I heard the policewoman say, before carrying on with what sounded like a rehearsed checklist. "But we're continuing with sweeps of the more open common land over towards the school and down to the town, and there'll be ongoing street checks by officers in cars and on the beat." She coughed nervously then continued. "Plus, officers have been doing house-to-house, and we've notified all the usual institutions."

"What's that, Officer?" asked Reg. "Institutions?"

"Oh, you know, hospitals and so on, it's standard procedure in a case like this."

"Ah yes, one of the other officers mentioned hospitals this morning," he said, nodding very deliberately in an effort to control his emotion.

"You can't call it off," shouted Michael's mother. "You can't, my boy's out there somewhere, it's going dark, I—"

"Please, Mrs Le Conte, we're doing everything we can."

"But he's only twelve."

"Come along," the policewoman soothed. "Our people are very thorough, so something may turn up at any time, and I'll stay with you for as long as you like. I'll just need to call the station for a lift when I need to go, and I could—" Marcelle interrupted with a loud sob. "I could make you a cup of tea if you'd show me where everything is," the officer continued, putting her arm around Mrs Le Conte's waist and walking her gently back into the kitchen.

I watched Michael's father, his face ashen, make a fumbling attempt to lead the way, then fall behind the two of them and stare at the floor, stock-still. Here, I thought, was a man used to being in control, to protecting his family, but now paralysed with anxiety.

"I thought someone, well, you know, might have called with some sort of ransom demand by now," he said, wild-eyed, without addressing anyone particular in the room. "Is there nothing more any of us can do?"

Listening to his tone, I felt the man to have given up hope. For myself, with everything I had heard that day, from Wilkins, the other boys and Mrs Magister, there seemed at least a glimmer of hope. It was simply too much of a coincidence that Michael had disappeared right now.

"I'm sure everything is being done by the police," I said. "But perhaps we could try to think of anything that might have been missed. What do you think, Reg?"

"We've told the police everything, I'm sure," he answered. "That Inspector Cooper asked us the same questions over and over again. In fact," said Michael's father, his teeth now gritted and banging his fist down, "I got the impression he thought we might have something to do with it."

"Don't take on so, Reg," sobbed his wife from the end of the table, where she had sat down between the WPC and Mrs Hart, both of whom had their arms around her shoulders. "I'm sure the police are just doing their job."

"But I can't believe the effrontery of the man," shouted Reg. "I should tell the chief constable, I mean, suspecting us, the parents, it's—"

"I know," I said as softly as I could, "that you've given lots of statements, but could you go over what happened since you last saw Michael?"

"As we told the police," answered Reg, his voice quiet again, "Michael was last seen around one o'clock on Sunday afternoon."

"Did he say where he was going?"

"To the town, he said, down past the school. Cyril was standing by the gatehouse and saw him walk down the road in that direction."

"Cyril?"

"Gardner and handyman. And when Michael didn't come home in the evening, we phoned the police."

"Did he have money with him?"

"Don't think so. Marcelle?"

"No, Reg, I'm pretty sure Michael wouldn't have had any cash.

I've kept the housekeeping purse locked up ever since we caught him stealing, remember?"

"Even if he did have money, it's standard procedure to check with the drivers on local bus and train routes," said the WPC. "So we'd know if he'd gone far. And we're appealing for witnesses who might have seen him talking to someone or getting into a car, but so far no luck."

"So," I said carefully, "most likely Michael sneaked off somewhere else instead of the town. Is there anywhere particular he might go, Reg?"

"We've told the police all the places we could think of." As he spoke there was a knock on the back door. "Is that you, Cyril?" The door opened slightly, and a bereted head appeared that I recognised as that of the lawn mower rider.

"Lawn's all done. I'll be knocking off now if there's nothing else."

"That's fine, Cyril."

"Oh, Mr Le Conte, any news on the lad?"

"Not yet, Cyril."

"Oh dear," said Cyril, shaking his head, then clearing his throat. "Ahem… and it's probably the wrong time, like, but I'd better let you know I found more of them crows."

"Where this time?" asked Reg, a shadow passing over his already strained face.

"Hung up on that big oak, the one by that old signpost on the path behind the back gate. Rotting there quite a few days, I'd reckon. Chucked 'em on the bonfire."

"Were they the same?" sighed Reg. "Enormous birds with grey, white and black feathers, like the others?"

"Aye, they were," said Cyril. "Shouldn't we report this, it happening so many times and all?"

"Not sure who I'm supposed to tell, but thanks."

"Wish I could afford a gardener," I said to Reg. "Although I imagine Cyril only does the gardening work, and you still have to get all the materials for the garden yourself?"

"No, as you ask," said Reg, looking slightly surprised by my question. "Cyril takes care of all that. I give him a budget and leave him to it. Does a sterling job." Cyril nodded with appreciation, said his goodbyes and the back door was closed again. The slamming sound had a finality about it, as if there was nothing more to be done that night, perhaps nothing more to be done at all.

Mrs Hart responded by looking at me and jerking her head towards the door. I prepared to stand up, wish the Le Contes well and then leave, but the same glimmer of hope I'd felt earlier made me think twice.

"I spoke to Mrs Magister at Saint Hildeburgh's today by the way."

"Ah yes," said Michael's mother. "We're very grateful for the help she's given Michael, especially this year." I felt a jolt at the words 'this year', realising the headmistress had lied about last seeing Michael the previous year.

"She, er... how did she help this year?" I eventually said, trying to hide my surprise.

"Oh, she encouraged Michael with his English. Lessons in the evening, every Tuesday, right up until last week."

"Yes," said Reg with a rueful laugh. "At least we know he didn't truant for those lessons."

"His schoolwork had been suffering since he went to the Manor Free," continued Marcelle. "But he's always been good at English."

"English?"

"Yes. Very keen on any writings about medieval stuff, magical lands, mythology and all that. And he seemed to like working with Mrs Magister, so we arranged the extra English tuition with her."

"Tolkien?" I asked, remembering the boys mentioning Michael joining their society.

"Yes, his favourite. I think his sisters bought him *The Lord of the Rings* a couple of birthdays ago."

Mrs Hart continue to gesture towards the door, but I needed to find out more.

"Michael has two sisters, doesn't he?"

"Yes, Claudia and Flavia. They're up in their rooms now. Both very upset."

"I'm sure, but would it be possible to speak to them? Just briefly."

"I don't see any harm."

Reg left the room, returning a minute or so later with the two girls. They both wore similar pairs of pyjamas and had their blonde hair in plaits. Their faces looked strained, so I determined to be as gentle as I could, introducing myself and Mrs Hart, explaining why we were there and that we would only take a minute of their time.

"Is there anything you can think of that might make Michael run away?" I then asked.

"Don't be ridiculous, the boy's perfectly—"

"No, Reg, let the girls answer," interrupted his wife. The girls both shook their heads.

"Has Michael changed at all?" asked Mrs Hart. "In recent weeks, say."

"Well," said Claudia, the elder of the two, "he has been a bit weird since, oh, I don't know, when do you think, Sis?"

"He's always been weird," Flavia replied.

"Yeah, but really weird. Might be the beginning of this half term."

"That would be the middle of February?" I asked.

"Yes," said the younger girl. "I know 'cos it was on Valentine's Day. Remember, Claudia?"

"What was?" the elder girl asked.

"When he went out into the woods, got obsessed with shooting all those crows, with his air gun, oh—"

"What's that, young lady?" shouted Reg. "Crows?" The girl burst into tears and placed her head face down on the table, Reg then pulling her up by the shoulders and staring into her streaming eyes. "Flavia, you say Michael shot the crows, the ones Cyril found hanging from the trees."

"I wasn't supposed to tell, Daddy," she sobbed. "He said he had to do it. To keep us safe."

"Safe?"

"Yes, he said he has to keep us safe so that he can stop something very bad happening."

"Oh," cried Marcelle. "How could our boy do something so brutal?"

"I'll give him brutal," said Reg. "I'll…" His voice trailed off and he released the girl's shoulders. "I'm sorry," he said softly to her, but she recoiled from him, eyes cast downwards.

"And Flavia, did Michael say why shooting the crows would keep him safe?" I asked, but she shook her head. "And did Michael tell you what the something bad was he had to stop?"

The girl said nothing, and Mrs Hart jerked her head towards the door again, this time very emphatically. I also felt it now really was time to leave.

"Michael's grandmother?" I asked as I stood up, noticing a portrait hanging on the wall by the door, showing (if the artist knew his craft, which I wondered given he had painted one eye blue and the other green) an aloof and humourless grey-haired woman of perhaps fifty, wearing a white blouse with a broad lace collar. 'Alita Bartholomew' was written in faded gold script on the bottom of the oval ebony frame.

"No, much older," said Marcelle. "That's Great-Granny Bart, my mother's grandmother."

"And we keep her hidden in the kitchen, Jack." Reg laughed, seeming to have temporarily forgotten Michael's disappearance. "The old bat was hauled up in court, for witchcraft no less."

"Witchcraft?"

"Oh yes, she was accused at Chester Assizes of pretending to communicate with the spirit world to extort money out of grieving relatives when their loved ones passed on. Refused an advocate, saying she was a chosen one."

"Reg, how can you say such things at a time like this?" said Marcelle, bursting into tears. "And Granny Bart protested her innocence until the day she died. Always claimed she had real second sight, a gift passed on through the generations."

"Didn't get handed down to you, Marcelle, or your mother, or even her mother as far as I remember."

"Well, Mother told me it can skip generations, but, Reg, please, not now."

"Oh… er, yes, sorry…" Reg whispered, his face dropping as his mind returned to the reality of his lost son.

"Michael was a talented artist," I said in an attempt to ease the tension, pointing at two sketches pinned to a cupboard door (and suddenly realising I had used the past tense). "He really is," I added quickly. The first sketch showed several coloured flowers, which on closer inspection could be seen to be floating, the water's surface reflecting the plants in what seemed to me an almost dreamlike way. A single word, 'Nellifers', was written underneath.

"Another name for water lilies, Jack," said Marcelle, presumably seeing the puzzled look on my face. "They grow in our garden pond."

"Very Monet, and Michael really is talented," I repeated, the flowers now almost moving in front of me. What sort of twelve-year-old could draw like this? My eyes wandered to the second sketch, another pastel drawing, this time of a large rocky outcrop surrounded by trees. It must have been drawn at dusk, as Michael had cleverly used shading to produce the dappling effect of evening shafts of sunlight penetrating the leaves and branches. Michael's name and a class number were printed at the bottom.

"Yes," said Reg. "And he won a prize for that one, it's—"

"Reg," said his wife in a sharp voice. "Did you mention the Face Stone?"

"What?"

"To the police. Did you mention the Face Stone?"

"My goodness, no."

"The Face Stone?" I asked.

"Yes," answered Reg, still gasping. "It's the rock in that picture, a place in the woods Michael likes. He's spent all day there sketching sometimes, and it's in entirely the opposite direction to the town and the school, over a mile away from here and hard to find. Officer," Le Conte shouted at the WPC, "we've maybe sent your search party the wrong way. Can you call them back?"

"I'm sorry, sir," she said, flinching at his voice. "No radio. But I can telephone the central switchboard." She walked over to a phone on the kitchen wall and began to dial, but Le Conte, now frantic, ignored her.

"Then we're wasting valuable time. Jack, would you come with me now?" I winced as he spoke, feeling the search to be pointless (wouldn't the dogs have picked up any scent leading to this Face Stone place?), but seeing the renewed hope in his eyes, I nodded all the same. "If that's alright, Marcelle?" Reg added.

"Yes, yes, Reg. I'll have the officer here with me, and Mrs Hart and the girls are here as well. Now go, please, and I pray... bring our boy back."

"Come on, Jack, there's a back gate to the woods we can use." The distraught father grabbed two torches from a cupboard and dashed out of the back door then round the side of the house, I following as best I could. Soon we were in Stapledon Wood, running down a winding path through thick trees and newly grown bracken stems that made visibility beyond a few yards in what little light remained near impossible. The ground was uneven, with unexpected dips and stones protruding from the clay soil making for even more difficult going underfoot, so that I struggled, my runner's knee causing me to almost stumble more than once. Undergrowth, ground and twilight combined with my already anxious state to make the journey disorienting, almost nightmarish, and we continued this way for about fifteen minutes, before our small path eventually joined a larger one, Le Conte shouting over his shoulder that we were close now. Then I lost him, until I turned a corner and saw the man standing breathless, hands on knees, underneath a massive sandstone outcrop.

"This is it?" I panted, trying to catch my own breath.

"Yes, this is the Face Stone. Now, look around. If Michael came here, he may still be close by. Look in the bracken, you go left." He began shouting Michael's name as he ran around to the other side of the rock, and I craned my head sideways as I walked, trying to peer through the vegetation. This carried on for about ten minutes, with both of us calling out and crashing through the woods around the stone, until we met again, still breathless.

"I'm afraid—"

"No, Jack, we must keep looking," Reg gasped. "You go back that way and I'll look further over here." He then disappeared behind the rock, his voice echoing through the trees as he cried out for his son.

For my part I still felt the search to be futile, but for Reg's sake I couldn't stop now so carried on beating my way through the undergrowth, coming to a line of birch trees and beyond these a small clearing thick with the dead brown stems of last year's bracken growth. I sensed an odour in the air, stronger than the general scent of the trees and bracken, a sweet and sickly smell that distracted me for a moment, and then, protruding from the carpet of dead vegetation, I saw it.

A shoe, definitely a shoe, and yes, a leg. And beyond that a whole body, lying face down, a rucksack still strapped on its back.

"Reg, come quickly, I've found him." In the excitement it took a few seconds for my mind to register that the body was still, perhaps even lifeless. I realised, just as Reg came crashing through the bracken, that this might be a tragedy unfolding in front of us. He saw the boy and ran to him.

"Oh my God, oh my God, oh my God, my son, my son," he sobbed, then fell to his knees, touching the boy's head and letting out a shriek that I shall never forget, a long wail that echoed despair through the wood. Then the wailing stopped.

"He's alive, Michael's alive," he screeched at me. At this the boy, now lying on his back, head cradled in his father's arms, opened his eyes, wiped his mouth (which seemed to have a dark stain around it), then muttered something unintelligible before lapsing into unconsciousness again.

"Shall I go back for help?" I asked, but Reg shook his head, so we sat in silence, for what might have been twenty minutes. Then came the sound of voices and dogs barking, followed by a line of police. Michael was placed on a stretcher and carried back to the house, where a police doctor pronounced him in shock but unharmed. And as we left the clearing, which was entirely surrounded by silver birch trees rather than the oaks and beeches that made up most of the rest of the wood,

I couldn't help noticing the red and white spotted toadstools that grew in a ring around the edge, their vivid colours still visible in the rapidly fading twilight. I bent down close to a cluster of the fungi and sniffed, coughing as I realised these were the source of the strangely sweet odour. For some reason, gut instinct, perhaps, I picked one, placed it into the paper bag that had contained my cheese roll from the Canteen, then slipped this rather odd package into my pocket.

*

"Well, Jack, that's an evening I won't forget in a hurry," said Mrs Hart as I drove her home (she had come by bus).

"Me neither." I laughed. "But all's well that ends well, eh?"

"Cliched but true." She laughed back. "It was such a joy to see the look of relief on Mrs Le Conte's face when they brought Michael back to the house. And when that police doctor gave him the okay. A bit dehydrated but otherwise good, he said."

"It was a joy, and apparently the boy was lucky we had such a mild night yesterday. Doctor reckoned he could have been unconscious for up to forty-eight hours, might have frozen to death."

"Did that doctor say what knocked him out, Jack?"

"I don't think he knew. Kept talking about a possible rapid drop in blood pressure, but he was clutching at straws, recommending further tests. Just wanted to give Michael the all-clear then get on home, I suspect."

After driving for a few minutes in silence, I asked, "What do you think of the Manor Free, Janice?"

"What, as a school?"

"Anything, really."

"Good academically, marvellous facilities, beautiful setting down near the sea, but elitist, I suppose, and a bit of a law unto itself."

"Johnson used those very words, 'law unto itself.'"

"Well, I say marvellous facilities," she went on, stressing the word 'say'.

"Looks pretty good to me."

"It's that Bolshaw House." She sniffed with contempt. "Place should be condemned. I'm on the case at the moment, in fact. Have you seen it?"

"Only from a distance."

"Well," she said, voice raised, "apart from anything else there's a rabbit warren of cellars underneath it that flood after heavy rain. I have the original old plans, and I think there may even be bricked-up cellars full of water we don't know about. Rising damp is a health risk." I recalled Paul Rylance mentioning the boys who boarded always being sick. "Place needs refurbishing, or better still knocking down. And there has been a grant made available, but whenever I try to talk to the school, I get no cooperation from Wilkins."

"Really?"

"Man's avoiding me," she added.

I now guessed why the headmaster had circumvented Mrs Hart that morning, pretending he thought she was sick and going direct to head office in Chester. Ironic, given his disapproval of Michael using the same excuse when truanting, but surely nothing more sinister than that.

"By the way," asked Janice, "what were you discussing with the parents just before we left?"

"I arranged to visit the Le Contes again tomorrow evening, to talk to Michael. Can you come, seven o'clock?" She exhaled with a slight moan, then went silent. "Is that a problem, Janice?" I eventually asked. "I'd hoped to interview the boy without the parents, and it would be best if I had a witness."

"I would if I could, but it's Geoffrey's darts night on Wednesdays, you see, and he doesn't like to miss it."

"You play as well, do you?"

"Oh no, I'll be staying in with the children," she said, with what sounded to me like despondent resignation. For myself, I felt frustration with her, then compunction. Not everyone had the luxury of being able to work odd hours. In fact, I thought, Sarah might say that I didn't either. "Perhaps we can postpone?" Janice added.

"Well, the police emergency may be over," I said, "but I'm no nearer to closing my original case, and I'd like to try and get to the bottom of things quickly. Apart from anything else, we must find out what he's been doing, where he's been going all this time. Can't have been outside much during February and March." She nodded. "I'll keep you and Director Johnson informed, of course."

"Do clear with him first that you intend to be alone with the boy." I nodded my agreement to what sounded like sensible advice but decided not to mention the reason I was in such a hurry. The events of the day were coming together in my mind like the pieces of a jigsaw, still only partially complete but already forming a picture. And although I couldn't have properly explained why, my overwhelming sense was that Michael, despite having been found alive and well, was determined to do something that would place him in the gravest danger.

*

About twenty minutes after leaving the Le Contes, we found ourselves driving slowly down a crescent-shaped street of modern semi-detached houses, in a far more modest (and less surreal, I felt, after the evening's events) neighbourhood than the Le Contes'.

"This is my house, number twenty-four, on the right with the rose bushes behind the wall." I pulled to a halt and she stepped out of the car. "Thanks for the lift, Jack, and good luck tomorrow with Michael."

"You're very welcome, Janice. That wasn't an easy evening, so it was good to have you there. Thanks."

"Oh, and I don't think your car is at all vulgar, Jack."

"I should hope not, Janice."

"Mrs Le Conte, I overheard her when you arrived. She said it was—"

"Ah, vulgar." I remembered Mrs Le Conte's comment. "You like cars?"

"Oh yes." Janice paused and stroked the side of the bonnet. "This is a beautiful car," she continued, in a soft, almost dreamlike register. "I could imagine riding in it through… in… yes, in Paris, with the hood down, in springtime. Lovely colour as well."

"Your husband, er—"

"Geoffrey."

"Yes, of course, Geoffrey. What does he drive?"

"Goodnight, Jack." She walked across the road to her gate before looking back towards me.

"Austin Eleven Hundred," she called over her shoulder. "Lime green."

SPY WEDNESDAY
9AM

"Can you pass the milk, please?" I asked, pouring a bowl of cornflakes.

The milk jug was placed silently in front of me.

"Thanks." More silence. "Look, Sarah, I'm sorry about last night."

"Did you really have to come back so late?" she said after a further pause. "I stayed up until eleven thirty."

"Things happened, one thing after another. When I finally got home it was past midnight. I didn't want to wake you."

"You could have called." She sniffed, looking away from me to try and hide her tears. "I went to bed worried."

"I'm sorry." I walked around the kitchen table and put my arm across her shoulders.

"I... I just don't feel part of all this," she sobbed. "When we married, you had your job with the oil company. I accepted it might take a lot of your time, but this thing with the Institute, it seems like, well..." She wiped her eyes and then stared up at me. "Like more than a job, as if it matters more than me."

"Of course it doesn't, I just—"

"I want to be part of it all, Jack, I want to help," she murmured, and

I continued to stand with my arm around her, neither of us speaking for a time.

"Okay," I eventually said, unable to bear the silence any longer. "Have you any lectures this morning?"

"No."

"Right, let's leave this lot then." I pointed to my half-eaten bowl of cornflakes and our teacups. "It's a lovely day, so I say we walk up to that cafe by the cathedral and I tell you all about it, over a proper cup of coffee, and if we want to be really naughty…"

"Yes, darling?"

"Maybe a toasted teacake as well."

"You're such a romantic, Jack," she whispered, leaning up and kissing me on the cheek.

*

"Did you know they call today Spy Wednesday?" Sarah asked me as we sat by the window in the Cloisters Cafe.

"Mmmm?" I mumbled, mouth full of teacake.

"You know, like Good Friday."

"Oh, why's that?"

"You've got a bit of butter, just there, darling." She looked at one side of my face.

"Would you?" I mumbled, still chewing.

"Because," she continued, leaning over and removing the offending butter from my cheek with her napkin, "the word 'spy' meant something more like 'ambush' years ago. Spy Wednesday was the day when Judas Iscariot was supposed to have agreed his deal to betray Jesus."

"My goodness, you know an awful lot, Sarah," I said, wanting to take any opportunity to show my appreciation after the upset at the breakfast table.

"Oh, Jack." She blushed, the obviousness of my flattery seemingly going unnoticed. "It's what I lecture in, what I studied, what I still study."

"No, you really do know your stuff," I told her, remembering a time in Jerusalem when we barely knew each other, when Sarah had first amazed me with her knowledge. "It was something I liked about you when we first met."

"You said it was my legs."

"They were the two other things I liked about you." I laughed. "But," I added, pointing out of the window towards the ancient building across the street, "I mean, how many of the people who've frequented that place over the centuries would know about something like Spy Wednesday?"

"Well, they're C of E and not exactly my brand of faith, so I couldn't say, but it's likely the whole crucifixion thing was anyway engineered by Jesus, you know, coming to Jerusalem on Palm Sunday with a big fanfare and making sure one of his disciples gave him away. The days of the Easter week are like a countdown to the big event. Jesus wanted it to happen so he could... excuse me?" She broke off to ask a passing waitress for two more coffees.

"Now then, I've waited long enough." Her manner told me (to my private relief) that I wasn't going to find out what Jesus did to engineer his own demise, at least not today. "You promised to tell me all about yesterday."

"Very well, Sarah. This is how my day started..." I explained how Johnson had dropped the Le Conte case on my desk out of the blue, my trip to the Manor Free school, the strange little 'Canteen' post office and its even stranger proprietors, the disdain of the police inspector, speaking to Sir John, visiting the Saint Hildeburgh's, and then my time at the Le Contes' house and finding the boy unconscious in the woods (I omitted the part where I dropped off Mrs Hart and added another three quarters of an hour to my drive home). "And that is how my day ended, Sarah, happily, I'm glad to say, but with more questions than answers, far more."

"Those two boys you mentioned, that disappeared last week. Are they from the same school?"

"No, local grammar school."

"That place they were last seen, by the marshes, we've been there, haven't we?"

"Yes."

"Well, it reminds me of a poem, in fact…" She scratched her head. "Yes, it was, it was written by a canon attached to the cathedral here."

"Which poem?"

"'O Mary, go and call the cattle home, call the cattle home, call the cattle home, across the sands o' Dee'…" She recited several verses, telling the story of a young girl who had wandered across the marshes and been caught by the tide, and of the fishermen who, discovering their nets had entangled her drowned body, still sometimes heard Mary's ghost calling the cattle home. "'And never home came she,'" Sarah said after the last verse, repeating one of the lines. "I wonder if those poor boys will come home?"

"Hope so, but it's in the hands of the police. It's this case with Michael Le Conte that's on my mind."

"Sorry, you just made me think of Mary and her cattle. Anyway," said Sarah, now leaning across the table so that her nose was almost pressed against mine, then leaning back again as the waitress arrived with our coffees, "did you talk to Michael yet?"

"Friends, teachers, parents, yes, but I haven't spoken to the boy himself. He was in no state to talk. I'll see him this evening, though, providing he's well enough."

"Was there any sign of a struggle, Jack?"

"What, with the boy? No. Doctor said he was unharmed, at least physically."

"Young boy missing, you always wonder."

"Nothing like that, Sarah."

"Thank goodness, but what could possibly have knocked him out for a day?"

"Doctor had a few theories but no firm idea as yet. I did find this next to where Michael lay though." I pulled out a crumpled paper ball from my pocket and unwrapped the red and white toadstool I'd picked in Stapledon Wood. Almost immediately, I sensed the sweet aroma I'd smelt in the woods.

"Ugh, don't touch it," cried Sarah, drawing away and grimacing. "D'you think the boy had been poisoned?"

"It's one explanation." I wrapped up the fungus again. "There were lots of these things growing near to where we found him."

"Weird."

"Sarah, that's a word I heard over and over again yesterday, whenever anybody mentioned Michael."

"That headmistress, the psychologist."

"Yes?"

"Weird sounds like the right word for her as well, darling."

"Definitely, and she wasn't telling me everything."

"How do you mean?" Sarah asked, making me remember I hadn't mentioned that Mrs Magister chose not to tell me she had been giving Michael regular private lessons, right up to and even during the time when he had been truanting from school. "Bit of side to the woman," said Sarah when I finished explaining.

"Yes, more than a bit," I said, sipping my coffee and realising I did actually feel better for having shared things. "I'll go back and see her once I've spoken to Michael." I also realised something Sarah had said might possibly have a bearing on the case. "You talked about a countdown."

"Sorry, darling?"

"The days of the week before Easter, with their funny names. A countdown to the big event, that's what you said."

"That's how I think of Holy Week, with its—" I raised my hand in a stopping motion. "What, Jack?"

"Hmmm." I rubbed my chin. "Just that..." I struggled to articulate my thoughts. "No, it's nothing."

"Tell me, please."

"Well, Michael's friends seemed to think he is working up to something, a proverbial 'big event', if you like." I thought further. "And Mrs Magister hinted that Michael might be fixated on something he felt he had to do."

"Yes, yes," said Sarah excitedly. "And that younger sister, er... Florence?"

"Flavia."

"Well, you say she thought Michael wanted to stop something bad happening."

"Shooting all those crows, though, Sarah?" I shuddered. "The boy's clearly cruel, perhaps even deranged."

"And you think he might be gearing up to do something far worse?"

"Don't let's think that." I shuddered again. "We'd be getting carried away by gut instincts without any facts to back them up." I lifted my cup to drink the last of the coffee, then spat out the dregs. "Phwrrr... coffee grounds." Sarah leaned over and wiped my lip. "Thanks, and if you want to hear something else weird," I laughed, "try this."

"Try what?"

"The boy's great-grandmother was tried for witchcraft."

"Surely not?"

"Apparently so. Makes you wonder what other influences there are on that boy."

"Is he intelligent, imaginative?"

"Yes, very, but also a known liar. Perhaps even a fantasist."

"So have you thought that he may genuinely believe all this?"

"What makes you say that?"

"Well, I'm not completely sure, and bear with me on this..." Sarah then told me about a case study she once worked on, of a teenage girl who was convinced she had lived a past life. She knew every detail of her previous incarnation, a serving wench from the sixteenth century. There was no explanation until a hitherto unknown published account of this wench's life came to light. It had an error on a key date, a typo, and the girl had made exactly the same mistake. Clearly it was more than coincidental, and she had somehow or other seen the account and memorised it, albeit probably subconsciously.

"So, you see, Jack, anything's possible."

"I'm sure, but I don't just want to go on instincts here."

"You told me once that instincts are everything."

"I didn't quite mean it like that," I said, trying to sound rational but unable to supress thoughts generated by the instinct currently

70

raging in my mind that something about the Le Conte case was very wrong.

"It's likely Michael's just a badly adjusted child who somehow managed to go missing and upset everyone around him, including the police. Now, come on, we need to go home via the office. I have to report to Johnson, it won't take long."

*

"I can hear singing, darling," Sarah said to me as we emerged from the cafe into the sunlight. "Come on, let's cross the road and listen through the door."

We walked over the narrow street that wound in an S-shape past the cathedral and then up to its main entrance, a grand archway ('that's a depressed archway darling, mid to late gothic') below high stained-glass windows and guarded by twin octagonal turreted towers. I had passed the place many times before but never really taken much notice. Now I could see that the entrance was made (as was the rest of the building) in red sandstone, a little soot-stained but otherwise identical to the stone I'd seen in the older parts of the Manor Free school.

"They must be practising for Sunday, isn't it beautiful?" Sarah whispered, as through the cathedral's massive wooden doors, which were thrown open wide, came the sound of choral music, mostly boy sopranos as far as I could tell.

"Mmmm. Do you know what it is?"

"Handel's *Messiah*. This was the first place they performed it, and did you know..." Sarah's voice was suddenly drowned out as, all at once, a car exhaust backfired and a raucous cawing sound echoed around the street. I looked up to see a turreted parapet on the top of the cathedral lined with black crows. More of the birds perched on the two guard towers, and several even stood on the broad stone steps leading up to the doors. After a few seconds the singing stopped abruptly, but the crows continued their cawing until the cathedral doors were pushed shut (giving the odd impression of moving by themselves, but presumably by people using handles on the inside). The crashing of oak-on-oak slamming together seemed to alarm the birds, which flew off all at once, their numbers sufficient to momentarily cast a shadow over the cathedral. The crows were still cawing as they went, eventually flying out of earshot and leaving us in silence, until the faint sound of the choir resumed, lilting again through the stained-glass windows.

"Do you know what they call a group of crows?" Sarah asked me, almost dreamily.

"Sorry?"

"The collective noun for crows, darling, you know, like a pride of lions or a flock of sheep."

"No, Sarah, I don't."

"A 'murder' of crows, that's what they call them."

Somehow the epithet seemed apt, and I was about to tell her when I felt a clap on my back.

"Jack, have you joined the flock?" I turned around to see the smiling face of Sam Youd, a long-time friend, confidant and by day the senior veterinary officer at Chester Zoo. "I'm sure the Bishop would be pleased to have you. Cynical old heathens like Jack Sangster converting to God probably earn him double Green Shield Stamps in Heaven."

"Less of the old." I laughed. "And don't worry, we're just walking up the road to the office, not Damascus."

"Morning, Sarah," said Sam, with an appraising look at my wife. "You look prettier than last time I saw you." He winked. "If that's possible."

"Oh, Sam, what are you doing in town?"

"What, apart from wondering why a young, intelligent beauty like you hangs around with this old fart?"

"If you're wondering why?" she replied, putting her arm around my waist and looking up at me. "It's because I can't imagine life if I didn't hang around with him."

As she spoke, I looked down at Sarah. Did I deserve her?

"So, Sam?" Sarah then asked, apparently oblivious to my emotions.

"Had to deliver some specimens, you know. To the lab."

"Specimens, Sam?"

"Pickled Humboldt's Squid, to be precise, they have nasty little beaks and they—"

"Um… thanks, Sam." I could see Sarah gulp when he said 'pickled'. "How's Sandra?"

"Oh, she's on good form, busy as ever. And you know, the wife was saying the other day it would be nice if you two could come over to the house. Perhaps," he said, scratching his head, "let me see, yes… how about Friday evening for a bite of supper?"

"Out of the question, I'm afraid," Sarah answered quickly, after which I then mouthed 'out of the question' to Sam with a smile. "I'm off to York tomorrow, visiting my sister. Jack's staying in Chester, though. Work."

"Ah, work, I see. Then, Jack, Miller of Dee on Friday evening, perhaps?"

"Pub sounds good, Sam," I said. "But I've got an odd case going on right now, so can I call you when I know for certain?"

"Of course, and I'm sure Sandra will let me off the leash. After all, it is going to be Good Friday. By the way, that really was a racket those crows made, wasn't it?"

"Horrible," said Sarah.

"It's been a funny year for them, in fact…" Sam became thoughtful for a moment. "There was a count at the zoo."

"You haven't got any crows at the zoo," I blurted out, before I realised he was talking about the zoo's work with local wildlife.

"Clever, isn't he, Sarah?"

"Ha, ha," I said. "But those crows did make a racket."

"What I was going to say, was that this year, the bird people have seen a lot more than usual."

"And who are the bird people?" I asked.

"Oh, ornithologists. Professionals, though. They specialise in tropical species most of the time."

"So there's been a proliferation of vultures in Cheshire?" Sarah laughed.

"No, the zoo works with native birds as well," sighed Sam, and for no reason other than the tone of his sigh, which almost exactly echoed that of Reginald Le Conte, I was suddenly transported back to the previous evening and Cyril telling us how he had found the dead birds hanging from a tree.

"Sam, those crows on the cathedral roof were all black, but tell me something."

"Yes, Jack?"

"Grey, white and black-coloured crows, bigger than those, are they to be found around here?"

"You have seen them yourself?"

"No, I was told about them."

"Then whoever said that was mistaken. You see, those birds we saw fly from the cathedral just now were common crows, and they have black feathers. For grey, white and black plumage you need hooded crows and they, well…"

"Sam?"

"They, er… simply don't live here. Scotland, Ireland, even the Isle of Man, but not in Cheshire. You'd maybe find jackdaws here, but they're much smaller."

"Could they migrate?"

"If you could bring me a carcass, I'd be able to answer that."

"Burned on a bonfire, I'm afraid."

"In that case we'll never know."

"Sorry, Sam," I said. "I won't bother you anymore. Just something to do with this current case. Anyway, all being well, see you Friday?"

"Of course," he replied, smiling, then touching Sarah's shoulder. "And as I say, Sarah, what you see in Jack is beyond me."

Waving to Sam as he went, we walked on, hand in hand past the cathedral, the street quite empty of people (school holidays weren't due to start until Good Friday) and on to Northgate Street and the non-descript three-storey office block that housed the Cheshire Department of Education.

"Did you know, darling, that this used to be called the Golden Falcon?"

"What, this office block?"

"No, before that. It was a hotel, or an inn or something. Anyway, Handel stayed at it whilst on his way to Ireland. His plan was to debut the *Messiah* in Dublin."

"Hmmm…" I was only half listening, still thinking about the crows. They bothered me, and I felt that somehow the dead birds were linked to Michael in a different way than just the gratuitous cruelty of a schoolboy.

"Well, Handel was delayed and so organised his work to be performed in the cathedral here. Hence the *Messiah* was first heard… Jack, are you listening?"

"Oh, yes, Sarah."

"Then what was I saying?"

"Sorry, Sarah, got distracted. Now, here we are," I said as we approached the director's office. "Shouldn't take longer than twenty minutes."

11AM

"Good morning, Mr Sangster, Mrs Sangster," said Miss Stephens, the director's diminutive and super-organised secretary. She was sitting typing, busy as usual behind her desk, which Johnson once confided in me was strategically positioned outside his office door to ensure nobody got in or out without her knowing ('makes for a quiet life, Sangster').

"There was a man called for you earlier."

"What, here at the office?"

"No, telephoned. An Albert Jackson, he left his number, here it is," she said, handing me a scribbled note.

"And you have meetings at the Manor Free School at three and with Mrs Hart at five thirty. You're meeting Mrs Hart at the Bell, by the way, it's a pub not far from the school. Here's the address."

"Thanks, now, is the old man accepting visitors?" I asked.

"Yes," she answered, resuming her typing furiously as she spoke. "And I think he's in a reasonable, you know…"

"Mood?" I asked with a smile.

"Yes, you can go right in." She nodded, smiling back. "And Mrs Sangster, if you would like to wait with me, here's a chair. Cup of tea?"

"Thank you," said Sarah, giving me a 'don't be too long' look as she sat down. She needn't have worried, I wasn't 'too long' at all, walking back out through the door about two minutes later.

"Come on, Sarah," I said, slamming it behind me. "We're leaving."

"Why, Jack?" She held up her teacup. "I heard shouting, but Mavis has just made me this cup of—"

"Never mind the tea," I growled, pulling her up by the arm. "We're off."

As I led Sarah away, Miss Stephens called after us, "Well, good morning."

"Is it?" I shouted before turning to the front door. Once out on the street, I walked to what felt like a reasonable distance from the office, then stopped and faced Sarah.

"Bloody cheek of the man."

"Jack, what happened?"

"Told me to back off the Le Conte case. Of all the—"

"Calm down, Jack."

"He always resented me. Right from day one."

"No, really, calm down."

"I am calm, I—"

"No, you are not," she said, stroking my cheek. "Now come on, deep breath and tell me slowly as we're walking."

I explained that Johnson had questioned why there should be any reason for me to continue investigating Michael now that the boy was safe and well. He had reiterated that he didn't approve of the Manor Free school, with its independence and elitist culture, and felt strongly that a senior investigator shouldn't be wasted on people who don't cooperate. I had retorted that I had only been sent the day before because of Wilkins' direct appeal to him for help, but his view was that Mrs Hart could handle the matter from now on.

It also seemed that Inspector Cooper had called him earlier that morning. Whilst ostensibly thanking Johnson for my assistance, Cooper made it abundantly clear that the police would tie up any loose ends and so didn't expect the department or the Institute to involve itself further. This suited Johnson, as apparently, there were several new cases pending where children might be in danger, serious cases where resources could be better spent, so I had therefore formally been reassigned to those, effective immediately. I'd argued that we were no nearer getting to the bottom of Michael's long-term truanting and that I anyway felt something to be amiss at the Manor Free. Johnson was prepared to listen for a moment when I mentioned suspicions about the school, but without evidence he had continued to insist we drop the case.

"I tried to tell him this is unfinished business, Sarah, and I'd have his evidence before long."

"I'm sure you did, darling."

"Do you know what he came back with?" She shook her head. "Well, pretty much word for word, he said, 'Perhaps it's unfinished for you, Sangster, a privately funded dilettante, but I can't allow you to indulge yourself in what's basically a hobby when we have genuine cases to chase up.' I told him I'd quit and walked out." At the word 'out', Sarah stopped walking and placed her hands on my shoulders.

"We're going back."

"What?"

"You say Johnson listened when you mentioned your suspicions?"

"Well, yes, he did. I think he wants to look under the surface of that school but doesn't know how."

"Then use that. Eat humble pie if you have to, darling, but pique his interest by letting him know you can find out more than his official people." I shrugged, but she persevered. "He'll feel guilty and you'll have more cooperation from him than before." I shrugged once more but she wasn't having any of it and grabbed my arm. "Now, no sulking, come on, let's go in again, you apologise and we get this case back on track."

Now I was the one being frog-marched, but this time back to the office, where a distraught-looking Miss Stephens was sitting with her head in her hands, her typewriter now silent. She sat up with a shocked expression at the sight of Sarah and me.

"I'm going back in to see Director Johnson," I said to her. "Don't try and stop me."

"Oh, Mr Sangster, I wouldn't advise it. He's in a terrible mood now, he, he..." By her almost hysterical tone I wondered if Johnson had been unduly unpleasant, perhaps even assaulted the woman.

"Mavis, what did he do?" coaxed Sarah.

"He asked me to make him a cup of tea."

"That's not so bad, Mavis."

"With five lumps of sugar? He never has more than two," she sobbed. "Mostly only one lump." I gulped and entered Johnson's office, muttering 'humble pie' under my breath.

*

"Apologies, Johnson," I said, walking straight over to his desk, "I was out of order just now."

The director looked up at me, his face, which was ruddy at the best of times, now flushed scarlet. He knitted his brow as I spoke, presumably deciding whether to accept the apology, then after a few seconds, stood up and held out his hand. As I shook it, he gestured to a chair, and we both sat down.

"Strawberry bon-bon, Sangster?" he asked, offering me an open packet of sweets.

"Er, no thanks." I then reached into my jacket pocket. "Are you open to bribes, Johnson?"

"Bribes?"

"Yes, I've got these." I pulled out the bag of sherbet lemons from the Canteen. "Peace offering."

"Ah," he said, peering into the top of the bag and licking his lips. "Sherbet lemons, eh? Well, in that case I'll, er... accept your bribe. Went a bit over the top myself just now." He laughed, then carefully placed the bag on his desk, next to several chocolate bars and packets of biscuits. "Got to keep the blood sugar level up. Wife claims it makes me a bit grumpy otherwise. Diabetes, did I tell you?"

"I thought that meant you had to keep off sugar."

"No, I've got the other one. Need a constant supply of glucose."

"Ah."

"Now then, Sangster. What was all that fuss about?"

"Look, I appreciate that there are more pressing cases than the Le Conte boy. You are right to prioritise, our primary responsibility is to the children, and I should let this case go. It's just that…"

"Just what?"

"Well, Johnson, yesterday was different. Something I'd never been through before. Felt like a whirlwind." I loudly drew in air through my nostrils for effect. "I suppose I became too invested in the whole thing, too close to it all. Sorry."

"Very well, Sangster," he said, his features visibly relaxing. "We all have our ups and downs. Ask Miss Stephens for the new case files and we'll say no more about this, er, blip."

"Thank you. And shall I brief Mrs Hart?"

"Please."

"Very well," I replied, and, with the humble pie having been successfully served, feeling it was time to offer Johnson a tempting dessert. "I'll explain my suspicions about the school and the headmaster's behaviour. She says she hasn't had much luck so far, but perhaps now…" I stood up to leave.

"One moment, Sangster. Could you tell me more about your suspicions?"

"Wilkins, for a start," I answered, sitting down again. "He seems paranoid about the school's reputation, doesn't want anyone to see the school's 'dirty washing', as he puts it."

"Understandable."

"Yes, Johnson, but I think it's a smokescreen. I think his real concern is to stop outside scrutiny of the school."

"Why?"

"Oh, little things he said, knowing looks with his secretary, that sort of thing."

"No, Sangster, I mean 'why', as in what's he got to hide?"

"Couldn't say for sure. Might be financial."

"What, embezzlement?"

"Possibly. Or some kind of neglect of the pupils, bad facilities."

"Private fees and state funding mean the best of everything at the Manor Free," interrupted Johnson. "Anything untoward and the parents or governors would blow the whistle, surely?"

"Well," I said, shaking my head for added effect (the 'dessert' seemingly to Johnson's taste), "there is that boarding house, it isn't—"

"Ah yes, Bolshaw House," he exclaimed before I could finish. "Mrs Hart has been compiling a report on that place. Wants it condemned. Oh, Miss Stephens?" The secretary appeared at the door. "That file of Mrs Hart's on the Manor Free, do you have it to hand?"

"Is this the one, Mr Johnson?" answered the ever-efficient secretary, handing a thick loose-leaf folder to the director only moments later. "I think you'll find pages seven, eight and eleven most interesting." This was all done so quickly that I wondered whether she had somehow predicted our conversation and got the file out in case it was asked for.

"Thank you," he said, leafing through the pages, frowning increasingly as he went. "Hmmm, Sangster, all sorts of damning stuff here, even a couple of recent cases of suspected typhoid, but..." He ran his finger along the page, murmuring to himself. "And she seems to think the school acts as a convenient dumping ground for a certain kind of parent."

"Certain kind?"

"Oh, people who don't really want their kids around for whatever reason. Quite common in minor boarding schools."

"That might explain why nobody's complained about the conditions."

"It might, but Mrs Hart says here she can't confirm her findings. Blocked at every turn."

"Well, Wilkins did pretend Mrs Hart was sick yesterday. Cut her out by calling you directly."

"Does he trust you?"

"Seems to like the idea that I'm not paid by the government, or your department. As I said, he's desperate to avoid coming under public scrutiny. And you know—"

"I would like to nail that place," said Johnson, in a slightly distracted voice and looking up at the ceiling before staring back at me. "Anyway, you were saying."

"I can't help thinking Michael Le Conte is somehow linked to all of this."

"Right," said Johnson, clapping his hands. "Let's reopen the Le Conte case. I'll give you carte blanche if you're game?"

"Carte blanche?"

"Indeed. One hundred per cent focus until we get to the bottom of things."

"And that police inspector, I mean, perhaps you should do as he instructed?"

"Certainly not, departmental matter. None of his damn business."

"But those other urgent cases you mentioned?"

"Oh, they can wait. Easter holidays coming up and so on."

"I'll need to interview the boy today if possible."

"Absolutely, Sangster. Sooner the better."

"And are you okay with me doing it without the parents present?"

"Yes, but take Mrs Hart with you."

"I, er... believe Mrs Hart is unavailable this evening."

"Then tread carefully, but let's not delay."

"May I take this?" I asked, pointing to the file and smiling inwardly at the thought that in this mood he would agree to almost anything.

"Of course, Sangster, and good luck."

"Oh, and Johnson?" I said as I stood up and walked to the door. "Yes."

"Do you know a Doctor Edith Magister?"

"Headmistress from Saint Hildeburgh's, of course. What of her?"

"She used to teach the Le Conte boy and I, er... would value your opinion."

"Well, Sangster, she doesn't do much headmistressing these days. Husband mostly takes care of the school management and teaching side of things, I believe. No, she goes in for all that highbrow research. Haven't seen her for a while now."

"So nothing special about her?"

"No, not really, I… wait, I tell a lie. I did see her not so long ago, at a lecture in Liverpool. Banging on about naughty children's brains being different."

"Really?"

"Yes, she said she would be publishing definitive proof before too long. Got laughed off the stage. Felt rather sorry for the poor woman."

"Anything else?" I asked, feeling I'd already got everything I needed.

"No, and if that's all, good luck again."

"Thanks, and bye for now," I said, walking to the office door as Johnson went to take a sip of tea before immediately spitting it out again.

"Pah, Miss Stephens," he yelled. "How much sugar did you put in this tea? Are you trying to poison me?"

I grabbed Sarah and we made a quick exit.

"Well, darling?"

"Worked like a charm. Apparently, I now have carte blanche."

"Was it the humble pie that did it?"

"Sherbet lemons actually."

Sarah didn't ask for an explanation, and we walked back home in grinning silence.

*

"So, darling, when do you expect to be home tonight?" Sarah asked me as we cleared our half-eaten bowls of cornflakes and cold teacups from the kitchen table.

"I'm due at the Le Contes' at seven, so about nine, I think. Late supper out somewhere if you like?"

"That's a sweet idea, but I've got such an early start tomorrow."

"Oh, yeah, I hadn't thought. York train leaves about six thirty, doesn't it?"

"Mmmm, so I'll make sure I'm all packed tonight. I can have something ready in the oven for when you come home as well. You, er… will be coming home before midnight?"

"Sarah," I said, wagging my finger, "don't start that again."

"Who's a prickly Jack?"

"I'm sorry, it's this case, and I'll do my best to be back at a decent time tonight."

"I know, darling, and I want to help. You'll know more after you talk to that boy, so I might be able to find something. After all, we've got enough books here."

"That we do," I said. "And for any really obscure local stuff, I can use the Manor Free's library."

"At the school?"

"Yes, Wilkins is very proud of it. Offered me free reign, I'm going this afternoon."

"Might be better to wait until you've spoken to the boy. Like I said, you'll know more then."

"Maybe," I said, "but I already made the appointment."

"Okay."

"Now I just need to make a couple of calls, cut a sandwich for the journey, then I'll be off. By the way, what are you up to for the rest of the day?"

"I'm going to a meeting at the Grosvenor. In about twenty minutes actually."

"For your degree studies, or to do with your lectures?"

"Neither, it's the WLM, North West Chapter."

"Oh God," I said, rolling my eyes in as exaggerated a manner as I could. "Not the Women's Libation Movement' again."

"The L stands for Liberation," she yelled. "And you know that."

"I thought you'd given up with that bra-burning women's lib lot?"

"Nobody ever burned bras, it's a myth surrounding the Miss America contest last year. If you want to know, what actually happened was—"

"Good, I always worried you might get severe injuries."

"Why?"

"Well, third degree burns at least."

"I think," she said, trying not to laugh, "that the idea was to take off your bra first, then burn it."

"So you do admit bras were burnt then?"

"No, just listen, it was a news reporter who said something like, 'Men burn draft cards and what next? Will women burn bras?' Got blown out of all proportion."

"No smoke without fire." I winked.

"Jack, shut up and make your calls. I'll do you a sandwich and a flask of coffee."

"You do spoil me, Sarah."

"Another word and I'll change my mind."

"You know I like you in a pinny," I said, grabbing her round the waist.

"Jack, I've only a few minutes before I have to go," she said, gently extricating herself from my embrace. "We're having a talk from the Secretary of State for Employment on—"

"Barbara Castle?"

"Yes, and she's talking about the odds of getting rid of the Marriage Bar once and for all, and I don't want to miss it, now, go on with you."

2PM

I ate a last piece of crust, crumpled the sandwich wrapping, dusted crumbs off my chest, reclined my car seat, then poured a cup of coffee.

I was parked next to a pub that overlooked the estuary, which here (less than ten miles upriver from the open sand flats that could be seen from the Manor Free) was choked with weeds that formed a vast marsh stretching almost as far as the eye could see, the waters of the Dee just a thin blue line in the far distance. I knew this place had once been a thriving port, but looking now I saw no hint of its illustrious past, a derelict building beyond the pub with a sign outside declaring it a condemned open-air swimming pool merely adding to the overall feeling of abandonment. The seafront promenade and the village behind me were pretty enough, though, and I'd parked in this spot more than once before to enjoy the solitude and the view.

Today, however, I'd chosen to come after talking with Sarah in the Cloisters Cafe, as it was here that the two missing boys from the poster in the Canteen had last been seen. Hard to believe, I thought, looking out across the quiet grass and mud flats, that less than a week before, a storm and a spring tide had carried the sea across the marsh to the village. This brought to mind the newspaper picture the Jacksons had shown me, with ferocious waves lashing the sea wall.

Winding down the car window, I sniffed the afternoon air, which was fresh with salt and colder than the day before when I had sat daydreaming on a bench by the beacon. The sky was blue with wispy clouds that scudded towards the horizon, riding an offshore breeze, and I felt momentarily overcome with a sense of intense loneliness, recalling Sarah reciting the poem about the lost girl.

'And never home came she.'

If children could disappear anywhere it would be here, I thought, even on a fine spring afternoon, let alone during a raging storm.

After several minutes staring like this I shook myself, wound up the window, and considered the afternoon and evening to come. I had arranged to see the Jacksons at half past two (Albert was insistent on the phone that I see him at the Canteen in person), then Wilkins at three and Mrs Hart at five. After that I would visit the Le Contes, and, I hoped, but with a slight feeling of trepidation as I thought about it, get to talk with Michael for the first time.

Then I smiled, remembering Sarah's reaction when I laughed about Barbara Castle and the WLM. In fact, I recalled the injustice of women having to leave permanent employment when they married (the so-called 'Marriage Bar') very well. Eileen, who worked in operations at the Admiralty during the war, had been subject to it when we married. She'd had to technically resign and take a new temporary contract to carry on doing exactly the same job as before. No such restrictions had applied to Sarah's lecturing post when we married, but I knew that the oil company still had this rule in place. It seemed even now, in 1969, enlightenment and fairness still had some way to go. My thoughts then drifted back to Eileen and the first time I saw her, moving little wooden models of Atlantic convoy ships and their Royal Navy escorts with a long pole, across an enormous map board in the 'Ops Room'. The memory quickly turned into a pang of remorse, and I was reminded of her strange comment in the arboretum at the asylum.

'Another world all around us. Things you wouldn't dream of. Outside of science and reason. Open your eyes, Jack.'

I shivered, feeling for a moment almost delirious, hearing Eileen's voice speaking out loud next to me in the car, her words mixing with my thoughts of the Le Conte case, almost as if the two might be somehow connected. I took a deep breath and the sensation disappeared as quickly as it had come. Then, with the car clock showing ten past two, I drained the last of the coffee, pulled my seat upright and turned the ignition key.

Driving away, as the road turned sharply inland, I looked back at the marshes, half-expecting to see the two missing boys climb over the sea wall, bedraggled but safe and sound. Then the marsh was obscured from view as the road wound up a steep bend. Alright, I thought, time to visit the Jacksons.

*

What on Earth do they want? I asked myself as the bell above the door to the Canteen announced my arrival with its usual rasping clang. Doubtless Michael's disappearance had made for an exciting break in the Jacksons' presumably very dull day-to-day routine, and I wondered for a moment, looking at a sign on the door showing the shop opened twelve hours a day seven days a week, how often they actually left the building. But as I entered the shop, my mind was set on other things, so that I was only half-focused on the conversations that followed.

"Thank you for telephoning," I said as the door closed behind me.

"Mr Sangster, thank you for coming," answered Fred and Albert in unison from behind their counter. Once again, both were dressed identically, this time in beige slacks and arran sweaters, and I struggled to remember which cousin was which. Was it Fred that wore the glasses, or was it Albert?

"I'm Fred," said the bespectacled one, clearly reading my thoughts.

"And I'm Albert."

"You do look very alike."

"People have commented."

"Well, as I say, thank you for calling the office."

"Yes, we telephoned rather than visited," said Albert. "We don't get out very much, tied up with the shop, you see."

"That's, er, quite understandable." I was now wondering whether any of the Jacksons ever saw the light of day. "So how can I help?"

"It's how we can help you, Mr Sangster," Fred replied.

"Indeed," said Albert. "You see, we were looking through our inventory after you had gone."

"The Le Conte boy," added Fred. "Thank goodness he was found safe, by the way; it was on the radio this morning." Fred looked at Albert, who nodded vigorously. "Anyway, when we heard the announcement, we did recall his purchases as being somewhat out of the ordinary."

"And," Albert continued, "when we checked the books, we thought it the responsible thing to call you."

"Very public-spirited of you."

"What we found was very odd, Mr Sangster."

"Very odd," echoed Fred.

"But what was it?"

"Well, let us show you." He took out a ledger from under the counter and opened the pages. "Here we have an entry for weedkiller." He pointed to a hand-written line item. "Then here for copper piping, wide gauge." He pointed to another item. "And most oddly, this order for sugar."

"Granulated," said Albert. "Not lump."

"Quite, and the orders were repeated, over and over again," Fred added. "Anyway, we thought you should know. We've noted the details down." He offered me a folded piece of paper. "Weights and measures, dates, prices charged, it's all there. Only last Friday he—"

"Yes, I'm aware of that," I said absentmindedly.

"No, what we mean is—"

"Well, thank you again," I interrupted, turning to leave and slipping the paper into my pocket. "That's, um… very useful," I then said, not wanting to offend the Jacksons, who were clearly very keen to help.

"But I must be going now, so I'll read it later, I have an appointment at the school. Good afternoon."

"Oh, and Mr Sangster," called Albert. "You were asking about the history of our shop last time we met."

"Yes," I said, thinking about the imminent meeting with Wilkins and wondering when I would finally be able to escape the Canteen and its eager-to-please owners. "It was very interesting."

"Well, do you know the school boarding house?"

"Yes, place at the back of the playing fields."

"That's right. Well, it seems some boys inadvertently kicked through a plasterboard wall there and discovered a sort of den from years ago."

"A den," said Fred, "with stone ginger beer bottles, sweet wrappers, cigarettes, even a copy of *Health and Efficiency*, which is how we can date the cache."

"Date it?"

"Yes, the magazine was from January 1901. I can imagine the boys enjoying a quiet cigarette whilst leafing through pages of scantily clad women. Must have been considered quite risqué in those days."

"Indeed," said Albert, "but the point is that we imagine the magazine and the other things were all bought from my uncle, Fred's father. He was noted for his magazines, you know."

"Fascinating," I said.

"Yes, and we hear the school has put it all out on display, in the boarding house. Ahem…" He coughed. "Talking of risqué, we still have that copy of *Parade* left if you are interested."

"Thank you, but no, Albert," I said. "Neither I nor my wife read it. Good afternoon."

3 PM

A minute or so later I was standing in the car park at the Manor
Free. Lost in thought for a moment, I jumped as I heard my
name (and former naval rank) being called.

"Commander Sangster, Commander Sangster?"

I sighed, recognising the earnest tones of Wilkins, who was
seated this afternoon on a scarlet-painted bicycle equipped with every
accessory imaginable, including numerous gears. I wondered why the
'Commander' rather than plain 'Mister'.

"Commander Sangster," Wilkins cried again, beckoning me to
cross the car park and pointing to a figure next to him dressed in full
naval uniform. "Come and meet our own Lieutenant Dawlish."

"Jack Sangster." I held out my hand in introduction to the stranger,
a man of about thirty-five with a full dark beard and thick glasses.

"John Dawlish," came the reply, along with a stiff salute. I saluted
back automatically, before thinking how odd the ceremony was in a
school car park on a Wednesday afternoon. "I head up the school's
naval training corp. I'm also head of history."

"One of the most popular arms of our Combined Cadet Force," added
Wilkins. "Not history, of course," he added with a rather forced guffaw.

"You're in the RNR," I commented, looking at Dawlish's double 'Wavy Navy' wrist insignias.

"Indeed, he is, Sangster," said Wilkins. "Indeed, he is. But Mr Dawlish hasn't seen action, or been in a war theatre, or even properly been to sea."

"You chaps in the Reserve do a sterling job," I said, noticing Dawlish looking to the ground.

"Thanks, sir," he said with a smile.

"Did you serve in the war, Headmaster?" I then asked.

"No, no, no," Wilkins answered, dismissing my question with a wave of his hand. "Reserved occupation and all that. Mmmm…" He paused from a moment, then held his finger up in exclamation. "Boy was found, we hear, safe and sound. Inspector Cooper visited this morning. Case closed, I believe. Jolly good news."

"It certainly is good news," I said.

"Anyway, Sangster, I believe you wanted to use our library facilities?"

"If I may."

"Well, you may, but I was meaning to call you to let you know I couldn't make our appointment. Can we postpone, until tomorrow?"

"Yes, I suppose so," I said, feeling frustrated but also remembering Sarah's point that the school library might be more useful once I had spoken to Michael.

"Jolly good. Ten thirty should fit my schedule, but I'll have Miss Lyons confirm with your office. Now then, I wonder if I might ask you a favour in return?"

"Happy to help if I can."

"Well, we are hosting a school cadet force get-together for the whole North West region, last day of the month, runs on through the evening. Great honour, perhaps wind of it has reached the department in Chester?" I shook my head. "Well, we need a speaker for the finale, someone interesting, someone who has seen action. In short, someone like you."

"Oh no, not me, Wilkins, I had my ship sunk. Left active service at the end of the war. I'm no role model. No advert for the Navy."

"Honourably discharged with a citation, as I understand it." Wilkins was clearly not in the mood to take no for an answer. "DSO and bar, and a distinguished shore career in naval intelligence afterwards, as well as occasional writer on naval history for Blackwell's magazine, isn't that correct, Dawlish?"

"According to the published Navy Lists, Headmaster, yes."

"So you'd be perfect," said Wilkins. "I'm sure the boys would greatly appreciate hearing you speak. We're training the next generation, you know." Of cannon fodder, I thought, but said nothing. He had me on the spot, and I wanted to stay in Wilkins' good books.

"Oh well, if it's not for too long, I suppose I could."

"Splendid, that settles it." Wilkins rubbed his hands, before bending down to put his bicycle clips on. "Now, give Dawlish a few snippets about your time in the Navy and your career afterwards for, who was it again?"

"Commander Sangster was with National Oil, Headmaster."

"Ah yes, anyway, Sangster, snippets for the programme, and Dawlish will fill you in about the evening's events. Meantime, I must be off to the playing fields, First Fifteen training, you see, final session of the season." Wilkins then flicked the bell on his curling drop handlebars with an exaggerated flourish and raised himself onto his saddle. "Now, where is that confounded first gear?" he muttered, fumbling between his legs for the bike's frame-mounted gear lever, before wobbling off across the car park, gown flowing behind. Watching him go, I smiled, remembering the Jacksons telling of boys discovering an old den behind a wall. Here was a chance to get inside the boarding house.

"Would you like to come inside, and we can go through things, sir?" asked Dawlish.

"Thanks, and please, less of the sir."

"Fine. Now follow me, please."

*

"So," said Dawlish, explaining how the evening would go as we sat in an empty classroom. "You're on at eight, last slot before the closing speech and drinks reception. You get introduced by the head, then just do your talk while I operate the slide projector."

"And you think my talk appropriate?"

"Royal Navy capital ships from 1906 to the present day? Yes, I'm sure everyone will love it."

That's good, I thought. This was the subject of a recent piece I'd written for Blackwell's, so preparation time would be minimal.

"Now, Dawlish, I wonder if you could help me?"

"If I can?"

"I heard from the owners of the post office that some boys had broken through a wall in the boarding house and found some items hidden since the turn of the century."

"Ah," said Dawlish with a smile. "The hole-in-the-wall gang."

"Pardon?"

"That's what the other boys nicknamed the lads who found all that stuff. The hole-in-the-wall gang."

"Ah, I see, and where is all this stuff now?"

"Oh, we put it in a glass museum case in the common room. Used to be full of stuffed owls, but they've been moved to the new biology labs."

"I, er, couldn't see it, could I? Sounds fascinating."

"Of course, we can go over there now if you like, though I need to be finished in about half an hour. Sea cadets this afternoon."

"Lead on."

We walked out of the school building and across to the corner of the yard, where a track led through some trees to the boarding house, which, up close, looked just as gloomy as it had from a distance the day before. I noticed the old school bell was permanently attached to one side of the rooftop belfry with rusting chains, unused and neglected.

"That place," I said, pointing past the boarding house to a square cottage with a steeply pitched roof and a tall chimney in its centre. "The headmaster's house?"

"Correct," said Dawlish. "Now then, here we are, let me open the door. I… Oh, hello, Matron."

"Mr Dawlish," said an enormous middle-aged woman in a nurse's uniform, complete with blue cape and hat. "Please be quiet if you're going in. I have three boys in the infirmary. All very poorly and in need of rest. Now, I must be getting on."

"Of course," Dawlish replied, as the matron brushed past us and headed back towards the main school. "Come on, Sangster, and quiet as mice, eh?"

We entered the hallway, the smell of which immediately struck me as stale and damp. Next to the front door, above the mantlepiece of an unlit fireplace, hung the portrait of a man with a long white beard, wearing a frock coat and stove-pipe hat, the man for whom the place was named:

'E.R. Bolshaw (MA Cantab)
Headmaster, 1856 to 1871
Established this boarding house in 1865'

Walking past Bolshaw, whose stare seemed to challenge my right to be there at all, Dawlish opened a pair of double doors that led into the common room, a large space filled with tables, chairs and several enormous leather settees. A TV on a wooden trolley stood in the corner, and in front of that was a small billiard table. The walls were largely lined with shelves, stacked with all manner of boxed games and books, as well as more random items like a single boxing glove, several non-matching golf clubs, a leather mitt I recognised as a fives glove, a bugle and a rusting piano accordion. Against the far wall stood the glass-fronted museum case Dawlish had mentioned, former home of the school's collection of stuffed owls and now, it seemed, the repository for the hole-in-the-wall gang's finds, which were arranged as the centrepieces in a sort of exhibition.

And the items on display were interesting, as the Jacksons had said. On the top shelf was a sign stating 'The Manor Free at the Turn of the

Century' and next to that several sepia-tinted photographs, showing buildings of the time, a picture of the then-rugby team and the cadet force lined up on benches. A faded copy of the school magazine from the period had been arranged next to these on a stand, open at its centre pages, which amongst lists of exam results also showed a picture of three boys standing to attention outside the boarding house. Someone had scribbled 'the Sods' in the margin, with an arrow pointing at the picture.

On the shelves below were the items found behind the wall. A row of at least twelve stone ginger beer bottles stood next to an empty carton of Players cigarettes, a pack of playing cards and numerous wrappers from now-defunct brands of sweets. In the centre, taking pride of place, lay a yellowed copy of *Health and Efficiency*.

"Nearest thing the boys would have been able to get to a nude mag," said Dawlish with a grin.

"I can imagine," I said. "I suppose you know from that exactly when they hid this stuff."

"Yes, well, certainly to the month. *Health and Efficiency* is the January 1901 edition. We had some records that showed there were works done at that time in the boarding house, so I suspect their den got walled up one day and the boys came back from lessons to find they couldn't retrieve their booty."

"Where is the den?"

"Down in the cellars."

"May I see it?"

"If you like, come on, quickest way's along past the boiler room."

I followed Dawlish down a steep flight of stairs and into darkness, before hearing him flicking a switch. The room was then dimly illuminated, to show a very big and very ancient heating system, powered by a coal-fired furnace that glowed behind an iron grate.

"That's a, er… venerable old set-up, Dawlish."

"Yes, although venerable isn't quite the word the caretaker uses when he has to top-up the coal every day. And to be honest, the thing is creaking at the seams and there are plans for a new one, I think. Anyway, the den is this way." We walked on, through several arched cellars, at one point passing a wooden door with a shiny-looking padlock on it.

"What's in there?" I asked.

"Not sure. Stores of some kind, I imagine, but nothing that would perish. These cellars are pretty damp." We walked further, eventually coming to a room at the end of the building that housed a water tank, as well as several thick drainpipes ('waste pipes from the boys' bogs, Sangster'). The smell of damp was now all-pervading, making the air thick and heavy so that I felt myself gag several times.

"Behind here, Sangster, look." Dawlish clicked his cigarette lighter and showed me the infamous 'hole in the wall', a jagged edged gap in the panelling about a yard wide and five feet deep. "Now watch your head." He bent down and entered the hole, lighter held ahead and sending dancing shadows across the walls and roof. I followed and, once inside, looked around to see a small brick-lined room with a vaulted roof, the air inside even more foul than in the main cellars.

"Not much to see, Sangster," said Dawlish. "Enough?" I nodded and went to leave, then noticed a small wooden box in the corner. I picked the box up (it had a rotten but still intact rope handle on top) and then stepped back through the hole, covering my mouth with my handkerchief.

"Can we get outside now?" I coughed.

"There's a back door here." Dawlish pointed to a small staircase by the water tank. "Lock's broken, so should be open. We can go out that way."

"Found this on the floor," I gasped once we were outside, taking several deep breaths of clean air before opening the lid of the box. "Newspaper lined, one more for your collection." The paper was yellowed with age and had suffered a little from damp, but the print was nevertheless still quite legible. "Date says twenty-third of January 1901," I read. "Let's see what the headline is. Oh."

"What?"

"Death of Queen Victoria, the day before this was printed."

"Worth something then. Collector's item, perhaps."

97

"Well, it belongs to the school now," I said, as my eyes fell on a smaller headline at the bottom:

'Quarry to close due to unstable rocks after rogue charges collapse caves. Two dead in tragic accident.'

I handed him the box.

"Thanks." He gingerly felt the newspaper then closed the lid. "Pretty fragile but stayed dry by the looks of things." We walked back across the playing field to the car.

"Well, thanks again for that, Dawlish, and I'll see you on the last day of the month, if not before."

"Looking forward to it," he said. "And give me a call if you need any help with your slides."

"Will do. Oh, and Dawlish, who were the Sods?"

"Ah, you saw the scrawl on the school magazine in the display case." I nodded. "Well, they were all expelled, three of them, for almost killing the headmaster and his wife."

"Killing?"

"Yes. Thought it would be funny to cut a sod of turf, then climb up and place it on top of the headmaster's chimneypot."

"Why?"

"So that smoke would billow back out from his fireplace. But the plan backfired, as it were."

"Oh?"

"You see the head at the time, a Doctor Beamish, was rather fonder of an evening drink than he let on, and so was his wife. The two were asleep in front of the fire and almost asphyxiated. It was pure luck one of the duty masters from the boarding house was passing and saw the smoke through the window. Rang the school bell and alerted the fire brigade just in time."

"Well," I chuckled, "I've seen all sorts, inner-city schools with some pretty desperate kids, but never children nearly killing a headmaster and his wife with a piece of grass."

"Just a practical joke gone wrong, but it made sure the Sods, as they came to be known, passed into Manor Free folklore. Anyway, Commander, I need to go," he said, giving me a quick salute.

"Until the thirtieth then, Dawlish."

5:30PM

"So, I did it," I said to Janice Hart as we sat in the 'snug' at the Bell, a rambling half-timbered inn just along the road from the Manor Free.

"Did what, Jack?"

"Managed to get into Bolshaw House without arousing any suspicion."

"Can we be heard in here?" she asked, looking around the little panelled room.

"Not unless someone else comes in."

"Good."

"Here's your file from head office." I placed the carboard folder given to me by Miss Stephens onto the table, whereupon Janice reached into a holdall and placed a similar file next to it.

"The complete school accounts, 1968, unaudited," she said flatly. "I was lucky they had a Roneo to make copies, mind you."

"Well done, Janice, but how did you do it?"

"Oh, very easy, I demanded the school's accountants hand them over. Cited the authority of the Department of Education." She shrugged. "No idea whether I have that authority."

"Seems neither did they," I said. "But did you find anything?"

"I believe I did, yes," she answered, opening the file and then pointing to two entries. The first described a receipt from the Department of Education for twenty-seven thousand pounds. The second was a series of withdrawals adding up to the same amount, made over subsequent days.

"So they received monies then immediately paid them back?"

"Not quite, Jack. Can you pass me your file?" She went through the pages and pulled out a document printed on headed departmental paper. "Look at this," she said, holding it up. 'A grant for the complete refurbishment of heating and sanitary facilities for residential pupils at the Manor Free School', said the heading. This was followed by various legal and practical details, including the date ('17th of April 1968') and a 'Consideration of twenty-seven thousand pounds sterling'.

"Plus," she added, "I already had these, so it all makes sense." She held up several carbon copies, faded but still legible, of withdrawal slips adding up to twenty-seven thousand pounds, all signed by TW Benton-Wilkins and countersigned by an EF Blount.

"Wilkins was a trustee for the school so had signatory power on the account, and this Blount person presumably had the authority to countersign."

"Was it usual for teaching staff to withdraw cash like this?"

"No, the accountants usually make payments to suppliers, and the only other person at the school allowed to withdraw cash is the bursar, Mr Venables, and he didn't sign for any of this. Now look at the dates."

"Er, twenty-first, twenty-second and twenty-third of April last year," I said, holding the withdrawal slips close to my eyes.

"Exactly, the same dates shown in the accounts for cash withdrawn to pay for the heating works."

"So?"

"But there were no works done."

"Are you sure?"

"Oh, you can go back over all the documents if you like, but you won't find anything. Plenty of other records for building works around the school, but nothing done at the boarding house bar a few minor repairs."

"I can believe it," I replied, remembering the ancient-looking furnace in the cellar. "Saw the boiler system this afternoon. Positively medieval."

"So, Wilkins must have pocketed the cash."

"That's an enormous sum to go missing. Surely someone would have—"

"No, Jack. They were doing all the work with the new teaching blocks between '67 and '68."

"And you're saying—"

"I'm saying there were hundreds of thousands flowing in and out of the school's bank account. What better time to steal twenty-seven?"

"Do you have proof?"

"Don't you think what we already have is enough?" she said, raising her eyebrows. "Unless Wilkins can explain what he did with the cash, produce receipts and so on."

"Then we must confront him, Janice. I'm going to arrange a meeting at the school, day after tomorrow."

"It's Good Friday."

"Can you not come as well? I'd be more comfortable if you were there."

"Well, it's Geoffrey, he likes to…" She paused, then continued, her voice raised. "No. I'll come."

"Thanks. Would you like a lift?"

"Oh no," she said, casting her eyes downwards. "I'll get there under my own steam." She was quiet for a moment, then looked up at me. "You know, Jack, this is the most alive I've felt for, well… I don't know when."

"You certainly are something of a Sherlock Holmes, Janice. All this forensic accountancy work."

"No, it's not that, it's, well, working with you, I suppose."

"A case like this is quite new to me too."

"But I was getting nowhere with all this until you came along."

"I suppose being independent means I can perhaps open doors that you can't, but you've done the clever work, made the connections."

"Well, thank you." She blushed. "But working on this together, confronting Wilkins, it is all so exciting, don't you think?"

"Oh yes," I answered, feeling a bit of a fraud given that now I'd discounted any link between Michael's disappearance and the headmaster, my main interest in pursuing Wilkins was purely to justify staying on Michael's case. "So, Janice, I know you can't make tonight, but I intend to see Michael again tomorrow evening. Do you want to come?"

"No, sorry," she said, eyes downcast again. "Thursday's Geoffrey's snooker night."

"I see. Can I give you a lift home?"

"No thanks, I'll take the bus. Doesn't do to, er... be seen."

"Very well," I said, deciding not to press her. "I'll say goodbye until Friday then."

"Goodbye." She stood up, then turned back to me at the door. "No, blow it."

"Blow what?"

"I would like a lift home," she said, placing her hands on her hips.

"Of course."

"And I'll take that lift on Friday as well if it's still on offer." I nodded. "Pick me up at two thirty, please."

"Er, yes," I answered as meekly as I could. "No trouble."

"And I don't care what the neighbours say if I'm dropped off or picked up in your Jag. Or Geoffrey, he can lump it as well."

The Bell was a labyrinth of small rooms and alcoves, linked by a narrow corridor that rambled through the building. As we walked, we passed other rooms, occupied mostly by couples, furtively talking (or so it seemed to me). I found myself wondering whether this time of day was when adulterers convened after work before returning to unsuspecting spouses.

"Could you hold on a minute, Janice?" I said, as we emerged into the main saloon bar. "Ah, excuse me?"

"Yes, sir?" answered the barmaid.

"Do you do rooms?"

"Rooms, Jack?" asked Janice.

"Yes, providing all this with Wilkins doesn't blow up too much, I'm supposed to be doing a talk in a few weeks at the school. Thought I'd stay the night here afterwards."

"We do," said the barmaid. "Bed and breakfast is three pounds per person, five pounds for double occupancy. Rooms ready at three, out by eleven the following morning and no music or pets." And no laughing, I thought to myself.

"May I book a double room for the night of the thirtieth then?"

"April?"

"Yes."

"I'll need a fifteen-shilling deposit," she said, opening a leather-bound reservations ledger. "Name?"

"Mr and Mrs Sangster." I handed her a note and coins in exchange for a chit.

"What's your talk on, Jack?" Janice asked as we walked out to the car.

"Oh, naval history. Battleships and things."

"Geoffrey would be keen to hear it. I must see if we can attend."

"If Wilkins is talking to either of us by then." I laughed.

"He may be on holiday at Her Majesty's pleasure." She laughed back.

"We'll see," I said quietly, remembering Miss Lyon's impassioned plea for mercy.

"Until Friday then, Jack," Janice said when we pulled up outside her house, just as a middle-aged man, bald and portly, opened the front door (Geoffrey, I presumed).

"You've done the most amazing job here by the way, Janice. There really is more to you than meets the eye."

"Oh, there is, Jack," replied Janice as she stepped onto the pavement. "Much more to me," she added, staring pointedly over at her husband, "if someone just bothered to look."

7 PM

By seven o'clock I was once again hearing the crunch of my tyres on the pebbled driveway that led to Kingswood House and, passing the gatehouse, saw Cyril wave from the doorway. I waved back, and five minutes later, I was sitting in the kitchen with Reginald and Marcelle Le Conte.

"Thank you for coming back, Mr Sangster," said Marcelle.

"Jack, please."

"Yes, of course, Jack, I…" She stopped and looked at her husband. "We are so grateful for your help last night."

"Yes, Jack," said Reg, placing his hand over his wife's. "Our family is whole again."

"Just glad I was there," I responded, not really knowing what else to say.

"And," Reg continued, "we had that Inspector Cooper visit us today. He said the police don't suspect anything untoward and have closed the case."

"Pending a medical report," Marcelle corrected.

"Of course, Marcelle, of course."

"And you must call the chief constable and thank him for all the police help."

"Yes, dear, I will," Reg replied, the much heavier than usual police effort to find Michael now making sense to me. "Anyway, Sangster, we had the doctor in earlier to look at Michael. Wants to run some tests but is fairly convinced him sleeping all that time was due to a condition where blood sugar level drops dramatically."

"Possibly to do with anaemia," Marcelle added. "Michael's been looking very pale of late."

"Well," I said, "I'm the last person to ask about medical matters, but if he's getting the best attention—"

"He is," interrupted Reg. "But we still need to get to the bottom of this truanting. I mean, six weeks or more?"

"Quite, that's what I want to talk to him about."

"Well, he's upstairs now if you want to go up, so—"

Marcelle was suddenly interrupted by the noise of a door opening, its creaking coming from a small archway in the corner I hadn't noticed before and through which I could see the sinks and plate racks of a scullery. "Hang on a minute, shoes off," she shouted. I instinctively looked down at my feet, then a moment later saw Flavia, resplendent in a Girl Guide uniform, enter in her stocking feet.

"Hi, Mum, Dad." She suddenly noticed me. "Oh, hello, Mr, er, sorry, I forgot your name…"

"Sangster."

"Yes, hello, Mr Sangster."

"Where's Claudia?" asked Marcelle, a look of panic on her face telling me she expected her elder daughter home now, panic I felt was fully justified given what had happened with Michael.

"It's okay, Mum, I have the most marvellous news, now, wait for it." She sat down in between her parents. "Claudia's been chosen for Queen's Guide."

"Oh," said Marcelle, her eyes watering. "That is… oh, after all this with Michael… that is marvellous, oh…" She began to cry, prompting Reg to lean over Flavia and put his arm across his wife's shoulders.

"She's going to meet Lady Baden-Powell in London. We can all go.

Miss Lyons kept Claudia behind in the Guide Hut after we broke up tonight, so I got the bus home."

"Would that be Eunice Lyons, the secretary from Michael's school?" I asked, trying in vain to imagine the school secretary pitching tents, singing around the campfire, cooking corned beef hash or otherwise embracing the Baden-Powell way of life.

"The same," said Reg. "Now, Flavia, will your sister walk home through the woods on her own?"

"No, Miss Lyons said she will give her a lift."

Marcelle, clearly still overcome by recent events with Michael, continued to sob.

"Do you think you'll perhaps get Queen's Guide one day?" I asked Flavia in an effort to up the mood.

"Oh no, Claudia's always been the best."

"Nonsense," said Reg. "You are just as good a guide."

"That's certainly a lot of badges," I added, looking at the arms of the girl's blue guide shirt, which were almost entirely covered with the round cloth patches.

"Mum sewed them all on for me, didn't you, Mum?"

Marcelle nodded and sniffed.

"What's that one for?" I asked, pointing to a badge with a brightly coloured bird motif, larger than the others.

"Oh, that's not a badge I won. It's for my patrol."

"Patrol?"

"Yes, I'm a patrol leader. We're the Kingfishers."

"Lovely colours, and that badge?" I asked, pointing to a smaller patch with a lion motif.

"Interest Badge, Commonwealth."

"You have a badge for the Commonwealth? Very impressive, and that one next to it?"

"Birdwatching."

"You have a badge for everything."

"Pretty much," said Flavia proudly. "Sixty-three badges so far, and as a Kingfisher, I'm expected to do a lot of birdwatching."

"I'm sure."

"That's how I knew what those birds were that Michael shot. Hooded crows, you can tell by the plumage." At this Marcelle, who had regained her composure, began to cry again.

"Flavia, no need to bring all that up," snapped Reg. "Look how it upsets your mother. What do you say?" The girl reddened but said nothing. "Then go on up to your room and change for supper." Flavia stood up and, head bowed, left the room.

"Sorry, Sangster," Reg then said more calmly. "Tensions are running a bit high at the moment. We're all—"

"I still can't believe he would kill all those birds," interrupted Marcelle. "I thought our son was brought up to be kind to animals."

"Let me go and talk to Michael now," I said as gently as I could.

"On your own?"

"If you don't mind. I'll try and be no more than half an hour."

"Then please, go ahead, but remember, he's very tired." Reg pointed towards the hall. "Left-hand landing, up where the front stairs split off to the west wing, then last door on the left."

I trod slowly up the stairs to Michael's bedroom, berating myself as I went for once again feeling trepidation at the thought of finally getting to talk with the boy that I had heard so much about. After all, this was just a child, and I was the adult, I said to myself as I mounted the broad staircase, its highly polished wooden bannisters glinting from the light of chandeliers high above. I took the left branch at the T-shaped mezzanine as Reg Le Conte had indicated, soon finding myself on a wide landing with numerous doors leading from it. The walls were hung with several portraits, each bearing the name of male family members and, by the styles of the dress, going back through the generations at least to regency times. Elsewhere were numerous paintings of ships, some sailing vessels, some steam. All the pictures looked, to my untrained eye, immensely valuable, as did the chandeliers, although the mere depth of the carpet pile beneath my feet was already enough to give a sense of wealth. Again, I found myself thinking this was hardly an environment to breed a repeat truanting boy. As I wandered over to the last door on the left and knocked, I determined to find out more about the source of the Le Contes' money.

*

Michael was sitting at a desk with his back to me when I entered. Then he stood up, turned and I drew breath, taking an involuntarily step backwards as I did so. The boy's face certainly looked unnaturally pale, but it was his eyes, I think, that shocked me most, wide open and of a piercing blue but, despite this, almost blank in their expression. I shook myself and appraised him. Tall for his age, with blond hair cut in a fashionable style over the ears, I could see why he was popular with the girls. But despite the good looks, I sensed strain in his face and general demeanour, as if perhaps he felt he shouldered some great responsibility. His white complexion rendered a faint growth of dark hair on his upper lip all the more visible, but there was no sign of the freckles that Mrs Magister had mentioned.

"You are the school inspector, aren't you, sir?" he asked in an almost monotone.

"Something like that, yes. My name is Jack Sangster and, if you don't mind, I'd like to ask you some questions. Is that alright?"

"Yes, sir. Please, take my chair."

"Very well," I said, and sat down. Michael walked over to the bed and sat down opposite me, whilst I looked around. Mostly a typical twelve-year-old's room, modern record player in the corner but with a somewhat moth-eaten looking teddy bear next to it, walls adorned with a poster of the winning Manchester United European Cup squad from the previous year, a picture of an Italian sports car and various current pop groups. There was also a large-scale model of the Saturn V moon rocket standing on the floor next to a wall.

"They'll be landing on the moon soon, sir," said Michael, seeing me looking at it. "And this week, NASA will pick the crew for Apollo Twelve as well."

"Apollo Twelve, eh?"

"It's going to be the second trip where they'll land."

"Going to the moon would have been science fiction when I was your age."

I continued to appraise the room. A bookshelf above the rocket model held standard younger children's reading fare (I saw the *Famous Five*, *Biggles* and *Narnia*), as well as more sophisticated fantasy such as Tolkien. Next to the *Hobbit* and *Lord of the Rings* volumes was a translation by Tolkien of *Gawain and the Green Knight*. I hadn't read it but nevertheless thought a medieval text interesting reading for a twelve-year-old. One book, laying on its side, particularly intrigued me, the spine stating *A Practical Guide to Codes, Pictograms and Cyphers* and, if that weren't enough, the next volume along was entitled *End of Days, Legends and Prophecies of the End Times*. This last book seemed familiar, although I couldn't for the moment place where I'd seen it.

The wall above the desk, however, was even more interesting, covered as it was with various drawings, some in pencil, some coloured with pastels. Michael was, as I'd seen first-hand with his drawing of the Face Stone and as Mrs Magister had observed, a remarkably talented artist.

One picture particularly caught my eye: a man, wearing only a loincloth and crude sash. He was crowned with what looked like a wreath of dead leaves, although it was hard to tell where his matted hair and long beard ended, and the wreath and sash began. He carried a large club and his skin, hirsute and scarred, was of an almost greenish hue. The style used bold lines with pale colour shading (Michael had presumably drawn a pencil sketch first and added the colours later). The subject's features were coarse, his broad nose flattened, his teeth blackened, but it was the eyes that were really noticeable, drawn with great passion by Michael as wild and staring. Behind the figure I could see a full moon, shining pale through the trees, and below that the outline of the Face Stone. If the proportions were correct, I judged the figure would have been at least nine feet tall.

"Who's that?" I asked.

"The King, sir."

"King of where?"

"Under the hill," the boy answered cryptically. "I don't know his actual name."

"A character from a book?"

"No, sir."

"And done at night, with the full moon."

"He's ruled by the moon, sir."

"It's a very good drawing."

"Thank you, sir."

"Michael," I sighed, "if we are to be friends, then perhaps you should stop calling me 'sir'. Jack, Mr Sangster, or nothing at all will be fine. Deal?"

"Yes, si… Mr Sangster." Michael had decided to keep his distance.

"When did you draw this?"

"A few weeks ago."

"Very good, as I say. Now, do you know why I am here?"

"Yes, I've not been going to school, and they've sent you to find out why."

"That's correct, Michael. And if you don't start going to school, you'll be expelled. Probably have to go away to a school where if you don't turn up for lessons they'll expel you again, and so on." At this, the boy's blank expression turned to one of fear, almost panic.

"You're not here to take me away tonight, are you?"

"No, lad, of course not." I made sure I smiled as I said this, the boy clearly needing reassurance. "But would it really bother you if I did, Michael?"

"No, as long as I can stay in this house for now," he answered, his face returning to blankness. "I can't leave yet."

"So, you wouldn't mind leaving, say, in September. Going away from home completely?"

"No, I wouldn't mind," he said with a shrug. "I just cause trouble for Mum and Dad. And Claudia and Flavia are embarrassed by me anyway. Claudia's boyfriend hates me."

111

"Hmmm," I said, suspecting he was telling me what he thought I wanted to hear. "I've seen your parents and I know that's not true, and so do you. Look, if we're going to work this thing out you've got to level with me. It's not a game, you'll be sent away." Michael said nothing, so I decided I would change tack. "So, how did you come to be unconscious in the woods?"

"Dunno."

"Well, what was the lead-up?"

"The what?"

"What did you do before you passed out?"

"Oh, I walked off in the direction of the town but climbed into the school grounds and hid behind Bolshaw House. Then I slipped out of the back gate there and went back over the hill and into Stapledon Wood." There was that name 'Stapledon' again. "I walked for a while, up to the old quarry and back, then sat down in the clearing by the Face Stone, with my packed lunch and sketch pad. I'd planned to wait until tea time, about five o'clock, then come back to the house as if I'd been in the town all afternoon."

"And?"

"Well, I must have fallen asleep, because the next thing I knew, my dad was holding my head and there were police everywhere."

"But you slept for two whole days."

"Yeah, they're going to give me a check-up at the hospital."

"Do you feel well now?"

"Mum's been saying I look pale."

"Was there a reason you walked to the old quarry?"

"I, um… there's an old house kind of place next to it, all overgrown, and a shelter, it's…" The boy hesitated, the first time I had seen him give any outward sign of discomfort when speaking, making me think the quarry must be important to him. "I just like it there, I suppose," he continued, now composed again. "Massive cliffs where they cut the stone away and lots of abandoned machinery, even what's left of an old tramway and an engine, everything overgrown now. Home to all sorts of animals, and there's a nesting pair of peregrines this season, have you been there?"

"No, but I'd like you to take me one day."

"Yeah, although I shouldn't, really."

"Why not?"

"It's out of bounds. Big, padlocked iron gates and all fenced off with high railings and barbed wire. Lots of signs saying its unsafe."

"But you get in anyway?"

"Yeah, been going there for ages, always on my own. There's a place behind some gorse bushes where the fence is bent and you can squeeze through. Don't think anyone else knows about it."

"And you say there are peregrines, Michael?"

"Yes, I didn't even tell my sister, with all her birdwatching."

"Why ever not?"

"They're very rare birds, I suppose you know."

"So I understand."

"Well, people might steal the eggs. Collectors will pay lots for them, so I didn't want to tell anyone in case it gets out. And anyway..." He went quiet, seeming, despite his bland veneer, to be struggling to express a genuine emotion. I wondered whether keeping his visits secret to stop egg-stealing was just a ruse.

"You were saying, Michael?"

"Well, it's just that, I feel like those peregrines are on my side. Did you ever feel an animal was on your side, Mr Sangster?"

"I had a dog once, when I was a boy."

The conversation stopped at this point, until, after a slightly embarrassing break, I spoke again.

"If you didn't go to the town, what did you do about eating when you were out on Sunday? The Canteen?"

"No, Betty made me a packed lunch."

"Does she pack you nice drinks?" I asked, remembering the dark stain the boy had wiped from his mouth, his first action when regaining consciousness. "I bet she does, like Ribena or Coke?"

"No, just orange squash. There's a spring in the woods as well, though. I like drinking from that." As he spoke, I noticed his eyes turn away from mine, not for the first time during the conversation. The 'distracted stare' that Mrs Magister had mentioned. I looked to where Michael was looking, towards the wall behind me.

"What is that, Michael?" I pointed to a brightly coloured painting of a red and white fungus growing by the stump of a tree. "Your work?"

"Yeah, a toadstool, from round here. They grow all over the woods, normally in the autumn, but this year they came early. Dunno why, but look." He opened a drawer in his bedside table and produced a slim oblong album (*Brooke Bond's Woodland Flora and Fauna*). "I collect tea cards. Here's the one." He pulled off a card (which had been glued to the page using a stamp hinge) and passed it to me. There was a picture of an agaric on the front and some information on the back.

"And that drawing, the bird?" I jerked my head towards a pencil drawing pinned to the wall underneath the agaric painting, showing a grey, black and white bird fixing its eye upon some unseen object, although Michael had chosen to draw the eye as a white-shining star. 'Badb' was scribbled on the top of the picture.

"A hooded crow." He turned the pages of the album. "I have a card for that as well."

"Thanks. Now that's a fine air rifle." I gestured towards a sleek-looking gun that stood against the bedroom wall.

"It's mine. Webley Mark 3, solid steel with a walnut stock, underlever action."

"Very nice. A point 22?"

"Yeah, delivers about eight foot-pounds at the muzzle."

"You know about foot-pounds?" I asked, vaguely remembering how to calculate this way of measuring a gun's firepower from naval college.

"I think it's the energy transferred upon applying a force of one pound-force through a linear displacement of one foot."

"Very good, Michael," I said, finding it hard to reconcile this with the dismal physics marks on the boy's school report. "But you used it to shoot all those birds, and you hung them up in the trees. Why?"

"I had to," Michael replied, staring straight at me in a way that made me understand why Mrs Magister had found him intimidating. "I needed to protect the house, the family, I didn't want us to be watched, I…" Suddenly, he jolted, as if to check himself, and his demeanour changed. "Actually, I should be ashamed of myself," he continued, eyes now cast downwards, voice quieter. "Killing all those birds just for fun. Dad's taken all my slugs away so I can't shoot anymore." He placed his hand across his forehead. "I do still feel weak, though, perhaps I should go to bed now."

"Well, as long as you're sorry." I felt Michael's acting wasn't as impressive as his knowledge of firearms, and, suspecting another ruse to deflect my questions, I decided it would be futile to ask the boy anything further right now. "May I borrow these two tea cards?" I said. "I'll return them."

"Okay, but please do bring them back, they're part of a set."

"I will," I promised, little knowing that it would be a long time before I would fulfil that promise. "Now, I think I've spoken with you enough for tonight." I stood up and walked towards the bedroom door. "I'll come back tomorrow evening for another chat, and if you can, I'd like you to think about why you don't go to school and what we can do to change that. And maybe try and remember more about what happened yesterday. Can you?"

"I'll try."

"Good," I said, my fingers closing around the door handle. "I'll—"

Suddenly Michael stood up and shouted, "No, please don't go."

"What is it, Michael?"

"Can I trust you, Mr Sangster, with something terrible?"

"Of course, and you can also trust your mum and dad. Have you told them about this 'something terrible'?"

"No, they wouldn't believe me. I spend my time getting into enough trouble as it is."

"You could try them." I sat down on the desk chair again. "They love you. I only had to watch how they were when you went missing yesterday to see that. And I know it's hard to believe, but your sisters as well. They're there to look after you."

"That's the worst thing, it's me who must look after them."

"Come on, Michael," I said, sensing real despair in his voice. "I'm sure they can fix things if you let them. Whatever you've done."

"It's nothing they can fix. I just thought you, being important and all—"

"I'm not that important." I laughed. "But try me."

"Well, is it true that the world's in a terrible mess. You know, like the worst it's ever been?"

I was somewhat taken aback by the question. "Er... let me see... no, I don't think so. I lived through the war, remember, with its bombs, threats of invasion, rationing. Pretty grim compared with now."

"Yes," said Michael, now looking straight at me. "But it's much worse now than then. Atom bombs, pollution, too many people. And there are still wars, like Vietnam."

"Where do you get all this from?"

"TV, reading, what I hear from grown-ups."

"Let me let you into a secret."

"Yes?"

"Every generation thinks it's time is the worst there's ever been. We did during the war, then there was the First World War and the times before that. Even great plagues that killed half the population."

"But they didn't have atom bombs, did they?"

"You have a good point there," I replied, feeling a little defeated. "Hopefully we have the sense to control the atom bomb now, though."

"There was that Cuban Missile Crisis."

"You remember it?" I asked, feeling further defeated.

"No, I was only little then, but I've read about it."

"Well, that was a close-run thing, but it worked out alright in the end."

"Mr Sangster," asked Michael, wriggling a little as he spoke. "What if... well, could someone, I mean..."

"Yes, Michael?"

"Could someone decide we don't deserve it all and take it away from us?"

"Take it away from you and me?"

"No, all of us. The Earth?"

"What, a dictator, like Hitler?"

"No, someone from outside, from somewhere else."

"Like a spaceman," I answered, a little relieved that the boy had presumably been influenced by science fiction, either stories or perhaps TV like *Doctor Who*. "Or an alien?"

"No," said Michael, vigorously shaking his head. "Somewhere else, but among us. With us. Under us?"

"Why under us?"

"It let him out, when the charges blew in the quarry." The boy looked up at the ceiling, and although his eyes were momentarily hidden from me, I was sure a brief look of terror passed across his face. "And I don't think it's atom bombs he'll use to end everything." He continued staring upwards, almost talking to himself. "No, it'll be something quite different."

"That's a bit of a riddle, Michael," I said, feeling a shudder at his expression, especially when he said the word 'quarry'. "Can you explain?"

He shook his head again, then looked downwards and muttered, "Doesn't matter. He takes a little from me every time I see him. I probably haven't got long now anyway. Nobody has, unless I can stop him."

"How long?"

Michael muttered something about days, then raised his head. "It's okay," he then said, once again speaking quite brightly. "I was just wondering. Stuff I've read, you know. It can be a bit frightening. Sorry to bother you with it."

"No bother, I'm sure," I answered, deciding to end this line of questioning for now and feeling all the more disturbed as I did so. What could he have meant by 'haven't got long now' and 'unless I can stop it'?

Stop what? I thought about the crows and the agaric. I needed to know more about the fungus and whether it could bring on the kind of hallucinations Michael seemed to be describing. I would take some expert advice, although I wasn't sure it would help. The only way to really find out would be to eat it myself, and that wasn't going to happen.

"Now, Michael," I said, standing up, "it's been very good for us to chat like this, but I really do think we've spoken longer than we should have." I looked at my watch. "And thank you for letting me into your confidence." I walked once more to the door.

"Goodnight then, Michael. Until tomorrow."

"Oh, Mr Sangster."

"Yes."

"That picture on the wall, of the King. I think I drew it from life."

"I know you do."

"And Mr Sangster?"

"Yes."

"I would like to show you the Face Stone, where I drew it. Maybe tomorrow?"

"This," I whispered to myself, drawing a deep breath as I closed the bedroom door and remembered my thoughts when I first arrived at the Manor Free the day before, "is looking to be just about as far from a run-of-the-mill case of sagging-off as it could be."

*

I felt a little dazed as I went down the stairs and entered the kitchen, where Reg, Marcelle and Flavia Le Conte, now joined by Queen's Guide-to-be Claudia, sat. I was about to say my goodbyes when Michael burst through the scullery door and ran over to his sisters.

"You didn't walk back through the woods, did you?" he shouted, shaking Claudia by the shoulders. "Tell me you didn't. Not at night, not on your own."

"Michael, get off me," she cried, struggling to get away.

"Tell me you didn't."

"I didn't, I got a lift home, now will you get off me."

Michael relaxed his grip, then turned and silently left the room, this time through the main door, as his family sat staring, parents and daughters apparently unable to move.

"I'm terribly sorry, Jack," said Reg. "He does this sort of thing sometimes."

"How did he get past me?"

"Oh, old servants' back stairs leading down to the scullery. West wing rooms like Michael's used to be all servants' quarters; east wing was where the family slept."

So, I thought, the boy could slip in and out of the house at any time and nobody would know.

"I'll show you to your car, Jack," Reg then said, and I bade the rest of Michael's family farewell before following him out to the driveway.

"By the way, Reg, I couldn't help admiring all those paintings of ships."

"Ah, you like them?"

"Yes."

"All belonged to the Line. All the way back to my great-grandfather's time."

"Sorry?"

"The Elderbank Shipping Line. Owned by a Le Conte from its founding until we sold up to Cunard a few years ago. You have a connection with the sea, Sangster?"

"Navy, joined as a midshipman after school. Ended up a commander for my sins."

"Impressive."

"Long time ago, but I do write a little on naval history. Just a side-line, but in fact," I laughed, "got shanghaied today into doing a talk at the Manor Free after Easter, for their cadet force gathering."

"I'll make sure Marcelle and I come. And Michael. He could do with joining a group activity, too much of a loner. By the way," he said, his voice suddenly slower, perhaps more serious, "you were up there with Michael for, what, almost an hour?"

"Yes, he talked a lot."

119

"Certainly a lot more than he does to me. Sounds as if you've established quite a rapport with Michael." He then looked to his feet. "At least more than I have," he added softly, before raising his voice again. "Anyway, my boy seems on the mend, and if we can just get Michael back to school then your job's done. And whichever way it goes now, I think we're over the worst of it."

"I hope so. I've some business to attend to tomorrow daytime, but I'll be back in the evening to follow up if that's alright."

"Of course, Jack. Until tomorrow evening then."

*

As I climbed into the car, watching Reg Le Conte walk back to the house and the welcoming light in the hall extinguish as he shut the door behind him, I felt a tinge of inner warmth, the sense of relief within the household having been almost a tangible thing. But that sense was tempered with an overriding feeling of unfinished business. Perhaps it was the disquieting aura surrounding Michael, the odd financial goings-on at the school or Mrs Magister's disingenuity, but one way or another I felt that the case of Michael Le Conte would become more chaotic and frenzied before the week was out.

9 PM

"What are all those?" I asked Sarah, as I entered the kitchen to see her leafing through a massive leather-bound book, whilst surrounded by piles of similar volumes.

"*Encyclopaedia Britannica*, or some of it anyway."

"Yes, I can see that."

"I'm researching."

"You've extended the table ends out to full length, are we expecting guests?"

"I need space."

"And dinner?"

"Got you a little surprise, darling, it's a curry."

"Mmmm. Used to love that in the Navy."

"On the side by the cooker." I looked over at the counter to see a plastic packet proclaiming itself a 'Vesta Beef Curry'. "I've already made the rice, so you just get the other ingredients and pour them into a pot of boiling water then stir. Sandra suggested it."

"Very exotic," I said, switching the kettle on then opening the packet to see a bewildering array of plastic sachets. "What do I do?"

"Oh, come here," said Sarah, pulling the packet away from me and cutting open the plastic bags one by one, before pouring them into a bowl along with the contents of the kettle. "Now, we just stir to taste and then…" She lifted a spoon up to her lips and pulled a face. "Ugh, would you like a cheese sandwich?"

I looked at the brown liquid on her spoon and, with little encouragement, set to work with a loaf, some butter, a jar of pickle and a block of Cheshire cheese, whilst Sarah poured the contents of the bowl into the bin and sat back down at the table.

"And Jack, could you pass me that volume, please? No, the far one, H to J. Yes, that's it." I handed her the heavy tome as I munched my sandwich, the smell of the 'curry' unfortunately still very present. As I ate, she frenetically turned the leaves of the books with one hand (constantly licking her finger to turn pages, as was her wont), whilst taking rapid notes with the other.

"I take it this is nothing to do with that awful Barbara Castle?" I asked, once the sandwich was finished, the plate cleared, the curry smell largely dissipated and a cup of tea sat in front of me.

"You've never forgiven her for the speed limit, have you?"

"Takes all the fun out of having a decent car."

"Or the breathalyser, darling."

"Now that was a step too far. Can't drive to the pub for a few pints anymore."

"Good thing too."

"So all this research is for your degree, or is it for your lectures?" She shook her head and continued writing.

"For you, darling. I've been looking into some of the things we were talking about this morning."

"You didn't need to go to all that trouble."

"It's no trouble. If you're going to understand this boy's mind, you need to understand the things that are troubling him, no matter how silly or obscure they seem."

"Alright, and I've got a lot more to tell you now I've spoken to him, but fire away."

"Okay. First of all, when you told me about that Great-Granny

Bart I just had to look up witch trials, and d'you know what?" I shook my head. "The last person convicted of being a witch was in 1944. Well... not for being a witch, that's legal, but pretending to be a witch for some sort of gain was a criminal offence."

"Oh."

"Anyway, that's by the by, but come here." I walked around the table to stand over her shoulder. "Look, hooded crows. Sam Youd was right, see..." She showed me the encyclopaedia entry, which was detailed, with a fine colour plate of the bird (although with less life about it, I thought, and certainly less malevolence, than Michael's drawing). The author confirmed the range did not include the North West of England, or anywhere particularly close to us.

"But they could still migrate, couldn't they?" I said, then explained that Flavia had told me Michael's birds were definitely hooded crows.

"Perhaps, but whether they belong here or not, what's really interesting is that these birds are closely associated with the End of Days. They're called 'Badb' in Irish mythology."

I jolted when she said Badb, visualising the title above the crow drawing on Michael's wall.

"What does it say?"

"It's horrible. Badb was a goddess of some kind associated with the end time. Seems the word itself originally meant 'rage', 'fury' or 'violence' as far as I can tell, and if it did, she was well named."

"Nasty girl, eh?"

"Yes, and this was the first of her prophecies, after the battle of Cath Maige Tuired it says in the entry. Anyway, here goes." Sarah picked up her notepad and read out loud:

'Peace up to heaven,
Heaven down to Earth,
Earth beneath heaven
Strength in each,
A cup very full,
Full of honey;

Mead in abundance,
Summer in winter...'

"That's not so bad, Sarah. Not so bad at all."
"No, but then listen to what she said next. It says here:

'She prophesised the end of the world, foretelling every evil, and
every disease and every vengeance.'

"And she most certainly did, Jack, listen."

'I shall not see a world which will be dear to me,
Summer without blossoms,
Cattle without milk,
Women without modesty,
Men without valour,
Conquests without a king,
Woods without mast,
Sea without produce.'

"Sounds grim."
"It gets worse."

'False judgements of old men,
False precedents of lawyers,
Every man a betrayer,
Every son a reaver,
The son will go to the bed of his father,
The father will go to the bed of his son,
Each his brother's brother-in-law.
He will not seek any woman outside his house,
An evil time,
Son will deceive his father,
Daughter will deceive.'

"It's awful, I mean, incest and lies all round, no fish in the sea, forests dying."

"It wasn't Barbara Castle who wrote that, was it?"

"Shut up," she said, turning away from me. "We had a wonderful talk today from her at the WLM meeting. Wonderful, as it happens."

"Sorry, Sarah," I said. "Only joking. And what's a 'Reaver' when he's at home?"

"I had to look that one up as well, Jack. It's someone who goes out raiding, intent on plundering, that sort of thing. Viking in times past, or a bank robber these days, maybe?"

"And now, welcome to *Call My Bluff*," I said, ruffling her hair and humming the TV show's theme music. "First up, we have the delectable Doctor Sarah Sangster. Sarah, you luscious young thing, you, please tell the audience what a Reaver is?"

"Don't be silly, darling," she said, pulling her head away. "You with your gnat's attention span. I've been working hard on this."

"Right." I nodded. "Sorry again, it's been a long day. Anyway, you're probably already one step ahead of me on some of it, but here's what I've found out." I related my visits to the Manor Free school and Saint Hildeburgh's, and my meeting with Mrs Hart.

"They sound a bit naughty," she said when I finished.

"What, Mrs Hart?"

"No, Wilkins and the secretary, silly. Mrs Hart sounds fine, and that psychologist woman's been a bit dishonest and a bad influence, but no, darling, I mainly mean that ridiculous old headmaster cavorting with the Brown Owl or whatever she is."

"Girl Guide and Ranger troop leader in the evening, and Manor Free school secretary on weekdays."

"And headmaster's bit of fluff weeknights and weekends."

"Ha, I'm sure she is," I said. "But I don't think that's got much to do with Michael's problems."

"Hmmm… maybe not. Hey, d'you think Magister might have been encouraging him to eat the toadstools?"

"Maybe."

"I looked them up in the *Britannica*." She pointed to a volume that lay open at the end of the table. "Screeds of general stuff if you're interested in fungi, but very little of it to do with the effect they have if you eat them. Basically, the entry just said agarics could be deadly poisonous and were to be avoided."

"I'm going to get one analysed quickly if I can."

"You won't find a lab open over the Easter weekend, surely?"

"Thought I'd ask Janie Dent, you know, the botany woman at Liverpool University."

"Yes, I know that, er… woman," Sarah growled, her face looking like thunder. "That," she grimaced, "old tart."

"Best in the business," I said as lightly as I could. "And if I hadn't met her that time at the club, I'd not be doing what I am today." This was a reference to a lunch I'd had with Doctor Dent (purely in relation to my oil company job, as I'd told myself), where a chance meeting with Sir John afterwards had resulted in my being invited to join the Institute. "Anyway, Sarah, her faculty's affiliated with the Granville."

"I'm sure her 'faculties' are affiliated to almost anyone who cares to have them," Sarah replied. "I remember her pawing over you at that Occidental Club charity thing we went to with the Youds. Sandra can't stand her. Huh." She pursed her lips. "Told me none of the other wives can either. Mutton dressed as lamb, that's what Sandra said."

"Well, this is professional, Sarah, purely professional. The Le Contes' house was really interesting by the way."

I then told of my conversation with Michael, about the drawings of the crow and the 'King Under the Hill', plus the boy's insistence that the end time was near and only he himself could stop it.

"My goodness, Jack," she said when I'd finished, all thoughts of 'that old tart' apparently banished. "Poor little boy must think he has the weight of the world on his shoulders. Let me look up the King Under the Hill." She scanned the books on the table with her eyes. "Pass me that volume, would you, J to L, at the bottom of the second pile?" I wrestled out the appropriate volume and she recommenced her furious page-turning.

I stopped her by placing my hand across the book, then kissed her full on the lips.

"What was that for?"

"Doing this with you, Sarah, right now, I feel, well, more... I can't explain it, maybe fired-up is the word, than I have since I don't know when."

"You're feeling alive, and I'm glad," she answered, looking up at me. "Now then, here we are, it says, er... for 'King Under the Hill' see 'King Under the Mountain'. Let me see... yes." She flicked over the page. "Ooh," Sarah exclaimed. "Look at the picture, Jack, macabre or what?" She pointed to a glossy plate showing a disturbing line drawing of a woodland scene with various supernatural characters. I recognised this as the work of Victorian children's illustrator Arthur Rackham (whose pictures had given me nightmares as a child).

"They've reprinted a passage from an old book on fairy tales. Let me read it to you, Jack."

'King in the mountain stories, which are common in folklore throughout the world, involve legendary heroes... sleeping in remote dwellings including caves on high mountaintops, remote islands or supernatural worlds... the presence of the hero is unsuspected, until some herdsman wanders into the cave, typically looking for a lost animal, and sees the hero. The stories almost always mention the detail that the hero has grown a long beard, indicative of the long time he has slept beneath the mountain... the story goes on to say that the king sleeps in the mountain, awaiting a summons to arise with his knights and defend the nation in a time of deadly peril.'

"And these sleeping kings aren't always heroes, see." I leaned over the table to read the page, but she pushed me away. "No, Jack, you're dropping bits of cheese onto the leaves. We'll never get it off, so let me read this bit out as well.

'Such sleepers may also be the antithesis of the hero, a "Chained Satan" best left to slumber for eternity, whose return would mean the end of the world.'

"Chained Satan?"

"Yes, and the author of this entry," said Sarah, pointing to a footnote, "also adds that the herdsman, or whoever stumbled on the sleeping hero, would, it says here, 'often be adversely affected, perhaps ageing and dying within a few days.'"

"So all in all pretty bad for your health."

"Isn't it, and this shows places with legends of underground sleepers." She pointed to a map of the world printed across two pages, with dots shown on almost every continent, including a number in the British Isles. "They're everywhere."

"Is there one in the Wirral?"

"No," she said, peering closely at the page. "Nearest is close to Manchester." She slammed the book shut. "And I think that's all we're going to find on our own. This encyclopaedia stuff's good as far as it goes, but we need more local detail, we'd... d'you know what?"

"Mmmm?"

"I was lecturing not so long ago, now, when was it?"

"Sarah?"

"January, it was then, I'm sure, and there was this Professor Horniman following on after me in the lecture theatre." She stopped and screwed up her eyes, trying hard to remember. "And I..." she said very slowly, as memories surfaced, "needed to tidy my notes after my session so stayed on sitting at the back while he delivered his lecture. Then we both went to a drinks reception. Yes, that's it."

"What's it?"

"Well, he's one of the foremost experts on this kind of thing, pagan gods and so on, and from what I remember, he's especially keen on the North West. I thought perhaps you could go and see him, darling." She looked at me, and, when I didn't reply, added, "Might help?"

"No time, I've got to see you off first thing, there are appointments tomorrow and then there's the long weekend. I need to wrap this up quickly, Johnson won't give me much longer."

"It's just that he had some ideas that might fit with all this. When are your appointments tomorrow?"

"I'm full up to about half eleven, then meetings start again at five in the afternoon."

"Lunch with the professor then?"

"It's a bit short notice for him." I laughed. "Anyway, Manchester's too far to go and be back for five."

"No, darling, Horniman was just visiting when I met him. He's based in Liverpool."

"Still unlikely to be available tomorrow."

"He might be for me," she said, in a soft voice that I knew well. "You see—"

"He took a shine to you, didn't he?" I sighed.

"Er… yes. Told me I looked like Liz Taylor, but he was disgustingly drunk by that time."

"That's a new one, they usually say Hedy Lamarr."

"Flattery indeed, Jack. We had a WLM talk about Hedy Lamarr not so long ago. She invented guidance systems for torpedoes, could have saved thousands of lives during the war, but the male chauvinists running the US Navy wouldn't let her—"

"Sarah, that's lovely, but do you really think this professor of yours would meet me?"

"Well, if I could call him first thing, I might be able to swing it."

"Swing it, eh? And how old is he?"

"Sixty-five if he's a day, and that's probably his belt size as well."

"Alright, lunch it is, if you can swing it." I laughed, then looked down at the open encyclopaedia again. "There's something else, Sarah, underneath that Arthur Rackham plate."

"Yes, Jack, it's a footnote, very small print." She leaned close to the book. "Says 'defend the nation' may also be interpreted as 'defend Mother Earth', and that we ourselves might be the enemy so that the

King must vanquish mankind in order to do so. And…" she said, leaning closer, "that his 'Knights' might not necessarily be an allusion to traditional chevaliers in armour but may be taken to mean the King's allies, not men, but 'warriors of nature itself'."

She sat up again, eyebrows now raised high and eyes wide open, placing both hands up to her mouth (we'd both come to call this Sarah's 'haven't a clue' look).

"Don't understand what that means, darling."

"Me neither, but I wonder if Michael Le Conte does."

MAUNDY THURSDAY
5:30AM

"Here we are, tea and your paper," I said to Sarah as I sat down beside her at a table in the station buffet. "Train should be here in…" I looked at my watch. "About now."

"Manchester Piccadilly, five thirty-five service, leaving from Platform One in seven minutes," came the announcement on cue.

"Almost on time, now, come on, I'll carry that tea for you." We walked out onto the platform, where yellow sodium lights shone weakly in the chilled darkness and the breaking dawn was still only a promise, to the now-waiting train, which hissed to us that its diesel engines were ready to roll. "Now, where's the first class?"

"I would say you were pampering me," yawned Sarah as we found the appropriate carriage and opened the door, "but it's too early." She yawned again. "And you seem to have such boundless energy," she said, stepping aboard; I followed her to a compartment, balancing the teacup and newspaper as I went.

"Take that and that, and let me get this." I placed the cup and paper in her hands then lifted her bag onto the overhead luggage rack. "Now then, all set?"

"Yes, darling, I'll miss you."

"Me too," I said, leaning to kiss her.

"Oh, and I'll call your office about Professor Horniman."

"Okay, just leave a message with Miss Stephens."

"I will, and—"

"Five thirty-five Manchester Piccadilly service leaving from Platform One in one minute," interrupted the station announcer. "Stopping at Newton Le Willows, Warrington Bank Quay..." He carried on, listing out each station on the line in an almost unintelligible drone that made further conversation impractical.

"Got to go," I shouted, shutting the compartment door behind me, then stepping back out onto the platform, only to hear Sarah's voice once again.

"Jack," she called from the carriage window. "Just remember, the professor didn't get that waistline by accident. Loves his food and loves his wine and really opens up after a few drinks."

"*In vino veritas*," I called back.

"So take him somewhere nice, and don't skimp on the booze," she shouted. "That should swing it."

"Okay, tell him to come to the Occidental for one o'clock," I yelled, watching her wave as the train began to move. "Got that?"

She nodded, and I waved back as the train gathered speed and the carriage disappeared from sight.

7AM

Not too long after seeing Sarah off, I was sitting once more at our kitchen table, but this time with steam rising from the sweat I had worked up during my morning run.

After talking with Sarah the night before, and thinking about the information she had uncovered, I now felt there might be just a hint of clarity beginning to disperse the fog around the Le Conte case. I was also excited by the day to come, convinced I would be able to clear more of the fog before too long.

And most importantly, I really did feel 'alive', as Sarah had so succinctly put it.

Thus stimulated, and sipping a cup of tea, I start to scribble notes, partly as an aide memoire, and partly to try and put some structure around those inklings of clarity I was starting to sense. Firstly, I wrote down four subjects to give to Wilkins. If his library was half as good as he claimed, that would be the place to find out what I needed to know. I then compiled a list of rapid actions I felt were needed to avert Michael falling into imminent danger (although exactly what kind of imminent danger I still couldn't say). After much crossing-out and rearranging, I felt the list was complete:

Contact Janie D re toadstool.

Organise analysis of same – how at short notice?

See Wilkins – research material as per list – do not confront!

Lunch Prof Horniman, maybe?

See Magister – confront!

See Michael:

>*Why Face Stone?*
>
>*Why crows?*
>
>*Why end of days?*
>
>*Visit Face Stone.*
>
>*Why truanting?*

I stared at the list for quite a few minutes, then idly scrawled at the bottom of the page:

Eat toadstool and you'll find out!

"Right, bath and then to work," I then said out loud. Half an hour later, I was back at the kitchen table, the clock on the wall showing eight o'clock. Time, I thought, for my call to Professor Janie Dent, head of the botany faculty at Liverpool University and the most knowledgeable person on fungi I could think of. Given everything going on I felt there was no time to wait and, calling her home number, hoped Janie wouldn't have left for work. It turned out (although I wondered if Sarah would have agreed), I was in luck.

8 AM

"Oh, Jack, it's you, how lovely," came the sleepy voice from the other end of the phone. "But, it's, er… what time is it, sweetie, it's early, could you call later, it's—"

"Yes, Janie, I know, it's eight in the morning. I've just come back from taking Sarah to the station, she's gone away for the long weekend. Anyway, I urgently need some information. Do you mind?"

"Not at all, sweetie, not for you, but," she giggled, "I'm, ah, in my birthday suit right now. Let me pull on a dressing gown." I heard a click as she put the receiver down, then the rustling of clothes. "That's better, now, what's so urgent?" she said faintly, presumably holding the receiver under her chin whilst she finished dressing.

"I need to know about fly agaric," I shouted down the phone. "Do you know anything about it?"

"Of course, sweetie," she answered. "No need to shout. Amanita Muscaria, grows near trees, evergreens."

Janie, I reminded myself, had a razor-sharp mind and encyclopaedic knowledge of her subject that belied by her looks (over forty but with peroxide-blonde hair and still wearing the shortest skirts and the longest lashes). She had a husky voice that seemed to load even the most innocent of sentences with innuendo, and something about her deportment would not only attract the attention of all the men when she walked into a room but also put their wives on high alert. She often said the world wasn't ready for a woman like her, and I tended to agree.

"Just evergreens?" I asked her, remembering the dell where Michael was found.

"No, sometimes deciduous ones as well."

"Like birch trees?"

"Probably."

"Go on."

"Well, it's common enough and looks quite spectacular. If you asked a kid to paint a picture of a toadstool, they'd probably do something that looks like an agaric. Red with white spots. Look, do we have to talk about—"

"What happens if you eat it?" I looked at the toadstool I had picked in the wood, now laid out on my desk, its colours as bright as when I first saw it, almost glowing. "I can't seem to find much out about that."

"Mainstream reference books do tend to be censored by the powers that be when it comes to freely growing psychedelic drugs."

"So?"

"Well, Jack, it usually just makes for a nice relaxing feeling. Could make you a bit ill in large amounts, I guess, and maybe the bemushroomed person might start seeing things."

"Is 'bemushroomed' a real word?"

"You did ask."

"How's it work?"

"Well, I'm sure you don't really want to know the chemistry…"

"I do, Janie."

"But Jack," she pouted down the phone, "there are so many more interesting things we could talk about."

"Please, just tell me the details."

"Oh, alright then," she whispered, in a tone that I could tell was now intended to sound both playful and sulky. "But it'll cost you lunch."

"Done."

"Okay, the main psychoactive ingredient is the compound muscimol, which mimics the brain-signalling chemical GABA, which in turn inhibits neuronal activity."

"And in English?"

"Oh, nothing I haven't already told you."

"Okay, you got me with that one." I chuckled.

"So, sweetie," Janie then asked, "what have you been doing with yourself this morning?"

"I dropped Sarah off at the station a couple of hours ago – she's visiting her sister in York for the weekend. Then I went for a run and had a bath."

"Mmmm, you'll be all clean then."

"How quickly would it work?"

"Pardon, sweetie?"

"The agaric, after you ate it."

"Oh, that again. Forty minutes, maybe an hour."

"And could it cause fatigue, pale skin, that sort of thing?"

"Not that I know of. Look, Jack, if you are feeling under the weather we can always meet and talk. You know, with your wife away for the Easter weekend and bad memories of the war and your ex, Eileen, coming back?"

"No, Janie."

"You don't need, er... stimulants to get by, do you?"

"The toadstools aren't for me, Janie. It's a child in a case I'm working on. I think he's been eating agarics."

"Of course." Janie laughed. "Silly me. How old is the child, by the way?"

"Twelve."

"And pubescent?"

"Er..." I thought about Michael for a moment, tall for his age and with a slightly 'dirty' upper lip. "Yes, I would say so."

"Hmmm... bad age to take a drug like this. All those hormones. Mind you, Jack, you won't find an agaric round here until the autumn, late summer at the earliest. If—"

"Is there any way they could grow in spring, Janie?"

"Well, not naturally."

"Thanks again, Janie, you've been more help than you know. And we will have that lunch when I've finished with this case. In the meantime, there's a favour I'd like to ask."

"Yes, Jack?"

"Could you have a sample of agaric analysed for me? The institute will pay any of the lab's costs."

"Of course, sweetie. But they're all the same, you know. Agarics, I mean, more or less. I don't want you to waste your money."

"Can you do the tests quickly if I have someone bring it over today?"

"No stopping you this morning."

"Janie?"

"Alright," she sighed. "Just send it in a parcel marked for my attention, and I'll have the folks at the lab give it the once-over straight away."

"Thank you."

"Oh, and Jack, sorry to be a bossy-boots, but before noon, or the lab won't do it until Tuesday."

"Okay."

"And it'll need to be a fresh sample for a full analysis, mind."

"Don't worry, Janie, it'll be fresh."

"I like fresh," she replied. "Now, Jack, may I go back to bed?"

I said goodbye, put the phone down and stared hard at the bright, sweet-smelling fungus in front of me.

8:30AM

Within twenty minutes of talking to Janie Dent, I arrived at the office, to find Miss Stephens sitting typing as usual behind her desk.

"Mr Sangster, good morning."

"Hello, is the old man in yet?"

"No," she said. "He comes in at half past eight, regular as clockwork."

"Good, I'll wait then." I looked down at a newspaper, lying on a chair next to her desk. "Is that your newspaper?"

"No, I guess one of the cleaners must have left it, but it's today's edition, I think."

"Any chance of a cup of tea?" I picked up the paper and sat down.

"Mr Sangster, I have a report to finish."

"But you do make such a lovely cuppa."

"Look," she laughed, "if you want to flatter me into making it, you'll need to do a lot better than that."

"Could I compare thee to a summer's day?" I retorted, going down on one knee. "Thou art more lovely and more temperate. Rough winds do shake the darling buds of May, And summer's lease hath all too short a date."

"Oh, alright." She waved her hands at me. "One cup of tea coming up, as long as you don't recite any more poetry. Promise?"

"Cross my heart and hope to die."

"And it starts 'Shall I', not 'Could I'."

"Whoops."

"Now up you get, Mr Sangster," she said, still laughing as I wrenched myself to my feet against the side of desk, feeling my left knee twinge as I did so. "And by the way, you have a nine thirty at the Manor Free school."

"Thanks," I said with a groan, before picking the paper up again.

'French President threatens to resign' exclaimed the front-page headline in enormous letters, with a few lines below describing the reason for the ultimatum, followed by an instruction to look overleaf for more. I opened the paper to see a bikini-clad young woman staring out at me, with a long-winded paragraph below explaining Tracy's passionate love of animals and, more bizarrely, origami and topiary. On the inside front page (I wondered if anyone except me had ever bothered to read it) was more verbiage on the French President's decision, followed by a short piece on the three astronauts chosen for the Apollo Twelve mission (just as Michael had said) and then a linked article that caught my eye, describing, with diagrams, a total eclipse of the moon due for the following night. What particularly drew my attention was the path of the eclipse, which was shown to pass across the Wirral.

"Ah, Sangster, here bright and early."

"Morning, Johnson," I said with a start.

"Did I see you take a fall just now?"

"Oh no, just dropped something on the floor."

"Good, thought you'd come a cropper. Now, Miss Stephens, is that Eleven Plus report ready to send off?"

"No, I was momentarily distracted," she answered, looking hard at me.

"But it was ready yesterday, wasn't it? Didn't you bring me the report last thing, and didn't I sign where you told me to sign?"

"That was just the signature page, Mr Johnson, I now need to type the report itself."

"Ah, well, just make sure it goes out this morning."

"Wouldn't you like to read it before I send it off to London?"

"Oh no, report's urgent, and I'm sure it will all be in order. Just include a note to the minister mentioning golf next time he's up in Chester."

"Golf?"

"Golf. Now come on in, Sangster, and Miss Stephens, one lump today, please." I followed Johnson into his office, catching Miss Stephens out of the corner of my eye giving a thumbs-up and mouthing 'One lump' with a grin.

"Now then, Sangster," said Johnson, hanging his jacket over a set of golf clubs that stood in the corner before settling into his chair. "Take a seat and give me an update. Ah, thank you, Miss Stephens." Teacups were placed before us, with the secretary pulling a fake grin and whispering 'lovely cuppa' to me as she exited. "Biscuit, Sangster?" Johnson then asked, offering me a half-opened packet.

"No thanks."

"Don't mind if do, do you?" he said, pulling out a gingernut and dunking it into his teacup before I could answer. "Now then, how's it going? Have you nailed that school yet?"

"No, but I think we'll have the answer soon. It definitely looks like money's going missing."

"Embezzlement, eh?"

"Seems like it, but I... sorry, we all need to be sure. I met Mrs Hart yesterday, and she now has a copy of last year's school accounts." I explained our suspicions that the modernisation grant for the boarding house seemed to have gone astray, and our intention to confront Wilkins with the evidence, at the school on the afternoon of the following day. My heart then dropped a beat when Johnson said he wanted to be there.

"Are you sure, Johnson, it being a bank holiday and all?"

"Wouldn't miss the opportunity to watch Wilkins grovel for all the tea in China, Sangster."

"Very well," I said. "I see Wilkins this morning, so I'll let you know the timing after that. I won't be giving him any forewarning today by the way."

"No?"

"No, I'll use a pretext to arrange the Friday rendezvous."

"Jolly good. And the boy's case?"

"Continuing," I said, standing up. "Bye now."

"Can't waste too many more resources on that boy, Sangster," Johnson called after me as I left. "There are other more deserving cases."

"Of course, but the boy's our pretext for catching Wilkins," I replied, closing the door behind me.

"Oh, Mr Sangster," said Miss Stephens, silencing her typewriter. "Your wife just called. From a platform at York station."

"Didn't she ask for me?"

"She had to rush for a bus. Asked me to tell you she has arranged lunch with a..." Miss Stephens looked at the ink blotter on her desk. "A Professor Horniman. One o'clock this afternoon at the Occidental Club, I've made your reservation. Oh," she added, whilst starting to type once again, "and your wife says the professor is also a member but to be sure it's you who pays the bill."

"Thanks," I said, wondering whether Johnson would accept the expenses for this meal given Sarah's description of the professor's appetites, before muttering, "What the hell, after this week I deserve a nice lunch."

"Pardon, Mr Sangster?"

"Oh, nothing," I said, looking down at the newspaper on the chair. "May I, er..."

"It's all yours, Mr Sangster."

"Thanks again," I said, and ripped the front page off, folding it into my pocket, then placing the rest of the paper back on the chair, page three side up. Miss Stephens looked down at Tracy and blushed.

"Now then, Miss Stephens, toadstools."

"I beg your pardon," she said, raising her hands high above the typewriter and looking up at me.

"I have a sample I need analysing, here." I pulled out the paper bag and showed her the fungus, which was still as bright and sweet-smelling as when it was first picked.

"Oh, what do want me to do with, er..." She held her nose. "That?"

"Mark it for this person's attention and have it taken by hand to this address." I passed her a note. "Can you do that by lunchtime?"

"Mr Sangster, you do make some odd requests." She looked at the note and scratched her head. "But, thinking about it, I bet there'll be no end of volunteers from the office to take a day trip to Liverpool with that package." She looked up and smiled. "So yes, before noon it is, but on one condition."

"What?"

"You wrap that toadstool up again. Now."

9:30AM

Half an hour later, I was at the Manor Free, being greeted by Miss Lyons on the school steps.

"Good morning, Mr Sangster, the headmaster and I are so glad the Le Conte boy was found safe and well. So glad."

"We all are, Miss Lyons."

"Oh yes, so glad. Now, come along, Mr Sangster, the headmaster will see you in the library." I followed her through the modern part of the school, past corridors, classrooms and galleries, until we arrived at what looked like a glass tunnel but set three storeys above ground and providing a bridge to the older buildings ('the Skyway, Mr Sangster, out of bounds except to staff, visitors and prefects, same as the main steps'). We crossed, passing several spotty-looking youths in gowns, who nodded to me as equals, then entered a door at the other end and, as far as I was concerned, into a dark and other world.

This was the ancient part of the Manor Free, its cloister-like corridors with low, vaulted ceilings and floors covered by stone flags that were concave from centuries of use, echoing our footsteps (especially Miss Lyons'), as we walked.

"Now then, Mr Sangster," she said, as we arrived at an enormous pair of doors, "this is the library where your meeting will be. I think the Reverend is still in the staff room, so if you'll wait here, I'll go and find him."

She clicked off and I looked around, disoriented, realising I had no idea where I was in this ill-lit sandstone maze. Eyes now becoming accustomed to the light, I saw that the walls either side of the doors were adorned with noticeboards, advertising everything from sporting fixtures to cadet force gatherings, chess, bridge and even debating societies. The latter society's notice (out of date) stated that to celebrate April Fool's Day, there would be a formal debate to decide whether 'A March hare in the hand is worth two nuts in May'.

I laughed to myself, conjuring up a vision of pompous teenage boys earnestly flexing their post-pubescent intellectual muscles in preparation for the Oxford Union or similar (and unfortunately, perhaps even Parliament), whilst congratulating themselves on their superior wit. My laugh was short-lived, however, when I looked across the corridor at a set of ornate gilt frames, all but one of which was filled with lists of names, each frame dedicated to a different conflict: Crimea, Boer Wars, World Wars One and Two, Korea, the Malayan Emergency and so on. The frame on the far right hung ominously empty, as if waiting for the next generation of lost boys to fill it. Each frame bore the same title:

'Nonne Frustra Moriar'

I was suddenly transported back to a sinking ship and the sound of men screaming, some trapped below, some jumping into flaming, oil-covered sea water and many calling my name.

That empty frame, I thought, whilst expelling my breath in resignation, wouldn't have long to wait to fulfil its purpose. Then, my feeling of sad inevitability was broken.

"Ah, Sangster," came the whining voice of Wilkins, even more high-pitched than usual. "Good morning. You haven't been in the old part of the school before, have you? Tell me, really, what do you think?"

"Er… very old. Medieval?"

"Some parts date back to the founding year."

"Oh yes?"

"1436, but we renovated most of those old buildings last year."

"And these are your fallen?" I asked, pointing to the lists of names.

"Indeed, boys and masters, over the years."

"I see."

"Now then, Sangster, come and meet some of my predecessors," Wilkins said, showing me into the school's 'Grand Library', as the sign above the oak doors stated. "This room was the school hall until we had the new teaching blocks built last year. Lucky to have such a space for our books."

I looked up at walls of the room, two storeys high, which were, save for windows and the door where I had entered, lined with books up to the ceiling. Except, that is, for a portion of one wall, against which hung a succession of more than life-size paintings, some portraits, some full-body, some bare-headed, some wearing mortar-board hats, all wearing gowns. The subjects' full names, dates of birth and death, years serving as headmasters, academic qualifications, and in a few cases military decorations, were printed on brass plates below ornate frames. In common with the current incumbent, many ex-heads seemed to have a double-barrelled surname and several Christian names, as well as numerous academic letters.

"These are likenesses of former headmasters. We each have one done when we retire. I, er… do hope my turn shall come." Wilkins paused in thought for a moment, then lowered his voice. "They have all passed on but still watch over the school," he said with a sweeping gesture. "Still doing their duty to the MF."

"Very impressive, Mr Wilkins," I said as solemnly as I could, then added for mischief, "And I am sure they're looking down on anyone who might take from the school at the boys' expense?"

"All Oxbridge men, of course," Wilkins said after what I thought might have been a guilty pause. "Anyway, we have less than an hour before the first library period, after which this room will be filled with boys for the rest of the day."

"I'll be as quick as I can."

"Good, but firstly, thank you again for agreeing to do our talk after Easter." I nodded in acknowledgement. "Now tell me, how may I be of service to you today?"

"You say you have a reference section on the immediate locality?"

"Yes, we do. Best you will find." He pointed to some bookshelves, lining one wall, leading up to a corner with several tables and chairs. "What in particular are you looking for?"

"Any references to the items on this list," I answered, handing him my pocket notebook. He read it out loud.

1. *Stapledon Woods,*
2. *Pagan rituals re sandstone outcrops,*
3. *Quarrying in West Wirral,*
4. *Writings of West Wirral, turn of the century or earlier…*

"Oh, and anything on End of Days," I added, to Wilkins' clear surprise.

"Let me see, hmmm…" mumbled the headmaster, pushing a wheeled ladder along the shelves. "Up here, yes, don't have anything on the woods, but, hmmm… do have a biography of Stapledon himself." The ladder was then pushed further. "Now then, where is the next one you want? Yes, here we are," he said, pulling down a moth-eaten volume with faded writing on the cover proclaiming *A Perambulation of the Hundreds of the Wirral in the County of Chester: With an Account of the Principal Highways and Byways, Old Halls, Ancient Churches, Situated Between the Rivers Mersey and Dee.*

"And now for the very early writings of the Wirral, I think the best we can do is *Gawain and the Green Knight.* It's just…" He peered at a gap in the row of books. "Ah, sorry, someone appears to have taken it out. Translation by Tolkien, you know."

"How would that book relate to this locality?"

"Oh, Gawain travelled to the Wirral on a quest, for no less than the Holy Grail itself." As he spoke, I felt the headmaster briefly looked (as Sarah had once described one of her ordained fellow lecturers) 'the historically enlightened religious academic'. But Wilkins didn't manage the masquerade for long, adding with a slight sneer, "Gawain didn't think much of the place or the locals, though, can't blame him, can you?"

"And something on the End of Days?"

"Let me look, I have a book in the comparative religion shelves." He somehow wheeled the ladder along whilst standing on it and talking, all at the same time (I was quite impressed). "Ah, sorry," he said, feigning disappointment to disguise actual pride. "That one's out as well. The boys at the MF do have sophisticated tastes, you know."

One boy has, I thought, and I doubt you'll find his library ticket in your borrowed books drawer.

"Now for the quarrying, I think…" He whizzed along on his steps again, this time to the far end of the room. "Yes, here it is, *Triassic Quarrying in West Wirral*," he called to me, opening a cupboard door high up and producing an ancient-looking leather-bound book that was covered in a thick plastic dust jacket with the words 'Not for lending' printed on the front. He then propelled himself back towards me, collecting another volume as he came, entitled *Pagan Rituals and Stone Outcrops*.

"Careful with the quarry book, Sangster," he shouted from his moving ladder. "As far as I know it's the only copy ever printed, privately bound and published. Not valuable but couldn't be replaced." The wheeled ladder then squeaked to a stop next to me.

"Now," said Wilkins, descending to the floor and presenting me with the pile of books he had gathered from the shelves, "let me leave you here whilst I take my morning RE lesson, and I'll see you at…" he looked at his watch and ran quickly to the door, "ten forty-five in my study, sharp, please. And do make sure you replace the books where we found them when you have finished. Follow the DDC. You can't go wrong."

"Pardon?"

"Dewey Decimal Classification system," he shouted from the corridor.

I gingerly touched the books and gulped. A lot of reading material, and I had forty-five minutes before the room would fill with boys. Pen at the ready for note taking, I took a deep breath and tackled the pile. Picking up the first volume, it suddenly came to me where I had heard the name Stapledon before. It was Olaf Stapledon, the science-fiction writer. A brief look at the introduction showed that he had lived nearby, the wood being named for him when he died, less than twenty years ago. So the wood, I reasoned, must have had a previous name, an older name.

I put the Stapledon biography aside, then picked up the next book, the one on Triassic quarrying. It was mostly technical detail in very small print, but there was a photo section in the middle which featured pictures of different quarries in the Wirral. I leafed through these, finally coming upon line drawings of the local quarry, shown as it had looked when fully working at the turn of the century.

"Yes," I shouted, banging the book down on the table with a thud that echoed around the empty library, worried for a moment I had damaged this rare volume and looking around to make sure nobody had seen or heard me. This, I said to myself, was definitely the incident mentioned in the newspaper headline from 1901 I'd seen in the Bolshaw House common room, the text underneath the etching mentioning the use of excessive explosive works, done to expose more beds of certain valuable rocks found there (called 'Helsby Sandstone' and used, amongst other things, to build much of the village close by the school).

The author then told how this dynamiting had inadvertently ignited pockets of methane within the rocks, resulting in much larger explosions than expected. The unfortunate side effect of all this had been weakening of the rock beds above a series of natural caves, making the geological structures unstable and forcing the closure of the quarry, apparently resulting in great financial ruin for the owners and job losses for locals. The two deaths were also a great scandal, it seemed, as the workers in the quarry had long known about the methane, which apparently caused hallucinations, with some workers reporting hearing voices, their complaints to the owners falling on deaf ears.

The legal fallout, plus the bankruptcy of the owners, resulted in long-running disputes that meant no equipment could be salvaged from the site. There was a final note explaining the engineers at the turn of the century had reported that the explosions uncovered evidence of ancient mining, perhaps pre-Roman. A major layer of sediment, likely due to a long-ago rockfall, was found to contain several human skeletons, lying in what appeared to be life-like poses.

I recalled Wilkins mentioning that controlled explosions had recently been used to make the area safe from subsidence and also remembered Michael's odd comment the previous evening.

'They let him out, when they blew the charges in the quarry.'

I checked my watch again. Fifteen minutes to go. I picked up the last but one book, *Pagan Rituals and Stone Outcrops*, which described inland and seaside rock formations in various Wirral locations. There were differing opinions as to the pagans' use of the rocks, with passages reproduced from Victorian researchers' books stating that these formations featured heavily in rituals, whilst the author, citing lack of concrete evidence, refuted this. I looked in the back index for the Face Stone and found one reference, a short paragraph that merely noted its position and described a door-like indent of unknown origin and use in its front.

I checked my watch again.

Five minutes to go, as I opened the last volume, *A Perambulation of the Hundreds of Wirral*. The book was fragile, so that the pages could hardly be turned without damage, but I eventually found what I was looking for. The author described a walk through a 'King's Wood' on a hill in West Wirral that featured a large stone outcrop with a door-like indent in its face. King's Wood was Stapledon Wood for sure!

And, "Oh," I said out loud to myself, remembering the name of the Le Conte's mansion, Kingswood House.

Just then a bell rang out, and a few moments later a surge of boys burst through the library door. They were jostling to get to the desks and shouting amongst themselves when their master entered. The room went quiet as the teacher walked over to where I sat and asked me if he could help.

"Actually, yes," I said, standing up then patting the books in front of me. "I've been doing some research for the headmaster and I'm hanged if I can get the better of this Dewey Decimal thing. You couldn't, er…"

"Put them back for you?"

"Yes, that's awfully kind," I said, then ran for the door.

*

The corridor by the library was awash with boys and masters, moving in opposite directions but somehow, despite a superficial chaos, able to pass each other freely and without collision. I flattened myself against the wall, until a second bell rang out, triggering silence within a few seconds as classroom doors were shut and lessons recommenced. I gave the roll call of the fallen one last respectful glance, then turned back towards the Skyway. After the noise of the class change-over, the vaulted ceilings and stone-flagged floors seemed to echo all the more, not just with my steps but of all who had walked before me. And not just the footsteps of those who fell before their time but those who lived out their days, good, bad or indifferent. I could imagine crowds of vague shadows passing me (much as the living boys had done in the corridor by the library), whispering as they went.

'We all matter' was what I intended them to say, but somehow my mind wouldn't obey, and all I heard was 'it doesn't matter in the end'.

"It does matter, it does," I shouted out loud, eyes narrowing and feeling slightly dizzy as I opened what I thought was the door to the Skyway, preparing my eyes for the light as I did so only to see through half-closed lids that I had gone into a toilet. Stepping out, I soon found the way into the brilliant sunshine of the Skyway, once again getting the sense that I had stepped into a different world (this time my own).

Momentarily dazed by the brightness, I blinked to see three gowned prefects standing in front of me.

"I'm sorry, sir?" said one. "You called through the door, but I didn't quite hear what you said."

"Oh, er... nothing, thank you," I muttered, trying to regain my composure.

"Are you lost, sir?"

"No, no. But thank you all the same."

"Very well, sir," the prefect replied, he and his companions giving each other knowing looks as they passed.

I walked on, arriving outside the headmaster's study, where the traffic-light sign was red, so I sat down and waited. Noticing a brochure on the table next to me, I picked it up (the effect of the surroundings made me fleetingly wonder if I was breaking school rules) and flicked through the glossy pages. The preface (written joyfully by Wilkins, pictured standing in front of the school gates in a silk-hooded gown and tasselled mortar board) extolled the virtues of the Manor Free, which was 'indisputably' (he claimed with his first line) 'an historic educational haven for boys, and best in breed for academic excellence, sporting prowess and pastoral care'. Moving on, I came to a section given over to boarding facilities, with pictures of boys in the peak of cherry-cheeked health engaging in various activities. Some tucked into sumptuous feasts, others relaxed in the welcoming common room (pre 'hole-in-the-wall', as the stuffed owls could clearly be seen in the background, on show in their glass case), whilst in a half-page action-shot, muddy but smiling boys participated eagerly on the playing fields and, in the last photograph, settled down into cosy-looking dormitory beds.

This brochure, I thought, whilst not showing anything specifically inaccurate, described something very different from the gloomy place I had seen the day before. The date on the front was summer 1968, so fairly current as well, but I wasn't given any more time to think, as at that moment the light changed to green, the study door opened and Miss Lyons appeared.

"The headmaster will see you now."

"So, Mr Sangster, you found everything you needed in the library?"

"Most of it, thank you, yes."

"I'll say once again that I, and the whole teaching staff, were very relieved to hear that the Le Conte boy was found."

"As we all were," I said, sensing something in his tone that told me his real concerns were other than Michael's welfare. "But we still have the unanswered question as to why he had been truanting in the first place, so I am mandated to continue with the case."

"And how are your investigations going?" Wilkins asked. "Found nothing, er... untoward, I hope?"

"Going well enough, and just a few loose ends now, but I don't want to be premature, Mr Wilkins. I think I will have my report ready before the end of the week, but I'd like to show you a draft. I know it's a bank holiday, but is tomorrow alright?"

"I'm taking a service in the morning at Saint Hildeburgh's."

"The prep school?"

"No, the parish church, in the town," he said. "But yes, if you can come after three o'clock, that should be fine. To my house, that is."

"The one in the grounds, with the big chimneypot, by the boarding house?"

"Indeed."

"Thanks, that's very accommodating of you."

"Say nothing of it, Sangster, glad to help expedite things. And we'll need your timely official sign-off so that we can, subject to Le Conte absolutely toeing the line, of course, have the boy back in class after the holidays. I spoke with his mother earlier by the way."

"That's wonderful news, Headmaster," I said, deciding to add some mild conflict to divert Wilkins from thinking too hard about the following day's meeting. "I am seeing Michael again tonight, so I'll be sure to tell him you are all gunning for him here at the MF."

"If by 'gunning' you mean giving Le Conte a second chance, then yes, but it's also his last chance."

"Mr Wilkins," I said, standing up to leave, "Michael is at a critical stage, and I would expect you to show him the utmost consideration." I stressed the word 'Michael' to show the boy was an individual with a first name. "If that were not to be the case, I would feel compelled to say so in my report."

"Oh, rest assured, Mr Sangster, I will take personal charge of Le Conte's… er… Michael's pastoral care."

"Then we understand each other. Until tomorrow afternoon then."

*

"Mr Sangster," called Miss Lyons as I walked towards my car. "Mr Sangster, may we speak candidly?"

"Of course."

"The education department's been investigating the school's financial affairs, hasn't it?"

"I really couldn't say," I answered, continuing to walk. "I'm independent, not formally part of things, you know—"

"Our accountants told me this morning they'd been approached by Mrs Hart. She was asking after the school's accounts again, just yesterday, they said." I nodded. "And they were obliged to hand the accounts over."

"I imagine so."

"And you want to see the headmaster about that tomorrow, don't you? Not about the Le Conte boy at all."

"Perhaps, but what do you want of me?"

"Leniency. The headmaster's a wonderful man." She looked downwards. "What I mean is, well, he does so much for the school, for the boys. It's his life. He doesn't spend much money on himself, doesn't have a car or own a house. No savings to speak of."

"Except for—"

"Yes, but if he gave the grant money back?"

"I don't think the law will see it that way, I'm afraid."

"But you could. You're independent."

"Yes, but not above the law. Now, I must be going."

She grabbed my sleeve. "You're different. I can tell. If we were to somehow ensure that the right thing was done from now on, wouldn't you…?" She tugged harder at my sleeve. "Couldn't you help?"

"And you?"

"I'm very close to Thomas, I mean, the Reverend Benton-Wilkins."

"I'm sure you are, and if I may say so, I don't understand why you try to cover it up, Miss Lyons."

"Can I trust you with a confidence, Mr Sangster?"

"I hope so."

"Lyons was my maiden name," she whispered. "I am actually a Mrs Blount."

"You are married?" I whispered back.

"In name only. My husband lives in London now but still refuses a divorce, and with the headmaster being a man of the cloth, well, we have to be discreet."

"Surely people would understand?"

"Mr Sangster, may I tell you a little story?"

"Er, yes."

"I have a divorced friend whose husband beat her over many years, then walked out, leaving her penniless with a child to support. My friend's devout, but the church now says she isn't allowed to take holy communion, has to sit in a pew at the back of the church while the vicar hands out the wine and wafers at the altar. So no, people would not understand."

"I see."

"But I'm sure I could do something, about the money, that is. And it would be for the benefit of the boys, the school, everyone."

"But the money is gone," I said, remembering the name Blount on the withdrawal slip Mrs Hart had shown me. "And you countersigned at the bank when he took it, didn't you?"

"No, he still has the money."

"You're sure?" She nodded, her beehive wobbling as she did so. "That's as may be, but how could I be sure?"

155

"I can't explain now, but I can assure you I know where that money is. If you can just give me a little more time."

"Then no promises, but if what you say turns out to be true, perhaps something can be done." She smiled, with what looked like relief. "Now, I really must be going, I've a train to catch."

12AM

"Return to Liverpool, please."

"Coming back today, sir?"

"When's the latest train that would get me back here for, say, four thirty?"

"Four-oh-five from James Street, sir. First class?" I nodded. "That'll be half a crown. Platform one in ten minutes."

Twenty-five minutes later the train finally arrived, as the tannoy bawled a garbled excuse then warned people that departure would be in two minutes. I sat down in the carriage and waited for the stationmaster's whistle to blow. As it did so, I relaxed back in my seat, while the train pulled slowly away on its journey around the West Wirral coast and under the River Mersey to Liverpool.

The ride was soothing, with the electric locomotive pulling the carriages quietly and at a leisurely pace, the rails clicking rhythmically below and the train rocking slightly as it passed fields and houses. I found my eyes drooping, and, with the carriage to myself, thought 'why not' to a quick nap.

But it was not to be. Although my eyes were closed, the pace of the week seemed to catch up, the events of the last few days swirling around my mind. Then, sleepy and not entirely in control of my thoughts, I remembered Sarah, waving at me through her carriage window a few hours earlier, so eager to help, to be part of my work.

Familiar guilt came calling.

Had I done the right thing by her? After all, when we met it had been, as they say in all the best love stories, a whirlwind romance, but she hadn't known about Eileen until I proposed. And as the carriage continued to gently sway, the circumstances that brought Sarah and I together, which were both exhilarating and also marred by a tragedy, came vividly to mind.

I had gone to visit friends in Kyrenia during the late autumn of '67, an ex-forces couple who had chosen to stay on in Cyprus after being cashiered. The trip afforded me the opportunity to fulfil a long-held ambition, a visit to the Holy Land and Egypt, and a short three-day cruise on a converted Baltic ferry now refitted as a passenger liner with proper staterooms, swimming pool, restaurant and casino, seemed the perfect way to do it. Somehow, the shipping line had managed to get dispensation from Egypt and Israel, with their uneasy peace only a few months old, to include both countries in the same itinerary.

The ship would sail from the southern port of Limassol, landing the following day at the Israeli free port of Haifa, before proceeding on to Port Said and then back home to Cyprus. The package included all meals taken on board, plus full cabin accommodation during each overnight stop (both countries, especially Israel, deemed too unsafe for any kind of long stay), along with guided day trips to Jerusalem and Bethlehem, as well as Cairo and Giza.

The ship's dining format was to allocate passengers to eight-person round tables, and one's seat was the same for the entire trip, although a place could be taken for the captain if he chose to dine on any particular table. As a result, I was asked if I would mind moving after the first lunch (which was with a group of retired hoteliers from Bournemouth) and that evening was relieved to find new company, very flattered to be the centre of attention amongst seven young, female research students, including Sarah. That meal, and the subsequent mealtimes and evening entertainment during the cruise (the restaurant also served as the night-time cabaret room), turned out to be delightful, although it was a little exhausting keeping up with my young companions, who between incomprehensible (to me) academic discussions, spent most of their time talking about or actually eying up men and being eyed up themselves.

Sarah was seated next to me for every meal, and we also sat together on the coaches during the day trips, her understanding of some quite arcane subjects intriguing me from the start. As the cruise went on, we got to know each other better and better, with the electric atmosphere of post-Six-Day War Israel adding to the intimacy. I remember the feeling when she held tightly on to my arm whilst walking around the old Jerusalem Bazaar, as we passed stall keepers sitting with rifles on their knees. In particular, it pleased me, almost as if she had been my daughter, that Sarah was as knowledgeable and enthusiastic as our guides about many of the holy places in Israel: the Church of the Holy Sepulchre ("It's just a twelfth-century Crusader-built thing, Jack, not that old at all"), the Wailing Wall ("Don't bang your head on that, Jack") and the Church of the Nativity in Bethlehem, which I was surprised to find was really just a suburb of Jerusalem ("Now this is properly old, Jack, can't you feel the antiquity?").

But my feelings for her were becoming far from daughterly, and I remember thinking how much I would miss the company of this fascinating young woman as the ship pulled out of Port Said on the last leg of its triangular journey back to Cyprus. The cabaret that night was billed as a musical 'extravaganza', including a show by 'Les Exotiques', a troop of dancers who performed in their ostrich feathers to a backing band playing current hits, Sarah seeming to know all the songs. The band played slower music towards the end of the show, and I finally plucked up the courage to ask Sarah to dance. She and I then moved together across the floor to the final number, 'The Last Waltz', sung by Engelbert Humperdinck, much to the giggling of the other research girls (none of whom had been asked to dance, it seemed). That slow waltz with Sarah was sublime, although the only music that evening I actually enjoyed for itself was a solo in the interval by the band's guitarist, who brought out a bouzouki and played the theme to *Zorba the Greek*, unaccompanied. I spoke to him afterwards and he said he had bought the instrument in Nicosia just six months previously. I shook his hand, acknowledging him as a quick learner and talented in a way I could never be. Cabaret over, Sarah and I then spent the next part of that final night in the casino, where I lost at roulette, whilst she impressed me with her skill at Punta Banco (I never did manage to fully understand the rules).

I realised sometime after the voyage that it must have been at one particular point that night when I knew this was the woman for me. Sarah, carrying the tiniest of clutch bags, was wearing a long, emerald-coloured dress with no pockets, and the moment she cashed in her chips for notes (Cyprus pounds), raised her skirt and tucked the wad of money into her stocking top, will be forever etched in my mind. That she did this unconsciously, and not for my benefit, was the thing.

We eventually said goodnight, after a spell on the upper deck watching the night sky, with me pointing out the constellations only to find she knew far more of astronomy than I did. Retiring to my cabin, I lay on the bed unable to sleep, repeatedly admonishing myself for imagining a young thing like Sarah could possibly be interested in someone like me. And as I stared at the ceiling, the ship now in utter silence bar the very faint drone of the engines, I suddenly heard raised voices outside my cabin window and pulled back the sheets, intending to look outside the cabin door. But as I did so the commotion, whatever it was, abruptly stopped. Climbing back under the bedclothes, I closed my eyes and thought no more of it.

The following morning, I rose early and walked out to the stern pool deck to take some air before breakfast, only to find Sarah there with her six friends, along with quite a number of other passengers. They were looking at the ship's wake, which was curved in a very broad arc, indicating the vessel was turning in circles. Then I saw other ships on the horizon and realised something was amiss. We were addressed very solemnly by the ship's cabaret compere, using his microphone, with the amplified voice out of place over breakfast and adding to the sense that all was not as it should be. It seemed that sometime after midnight the guitarist (whose playing I'd liked so much and whose name I never even knew) had an argument with one of the dancing girls that resulted in him somehow falling over the side. She hadn't reported it for two hours, but now there was an all-out search. And as the compere was speaking, I saw the girl being escorted by several crew members past the restaurant room, shoulders covered in a blanket, her face literally ash-coloured, her body bent. With my practical naval mind, I wondered what would happen to her. Would the Cypriot police charge her, or the Egyptian authorities, or the British; would the shipping line prosecute, or would she go free as the incident happened in international waters?

In any event, as a result of all this, the passengers spent the rest of the day on the ship (food and drink compliments of the cruise line) until late evening when the search was called off. And if the ship had docked as planned, just after breakfast, then I suppose Sarah and I would have gone our separate ways, but as it was, we spent that unexpected extra twelve hours on board together and agreed to meet when we both got back to England (she was in her final year studying for a doctorate at Manchester University). We were engaged by Christmas and married the following summer.

*

"James Street, James Street underground station next stop," blared the tannoy, interrupting my daydream as the train drew very slowly to a halt. I stepped through the sliding doors and onto the platform, the only passenger alighting there, then watched the carriages disappear down the tunnel before turning towards the exit.

1 PM

"So, Mr Sangster, your health," said the bearded and bespectacled man opposite me. He wore a brown, checked, three-piece suit (the waistcoat buttons of which strained to contain his ample girth) and a red and white spotted bowtie with matching pocket handkerchief. We were sitting in a private dining room at the venerable Occidental Club (a haven for fine dining, wine and solitude founded by Liverpool's great and good in times past), having finished a lunch of steak and kidney pie and mash accompanied by claret, which, according to Horniman, was 'a robust chap, Sangster, this particular Bordeaux'. As I watched his eyes twinkle (from the lighting or perhaps the claret), I smiled inwardly at him calling me Sangster from the point we first met, whilst insisting that I address him simply as 'Professor'.

There was a knock on the door and a waitress entered, wheeling in a selection of sweets and cheeses. Horniman, to my surprise, declined to take pudding ('even from the most seductive of trollies', as he put it), patting his waistline and telling me he didn't really have a sweet tooth anyway. We compromised (if such a word can be used to describe the amount of cheese he eventually ate), with Stilton spooned from the half-truckle, washed down by a tawny port (from a full decanter left on my instruction by the waitress). As she cleared the cheese and served coffee, I looked across at Horniman, who was trying to simultaneously wipe his mouth whilst shoving in any last remaining morsels of cheese lying on the tablecloth. Seeing this tableau, I felt my guest was clearly relaxed and ready to 'open up', as Sarah had said he might. Horniman raised his glass and clinked mine, then we both took a deep draft of the sweet, almost blood-red liquid.

"Thank you for coming at such short notice, Professor." I raised my glass and returned the toast. "I really do appreciate it."

"Your wife suggested the venue, and how could I refuse? Member myself, best kitchen in town."

"That's good."

"Handsome woman, your wife, I met her whilst giving a lecture on, er... what was it now?"

"Pagan deities of the North West, I believe."

"Yes, that was it, in Manchester. Your wife was lecturing before me and stayed to do some work in the theatre while I addressed my students. We had drinks afterwards." Here he put his glass down and looked me up and down. "Younger filly, isn't she?"

"Yes, more than twenty years younger than me." I cringed at the thought of what Sarah might say (or do) to Horniman if she heard him label her with that epithet.

"And as I say, lovely creature. Reminds me of a young Elizabeth Taylor."

"Yes, Professor, people tell me I'm a very lucky man."

"So you are, Sangster, so you are," he said, mannerisms and turn of phrase, albeit with a more rich and measured tone of voice, reminiscent of Wilkins. Were these older academics all built to a standard design?

"Now then," Horniman continued, "I'm sure this lunch wasn't purely social, and I can't imagine what you can do for me, so what can I do for you?"

"Bluntly put," I said. "May I tell you?"

"You may," he answered, reclining with hands placed palm-down across his considerable abdomen.

"Professor Horniman, I am told you are one of the foremost experts on pagan deities in the land."

"Perhaps," he nodded. "Professor Emeritus of Ancient Faiths, Durham, sometime travelling lecturer based out of Liverpool University, now occasional speaker and consultant. Liverpool's my alma mater, you know. Graduated in 1924."

"And I am looking for your help, but first, please do have some more of this excellent tawny. Oh." I looked down to see the decanter already empty. "Let me ring for more." I pressed a buzzer on the wall and the waitress reappeared.

"Could you refill us, please?" I asked, holding up the empty vessel.

"The thirty-year-old Ferreira tawny again, sir?"

Horniman sat silently, fidgeting, before she returned a few minutes later with a full decanter.

"Thank you," I said to the waitress. "And don't worry, we'll pour." I recharged Horniman's glass, left my own empty and sipped some coffee.

"So," he then said, sitting back again. "Proceed."

"Well, please bear with me if I ask what seem uneducated questions, but I'm interested in learning more about ancient pagan gods."

"Ah, pagan gods, Sangster." He reached into his jacket and pulled out a curling white meerschaum pipe, the bowl of which was carved into the shape of a man's head covered in leaves. He then tapped this against the ashtray before producing a tobacco pouch and matchbox from his waistcoat pocket. I couldn't help staring at the pipe.

"Pagan is a very broad term, very broad," he continued, whilst opening the pouch and stuffing the pipe bowl with tobacco in a single flourish, doing this with surprising elegance given the thickness of his fingers. "You need to be more specific." He struck a match, lit the pipe then sucked several times. "You see, 'pagan' is from the Latin 'paganus', which literally meant something like, let me see now." He sucked again. "Rustic, I suppose. It was just a Roman catch-all term used for any non-Christians. We still have people calling themselves pagans today."

"Ah," I said, experiencing that trap of needing to already know most of the answer to ask the right question. "So what specifics do you need?"

"Hmmm..." He sucked even harder on the pipe, which seemed not to want to light properly. "Time period, place, which aspects of the ancient faith you are interested in, that sort of thing."

"That's a nice pipe, Professor," I said, unable to stop myself staring at the pipe as smoke eventually curled out from the leaf-faced bowl.

"Ah, yes, my meerschaum. Gift, you know, devil to light. Depicts the Green Man."

"And is that Green Man a very ancient or magical name?" I asked, remembering it was the title of a ghost story Sarah had recently been reading.

"Green Man's a twentieth-century term, I'm afraid, although these images have been around for a while. Give you an example," he said, holding up the pipe. "This meerschaum is copied from a thirteenth-century carving inside a Bavarian cathedral."

"But, Professor, did this image, whatever they called it, represent a sort of pagan woodland spirit?"

He puffed away, then regarded the pipe bowl. "Romantic idea, but I'm afraid not, Sangster. Again, like the name, a modern notion. These leaf-covered faces represented sin and mortality to the ancients." He tapped his pipe on the ashtray again. "Not that our pagan ancestors didn't believe in woodland spirits, far from it, but I digress. As I was saying, give me a place and a time period."

"At least two thousand years ago, perhaps much longer than that."

"So, pre-Roman, perhaps Bronze Age?" He looked down pointedly at his empty glass, so I leaned over with the decanter.

"And the south-west part of the Wirral," I said whilst pouring. "Specifically around all those woodlands and sandstone hills."

"Interesting." He swirled his port, gazing at it with a distant look before putting the glass to his lips. "Very interesting. And what in particular makes you ask about these Bronze Age pagans of Cheshire?"

"A case I'm working on. Could you, er, give me some background?"

"We know little of the very ancient faiths of the British Isles," Horniman began. He then explained, pausing now and again to sip his port and have his glass topped up, that the first religions involved worship of ancestors. But, he said, once people turned from a nomadic hunting life to crops and livestock, and settled down in one place, the land became more important and so beliefs changed.

"The air, the sea, the land, all were divine to the ancients. A tree, Sangster, a rock, a cave, might all harbour a spirit, equal or greater than a man, with equal or greater right to the world around us."

"And these were pagans?"

"No, animists, Sangster, animists."

"What's the difference?"

"Oh," he mumbled. "Not sure."

"But these animists practised here, in the North West, and perhaps in the Wirral?"

"Oh yesh." Professor Horniman was now slurping audibly.

"So," I said, refilling his glass once again, "how would these animists have communicated with their gods?"

"Only the chosen ones would have communicated, Sangster, those considered to have been born with a gift, conduits from the spirit world to the natural world."

"Who?"

"Some called them druids," he said. "Julius Caesar himself had a lot to say about that."

"I thought all druids were Welsh."

"Oh, no."

"So how would one become a druid. Training?"

"Phwoar," guffawed Horniman, spraying port from his lips. "More likely drugs, just like these hippies take today."

"They had drugs in those days?"

"Oh yes, made from whatever they had available. Herbs, animal parts, fungus and so on. Being a pagan meant enjoying yourself."

He sighed and began to recite what sounded like the opening to a poem.

"'The World is too much with us, late and soon, Getting and spending, we lay waste our powers, Little we see in Nature that is ours'... How's the next bit go, Sangster?"

"Don't know that one, Professor."

"Ah, I think I have another bit, yes. 'Great God, I'd rather be, A pagan suckled in a creed outworn, So might I'... Lovely verses," he whispered, looking to the ceiling, "but blessed if I can remember the rest."

"Tell me, Professor, would these ancient gods have been very local or more widespread?"

"Oh, very local. Remember, unless you were something like a soldier or noble, you didn't tend to travel far from where you were born in those days."

"So the pagans didn't believe in a worldwide religion, like Mohammedans or Christians do?"

"Oh, they did. To them, everything was linked, you see, interconnected. Your local god would have communed with others across the Earth, giving them power that was to be respected, feared even."

"Do we know how these ancient pagans appeased their gods?"

"Plenty of evidence that they sacrificed livestock and even humans."

"Human children?"

"Sometimes children, but an adult man, willingly sacrificed, was considered by many as best to make the gods do your bidding." He tapped his pipe and screwed his eyes up in concentration. "Now, how did they put it in one old account I read, yes... 'A full man, come eagerly to his fate.'"

"Were there other ways of controlling these deities?"

"Oh yes, human sacrifice would be for short-term, immediate effects. In the main, these ancients believed the gods were subject to natural forces."

"Such as?"

"The moon was the strongest," he answered, bowtie slightly askew as he helped himself to the port, superficial niceties having been forgotten as the dark liquid performed exactly as I had hoped it would. "They were ruled by the moon."

"And the seasons, how did they name the seasons?

"Not seasons, but times of the year."

"And this time of year?"

"Er… April the, er…"

"Tenth," I said, reaching over and steadying Professor Horniman, who, with bowtie now drooping even further, was leaning precariously to one side.

"Ah yes." He sat upright again. "Then we would be between Ostara, that's the vernal equinox, and Beltane, a time over the last night of April and May Day."

"I'm sorry to keep asking all these questions," I said, keen to find out more while Horniman could still talk coherently.

"S'quite alright, Sangster. With port wine as good as this you can ask till the cows come home."

"Well, I wondered if you would know any important pagan sites in the Wirral? Stone outcrops and the like."

"There were a few, but most have been built on now. Mind you, it was places like that which led to my interest in the ancient faiths, you know." He then stopped, apparently lost in thought, so I prompted him with another top-up.

"Professor?"

"These wild places are fast disappearing, Sangster. Towns and villages encroaching all around, sacred places now in isolated pockets, like those hills, rocks and woodlands in the Wirral you mention. People living in little rows of houses where once the gods could walk from river to river, under the trees and without seeing the works of man." He looked distant, almost wistful, and I wondered if a lifetime of studying ancient faiths (with a little help from fermented grapes), had gradually turned Horniman's beliefs towards the pagan way. Perhaps, but whatever his state of mind, I realised this was my last chance today for any more information.

"And the Face Stone, do you know of that?" I asked.

"Name rings a bell," said Horniman, taking out the pocket handkerchief and mopping his forehead. "Now, where's that port decanter?"

"I'll pour another, you just try and remember the Face Stone, Professor."

"Read it somewhere, perhaps." His head lolled, bowtie now completely askew. "But no, it was when I was very young." Eyes half-closed, he now talked, in almost delirious whispers, of a midsummer night, with undergraduates running naked together in the woods and dancing under the full moon around a great stone.

"We could sense it, alive, in the trees, the rocks, all around us. We could almost hear it speak." He sat up and raised his voice. "Do you think it will really let us keep crawling all over the precious Earth? Time will come when the Earth will say, enough," he shouted, glass raised a little too excitedly so that the port splashed his suit. "Oh dear, sprayed meself. Anyway, got carried away there, what was I saying?"

"You were telling me about your undergraduate days, Professor."

"Wash I now," Horniman murmured, head lolling again.

"Yes, you have been a great help and thank you for your company at lunch. I have to dash but please do stay and finish the port. Good afternoon." I left the Professor Horniman muttering, "Don't mind if I do," before leaning back in his chair and starting to snore, his elbow nudging over his still full, but now quite cold, coffee cup. I mopped the table with a napkin, gently placed his smouldering pipe in the ashtray and then left, asking the waitress on my way out to wake him at five.

3 PM

I stood on the steps of the Occidental Club and breathed in the afternoon air. Whilst Professor Horniman had drunk almost all of the claret and port served at lunch, my own few glasses still left a slightly soporific effect, and there were two more meetings to go on what had already been a very long day.

Walking down the road, I heard the blast of a ship's foghorn and decided, rather than using the nearby station, to take the ferry over the water and join the train from there. I couldn't think of anything better than a trip across the Mersey to wake me up.

I carried on, past the Liver Building with its clock-faced tower and statues of rampant green birds, along with the Liver's stone-clad sisters, the Cunard and the Mersey Docks and Harbour Board buildings. Together, they made up the 'Three Graces', enduring soot-stained survivors of better times in Liverpool and now surrounded by decay on all sides. Indeed, as far as I could see along the riverside there were derelict docks. Built, no doubt, by confident maritime entrepreneurs to service every cargo imaginable, from sugar to slaves, these havens were now unfit for the modern age and condemned to rot, perhaps (I thought with some emotion) like the once (and future, I hoped) great city they had served so well.

Walking across to the ferry terminal (a wooden building, painted a virulent shade of green that after the lunch with Horniman almost turned my stomach), I paid at a kiosk and pushed through a turnstile to the sound of a ship's hooter.

"Ferry's leaving in a minute," shouted the ticket collector, and I ran, down a covered walkway that inclined steeply to a floating landing stage (it was low tide), where the ferryboat lay moored.

"Come on, mate," called a shore-hand, lifting thick, looped ropes from several dockside bollards. "Jump on quick."

I jumped, a boatman pulling across a metal gate behind me, while the shore-hand stepped back onto the landing stage and made a thumbs-up signal to the bridge. A hoot from the red and black funnel blew out once again, after which the flat-bottomed ferry turned on itself by ninety degrees, the boat's propellers causing water and mud to kick up from the shallow river and spray against a row of fenders (made of car tyres) that hung on the side of the landing stage. I laughed as the shore-hand, drenched up to his chest, jumped backwards and shouted something up to the bridge, his voice, fortunately for the passengers, I guessed, inaudible over the ferry's engines.

Climbing up to the top deck I leaned against the side rail, staring at the murky water below as the boat steadily plied its way across the river, navigating around several larger ships that lay moored in the Mersey roadstead. The breeze was fresh, and much stronger than it had been on land, so that the effects of the wine, steak and kidney pie, and cheese, so recently taken with Professor Horniman, were soon replaced by a clear head. Pulling out my notebook and pen, I scribbled a few lines.

Green man – sin and mortality, wood spirit?
Prof H's pipe looks like Michael's King under the Hill sketches?
Ruled by the moon?
Conduits, druids, animists, drugs of herbs and fungi
Prof H dancing around stones!!!

If Horniman could acquire all this knowledge, I thought, then so, at least in theory, with access to the Manor Free library and who knows what other sources of information, could Michael Le Conte. If that was the case, then perhaps, like Sarah's reincarnated serving wench, Michael really did believe in the King Under the Hill, and if he had been eating agaric mushrooms, then the delusion would doubtless seem all the more real.

I felt sure Mrs Magister knew far more than she had let on and watched as the shoreline of the Wirral, as well as my meeting with Michael's erstwhile headmistress and now private tutor, drew nearer.

5PM

"Mrs Magister, thank you for seeing me again. I'll try not to take too much of your time."

"That's quite alright, how can I help?"

"I just need some last pieces of information for my work on the Michael Le Conte case."

"I wonder if they will be the last," she said, smoke rising from her ever-present cigarette holder. "But do tell me."

"The condition you ascribe to Michael. Would it cause him pain, mental pain, inside, I mean?"

"Yes," she answered, "I do believe so. He must spend his days in uncertainty. Will he be able to sit still in class, will he get into a fight, will he let himself down by lying and getting deeper into the lie, will he just wake up feeling emotionally different to yesterday? He cannot even trust his own mind. He may wonder who he really is. So many unknowns. And a perceptive boy like Michael often worries about more abstract things. Bad news on the TV, say a programme on nuclear war. Who wouldn't feel pain, Mr Sangster?"

"And is there any way of respite?"

"As I say, in adults, alcohol gives temporary relief, and there are tranquilisers, amphetamines and so on. But," she said, shaking her head, "drugs leave the child in a state of perpetual drowsiness. The baby goes out with the bathwater, as it were."

"Would there be delusions? Hearing voices, seeing things that aren't there?"

"I've never actually read of the condition causing such delusions," she answered slowly and appearing to choose words carefully, whilst flicking ash in her tell-tale mannerism of discomfort.

"And you say this condition may be physical."

"Yes."

"In what way?"

"Most people believe these children's brains are overactive, resulting in intelligence but also restlessness and erratic behaviour. I disagree. I suspect their brains are underactive."

"How so?"

"I can only guess, but I believe that most of us have filters in our brain, filters that are somehow switched off in subjects like Michael. Filters that keep us stable, that prevent information overload."

"And what would it take to turn those filters back on?"

"Not surgery, that's for sure. The solution will be at a biochemical level."

"Sorry?"

"A drug of some kind, as yet unknown. Perhaps it occurs in nature and is staring us in the face, like penicillin."

"You want to give these children penicillin?"

"No, no, no, not antibiotics per se, I just meant something natural, hiding in plain sight, waiting to be found. But for now, as I said to you before, Mr Sangster, Michael remains a complex and insoluble case."

"Perhaps," I said, leaning back in my chair, "not so insoluble.

"How do you mean?"

"You told me you hadn't seen Michael for almost a year."

"Er... possibly, I don't recall our exact conversation."

"The Le Contes say you have been giving Michael regular tuition, right up until last week."

"Er... yes," she said, flicking ash and looking from side to side. "I must have forgotten to mention that. English lessons. He's very talented, as I said. I even organised a pass for him at the Picton."

"Sorry?"

"The Picton Library in Liverpool, next to the museum and the art gallery. Probably the best in the country, after the British Museum, of course."

So, I thought, Michael had doubtless been using some of his time off school to visit this place, but he must have been going somewhere else as well. Did this woman know?

"Mrs Magister," I said, standing up, "I need you to be open with me."

"Open," she whispered, looking up at me with what I thought was the realisation that I knew she had lied about Michael, before speaking more loudly. "Of course."

"Then tell me, that book." I pointed to the *End of Days* volume on her shelf. "Michael has the same one in his bedroom, and the book next to it on your shelf, *Mycology and the Hallucinogenic Effect*, why would you want that?"

"I, er..."

"Please," I said, sitting down again. "Just let me know what you've been doing with Michael. The boy is clearly ill and very possibly in some sort of danger. I'm not a school inspector and certainly not a cop. I won't judge you."

"I'm sorry..." She dabbed her eyes with her trademark black lace handkerchief. "They were books I bought after some of the sessions with Michael – let me explain from the beginning."

"Please."

Mrs Magister then told me that during her research on hyperkinetic disorders amongst children, she had come across accounts of certain ancient Siberian communities successfully treating what sounded like similar symptoms with fungi. Convinced as she was that such disorders were the result of physical differences in the brain, rather than the accepted idea of pure bad behaviour, environment or upbringing, the idea that there might be a natural remedy was of great interest. Michael had been receiving regular private tuition for some time when two events coincided to make her decide to use the boy, whom she knew suffered badly from the condition, as a test subject.

The first event, Mrs Magister said, was a talk she gave on her theories at Liverpool University, where she was laughed off the stage (presumably the same speech Johnson had mentioned). The second event was Michael showing her a drawing he'd made of an agaric. She had already realised the fungi used by the Siberian shamans was likely to have been fly agaric and so planned to persuade Michael to eat some and record the results.

But the results, as she discovered to her dismay, were not as expected.

"He was always deeply imaginative, and perhaps far less secure than he seemed on the surface, you see."

"Less secure?"

"Mr Sangster, last time we met, I think I may have told you I didn't hold with Freud."

"You did," I replied, wondering where this was leading.

"And no more I do, but that doesn't mean we can't attribute childhood issues to family. With Michael, well, his father…"

"You don't mean?"

"No, no," she answered quickly. "Nothing like that. Just a distance, so that the boy won't confide in his father and actually tells me he worries for his parents' welfare instead. In Michael's mind, that means he takes on responsibility where he should find succour, and for a twelve-year-old, that's a terrifying reversal of the parent-child relationship." She dragged hard on her cigarette. "In the boy's mind, of course."

"I can see that. But the results. Different than you anticipated?"

"He became extremely obsessive, Mr Sangster. And his health deteriorated."

"Yes, I saw him last night and he certainly doesn't look well. Doctors suspect anaemia."

"I told him to stop using the agarics, I tried, but it was as if a floodgate had been opened. He couldn't stop. Or wouldn't stop."

"Addiction?"

"I'm not sure, more likely the result of the hallucinations. Perhaps I had better show you my notes." She opened a drawer and brought out a notebook. "I have several notebooks on Michael, but this one contains the entries I made since February," she said, then placed the notebook on the table, side on so we could both read it. A label on the front bore Michael's name and details:

Subject Michael Le Conte

Male, aged twelve years five months.
Displays severe hyperkinetic disorder symptoms.
Regular hour-long one-on-one sessions.

"He we are." She opened the file and turned several pages then pointed to the date on the first entry. "This was the first time he mentioned the agarics."

February 7th – Subject reports agarics growing in woods close by his home. Have suggested he ingest small amount to see if symptoms are alleviated.
February 14th – Subject reports merely licking agarics eases feeling of anxiety and restlessness – success?
February 21st – Subject continues to report reduced anxiety – encouraging!
February 28th – Subject clearly hallucinating. Continues to report voices and now reports visions.
March 5th – Subject appears paranoid. Is convinced crows around his house are watching him. Has shot many of the birds and hung them in the woods as a warning to, quote, 'other birds like them and their master'. Who is this master?
March 26th – Three weeks since last session. Subject still

convinced of delusions. Subject appears to be physically
weakening.

"It was at the time of this last entry, Mr Sangster, that I became extremely concerned for Michael's wellbeing."

"Why didn't you alert the authorities, or his parents?"

"I've been very remiss, I admit." She dabbed her eyes again. "But I was getting so close with my research. I wanted to carry on, show those fools who laughed at my theories that the condition was physical and could be treated with drugs like any other ailment. I was selfish, as I realised when I saw Michael for the last time. Look."

April 3rd – Subject appears further changed. Pale and obsessed.
Pleaded with him to cease eating the agarics. Subject refused. Is
suffering from delusion that the end of days may be upon us, and
only he can stop it. Is now hyper-focused on this one goal. Hasn't
been attending day school since February, spending time devising
plan to thwart end of days. What can plan possibly be?

"But still you didn't say anything?"

"No, I didn't. I'll understand if you feel compelled to report me to the authorities."

"Not right now, but your deliberate misconduct is a very serious matter, and I'll call you tomorrow to discuss it further. I assume you can make yourself available on a Good Friday?"

"Yes," she whispered.

"Very well, mid-morning then, but I have to ask again, why on Earth didn't you tell someone what was happening?"

"It all spiralled," she said, continuing to dab her eyes. "Got out of hand. I should have reported it from the outset, but when I let it run on and Michael was clearly degenerating, I panicked." She paused to light a cigarette, her hand trembling as she did so. "Plus he has a way with him." She drew smoke in deeply between words. "He demanded I keep quiet, threatened to report me if I spoke out. What else could I do?"

"Well, he's a child and has no hold over me, so I intend to stop all this now. Is there anything else you can tell me that might help?"

"Do you understand the nature of obsession, Mr Sangster, of compulsion?"

"Well, my wife says I'm a bit of a bore about cars, but…" I saw an angry look in her eyes and stopped speaking.

"Then let me illustrate with a very local legend. You saw a long sandstone wall opposite the school?"

"I saw a lot of sandstone walls, but yes, I think I know the one you mean."

"That was the boundary of the old manor, the one that the Manor Free school is named for. Knocked down after the war."

"I see."

"If you'd look carefully you really would see."

"See what?"

"An inverted stone heart, set in the middle the wall, about half-way down the hill." She then told me how, in the last century, the builder of the wall, in fact the builder of the numerous sandstone walls in the area, had fallen in love with the beautiful daughter of the master of the manor. The girl would not go against her father, who refused the match, and from then on, the builder, heartbroken, became driven to complete his walls, a man obsessed, working day and night.

"And on one night, he embedded an inverted heart into the wall surrounding the very house where his beloved dwelt, setting her betrayal in stone forever."

"That's, er… an interesting story."

"Don't you see my point, Mr Sangster?" I shook my head. "The man became utterly and unnaturally fixated due to intense emotion, to the point where he built more walls than it should be possible for one man to build in one lifetime. Just look around this town if you don't believe me."

"And Michael?"

"I sense something similarly intense brewing with Michael, something that he is driven to finish." She dragged hard on the stem of

179

her cigarette holder. "And despite his, er... tender years, if he can he'll remove any obstacles that may get in his way to achieve it, regardless of the cost to himself or others."

"What exactly?"

"I honestly don't know, Mr Sangster, but possibly something quite dreadful and quite imminent."

5:50PM

My car clock showed ten to six, so well over an hour left, I thought, before meeting the Le Contes. Driving past the Manor Free, I was wondering how to fill the time, when I noticed a lane on the right. Next to the entrance stood a wooden sign, some of which was rotted away, although the word 'Quarry' was still clearly marked, along with instructions from the council about the area being unsafe. Surely this was the track leading to the very same quarry I had been reading about, and the place that Michael had mentioned?

Pulling up with a screech (and apparently to the chagrin of the driver behind me, who honked his horn and offered a 'V' sign several times to me through his window as he passed), I pushed the gear lever forward and to the left, slamming the car into reverse, then, after fifty yards, changed up again and turned into the track, a narrow green lane lined either side by gorse bushes.

My car, with its low clearance, struggled with the rough terrain, and I bumped along, driving slowly in S-shape patterns to avoid potholes and deep ruts on either side, before passing a further sign stating that the tipping of rubbish was prohibited (which didn't seem to have dissuaded locals from discarding everything from car tyres to washing machines amongst the bushes). After a hundred yards or so, a small clearing came into view. I looked ahead and, seeing thick bushes, realised I couldn't drive further, parked and stepped out of the car, noticing a series of metal wands driven into the ground with tape linked between them, as well as a wooden sign on a pole, which bore a grinning skull-and-crossbones.

'DANGER' exclaimed the print under the death's head, in large red letters. 'Rylance & Partners. Explosive safety works underway, flammable gases, do not enter. 7 February to 14 February inclusive'.

Stepping carefully over the tape, I continued on foot up the path ahead, which, after a further few yards, forked. Taking the track on the right I quickly came to a tumbledown wire fence and, climbing over this, saw a white-walled, flat-roofed building through the bushes. Close up, I could see the walls were covered with decaying plaster, in some places heavily cracked, in others missing entirely to expose patches of dull underlying metal, conveying a flimsy, temporary look so that I imagined the whole edifice might collapse given a push in the right place. "A prefab," I said out loud, and walking through patches of nettles and other weeds to the back of the building was unsurprised by lettering on the wall above a pair of steel doors stating, 'Ministry of Defence Property'.

This place would be one of many such facilities, hastily erected during the war and hastily abandoned afterwards. I pulled at one of the doors, which creaked on its hinges but opened surprisingly easily, and entered a chilled space, ill-lit by small iron grated windows, each with its panes of glass long since broken. The air inside was thick with dust, which could clearly be seen suspended in the few rays of penetrating sunlight. Here and there amongst the dirt-stained remnants of linoleum tiling, discarded rubbish (mainly old newspapers, rusting tin cans and empty bottles) littered the uneven concrete floor. Against a side wall, covered in graffiti (including the life-sized figure of a young woman dressed only in stockings and high heels, and actually rather well drawn in charcoal), I noticed bare wiring and other remnants of a military radio installation, along with what must have once been metal shelving and filing cabinets, now warped and almost unrecognisable (presumably from having suffered the attentions of destructive youngsters over the years). No, I thought, this forsaken relic of the past wasn't what I'd come for, and was turning to leave when I saw it, the answer to a question that had been vexing me since my first meeting with Wilkins.

What had Michael Le Conte been doing when he truanted, rain, wind or shine, for six whole weeks?

At the end of the room, in one particularly dingy corner, I recognised a sketch of the Face Stone pinned to the wall. Below this were several wooden packing cases, arranged to make a table, on top of which were a tilly lamp and several thick sheafs of papers held in place with rocks serving as paperweights. One upended box formed a seat, around which sweet papers and empty pop bottles were strewn on the floor. A paraffin heater and metal drum of fuel (judging by the smell) sat close by, all this making a cosy-enough lair for Michael to spend his days.

I shook the tilly lamp, feeling the slosh of oil inside, and, taking a match from a box next to it, lit the wick, whistling as the hidden secrets of this darkest crook of the room suddenly came to light.

The first thing I noticed was a book, *The Moon and Her Phases*, as its grey dust jacket told me in a semi-circle of fancy script underneath images of the lunar cycle, from crescent to full disc and back again. Below that was a label declaring the book to be 'Property of the Picton Library, Liverpool – To remain in the Reading Room, reference only', and next to this volume, a sheet of notes, written in a spidery and rather immature hand that I recognised as Michael's from the wording on the picture of the Face Stone in the Le Conte's kitchen. But the text itself seemed gibberish, with apparently random letters, numbers and odd symbols, all meticulously laid out in rows, now and then interspersed with equally meaningless diagrams showing intersecting circles and lines. I thought of *A Practical Guide to Codes, Pictograms and Cyphers* lying on the bookshelves in Michael's bedroom and presumably also stolen from the Picton Library, then folded the notes sheet and put it into my pocket. Flicking through the rest of the papers, I found that they were all sketches, some of animals and birds, others of landscapes, including various woodland scenes (with several more of the Face Stone), as well as numerous drawings of a place with high cliffs and an expanse of water. Was this the old quarry I had come to see?

I looked at my watch. Six fifteen. Now I knew where Michael had been spending most of his time ('there's an old house kind of place next to it, all overgrown, and a shelter', I remembered him saying), and with nothing else of interest in the place as far as I could tell, I decided to carry on towards the quarry itself. As I came again to the wire fence I noticed what at first looked like an oblong-shaped pit in the grass but on closer inspection proved to be a set of grass-covered stone steps, some of that grass flattened by what must have been recent footsteps. Michael had mentioned a shelter, so perhaps this was it, built to protect the occupants of the facility from air raids a generation before and now hiding who knew what.

I was tempted to investigate but, with not long left before my appointment with the Le Contes, decided to leave the shelter for another time. Backtracking along the path, I now took the left-hand fork, coming in due course to a pair of high and heavily padlocked metal gates, either side of which stretched a metal fence topped with barbed wire. A heavily weathered sign on the gates reminded me that 'Trespassers will be prosecuted, by order of the Urban District Council'.

'There's a place behind some gorse bushes where the fence is bent and you can squeeze through,' Michael had said, and, looking around, I noticed a single clump of gorse, a few yards to my left. Pushing behind the bushes (which aggravatingly caught on both my jacket and trousers), I saw the gap in question, where one railing was missing and another twisted sideways. Enough room for a twelve-year-old boy, perhaps, but for a man?

I bent down and heaved my shoulders between the metal bars, eventually bursting through the other side and staggering forward, just managing to avoid falling. Going back to the path, I noticed the track was now lined with metal rails where there had only been ruts before (presumably the lines from the old tramway Michael had talked about).

As I walked on, I saw dark shapes in the undergrowth on either side, remnants of rusting and now-unnamed machines that I supposed must have been abandoned when the place was closed, almost seventy years before. One shape, with what looked like a funnel and dome sitting atop a cylindrical boiler, was more recognisable. I guessed it to be the remains of a small open-cab steam locomotive, now entirely given over to nature, with a birch tree growing up through the footplate and gorse bushes surrounding it. All this evoked an overriding feeling that the quarry had been abandoned in a hurry, presumably after being declared unsafe, and, for whatever reason, the equipment there left to decay.

After a time, the birches and oaks (which had been so thick and tangled as to make visibility beyond a few yards all but impossible), thinned out and I found myself looking at a broad pond, surrounded by a horseshoe of spectacular cliffs, just as I had seen in Michael's sketches.

The pond water itself was black and calm, a mirror that perfectly reflected the cliffs, which towered above in a series of red chimneys (almost, I couldn't help thinking, like the sponge fingers surrounding a sherry trifle). One chimney escarpment, almost perfectly cylindrical with a serrated stone top, stood higher than the rest (which were themselves already well over two hundred feet high), but despite this, the general evenness of the cliffs, their height and shape, clearly indicated the work of men rather than nature.

Looking carefully towards the far end of the pond, my eyes accustoming to the dusk (due to their height and east-facing aspect, the cliffs were already in shadow, immune to the evening sunshine), I saw metal scaffolding, even at this distance clearly in a neglected state of repair. These rusting frameworks were effectively ladders leading to different heights, and at the top of each iron 'ladder' was a metal platform next to a gap in the rocks, an entrance that followed the natural fault lines, perhaps a narrow aperture like a throat in one case, or a gaping mouth in another. The platforms were linked by horizontal walkways, some of which had collapsed, but for the most part were still intact. At the bottom of the cliffs were piles of rubble and surrounding the bases of the ladders (which were placed approximately fifty yards apart), iron railings had been erected, obviously by their glossy paintwork, newer than the quarry machinery and the ladders, with each set of railings bearing a sign from the local council declaring the cliffs unsafe.

Looking down at the pond again, I noticed a metal pylon protruding from the water and, upon inspection, made out the largely ruined and half-submerged remains of a cab beneath. Altogether, this must have been a substantial crane in its day and, like the other machinery I had seen, not something to leave here without good reason.

Other than a small gravel area leading to the water, bullrushes surrounded the edges of the pond, the sides of which sharply met the base of the cliffs, leaving no place to walk. And besides these rushes I saw no plants of any kind by the pond, except, that is, for a willow tree, which lay almost horizontally across the surface of the water. The trunk, which I judged must have been at least sixty feet long, was bent in what looked like a natural right-angle close to its roots, so must have grown to be the way it was rather than fallen in some accident. The tree was also clearly still alive, with green shoots protruding from its thick, gnarled bark. I fancied anyone with a good sense of balance could have walked across the pond over this tree-bridge to access the far end of the quarry.

The whole scene, with the cliffs, the spindly frameworks lying against them, the pond, the strangely fallen willow trunk and the abandoned machinery, was evocative enough, but as I tried to take it in, the silence of the place was suddenly broken by a gurgling and splashing sound. Of all things, the noise put me in mind of a submarine I'd once watched break the surface of a calm sea, its ballast tanks pumping out air and spray. I jumped back from the water's edge as the flat surface of the pond broke with a series of enormous bubbles followed by a jet of water rising perhaps six feet into the air. As the jet subsided, I heard a deep, metallic groan reverberate around the quarry, as the crane pylon shifted in response to the disturbance.

This is an unstable place, I thought to myself, as the crane settled and silence returned, only to be broken once again a few seconds later.

'Kak kak kak.'

I looked up to see a bird flying high above the cliffs, hovering in the way that only a falcon can, then dropping like a stone, almost too fast for the eye to see, before colliding with a much larger bird. The two tumbled together in the air, as another falcon appeared from a crack in the jagged rocks at the apex of the tallest chimney, flying directly into the two. Within a few seconds, a mass of feathers fell to the ground, almost at my feet.

It was the body of a crow, bloodied and very much dead. Before I had a chance to look at the carcass properly, I heard another 'kak kak kak' and watched as one of the falcons alighted on the willow trunk, not ten feet away. It held me in its gaze for a moment, head turning to one side, then looked down at the crow, before flying away, seemingly satisfied the creature was indeed dead.

Looking upwards again, I saw the two small falcons flying together as another crow circled close to their lofty nest. They menaced the ungainly larger bird with a series of loops and swoops, after which the crow, thinking better than to meet the fate of its comrade (I supposed), retreated into the distance. The two falcons followed for a few seconds, then turned back, clearly content that the danger had passed.

I kicked at the dead bird's carcass, which I judged to be much bigger than the crows I had seen outside the cathedral, turning the creature's breast to the soil so that I could better see its plumage. Black, grey and, where blood hadn't stained the feathers too much to tell, white. Its lifeless body gave me an unpleasant, almost nauseating sensation, and as I looked down, a cloud obscured the sun and, despite the calm evening, a chill wind blew, bending the rushes and ruffling the surface of the pond. This unexpectedly dark zephyr brought on an instinctive feeling that I was not welcome in this place, and, looking at my watch (perhaps a subconscious response to bring some normalcy to the situation), I saw that it was six forty-five, time for me to drive to the Le Contes. I was turning to leave when I remembered Sam Youd's words the day before.

'If you could bring me a carcass, I'd be able to answer that.'

I felt in my pockets and pulled out a white handkerchief, then bent down and picked up the dead bird by its feet, surprised by how light it felt, despite the size. Carrying the carcass thus, I ran down the track, the trees now claustrophobic and the rusting machinery either side seeming almost threatening. I pushed, almost in panic, out through the iron railings, and continued running, down the lane and past the fork, until I found myself back at the clearing, where (for no rational reason) I was relieved to see the car still stood parked.

Breathing heavily, I laid the crow on the ground and took out a tarpaulin that I normally used to cover the car's luggage rack, wrapping the carcass as tightly I could to avoid any bloodstains and then placing the package carefully in the boot. I let out a sigh when I finally sat down, turned the key and heard the engine fire, and an even louder sigh when I came to the end of the lane and drove out onto the main road.

7PM

Fifteen minutes after leaving the quarry, I arrived at the Le Contes' house, which was really quite close as the crow flies but a few miles away by road. Pulling up at the head of the drive, I saw Reg talking to Cyril the gardener by the front door.

"Ah, Jack, come over here, please. Cyril's saying he was on one of your ships."

"Oh, really?" I walked over to them whilst trying to remember if I knew the man.

"*Victorious*, sir," said Cyril.

"And may I ask your surname, rank?"

"Able Seaman Blacoe, sir."

"Well, Blacoe, I'm afraid we had over twelve hundred men on *Victorious*, and I only looked after one part of the ship. Which years did you serve on her?"

"'41 to '44, hangar deck."

"Lots of action then."

"Oh yes, sir, and we saw off the *Bismarck*, didn't we?"

"And did that take a lot of lives?" came a voice from behind, and I looked round to see Michael, standing pale in the doorframe.

"Come and join us, Michael, please," said Reg. "Jack, you can answer that question best, I think."

Michael walked out onto the drive, looked at each of the three of us in turn and then spoke again. "So how many died?"

"About three thousand, maybe more," I said, roughly adding up the combined losses from German and British ships during the hunt for the *Bismarck*.

"And why?"

"Because, lad," said Cyril, "they were the enemy. The Nazis."

"Why were they the enemy?"

"They were Nazis, lad," said Cyril, spluttering. "Bad people."

"But how many of those three thousand did we kill?"

"About half," I said.

"So, Mr Sangster, you are saying we had to behave badly to stop even badder people. Is it that?"

"Michael," Reg said to his son, "when you are older, people will tell you not to put words in their mouth. Do you understand?"

"I understand," said Michael, still looking at me. "Mr Sangster, you said you were coming to talk to me?"

"Yes."

"Then can we do that. Perhaps in the kitchen, Dad?"

"Of course, Michael," said Reg. "You go in and Mr Sangster will follow presently." Michael then walked away, whilst Cyril, saluting, left as well, leaving Reg and me alone.

"Wonderful chap, Cyril, salt of the earth."

"I'm sure."

"He and his wife have done for us for, oh, at least twenty years, and Betty, Mrs Blacoe, that is, her mother worked for my parents years before that. They live in the gatehouse."

"Yes, I saw Cyril there yesterday."

"But as I said before," Reg continued, "you seem to have a rapport with my son, Sangster. Marcelle says he's been talking about you on and off all day."

"He may have imagined I'm some sort of authority figure." I

laughed. "Far more important than I really am, but I did take to him. He's an interesting boy."

"My wife would agree, but what I'm trying to say is that he's taken to you in a way…" Here Reg slowed his voice and looked downwards. "A way that he never has with me. I don't know what I did wrong, but anyway, come inside and have a drink."

I followed him into the kitchen, and then through to the lounge, where Marcelle sat, curled up amongst pillows on a chaise longue.

"Sit down, please." He gestured to a wing chair next to her. "Betty," he then called, a small, trim woman in an apron and hairnet appearing at the door seconds later. "Could you bring us both a drink? Scotch, Jack?"

"Well, a small one."

"Water?"

"No thanks."

Betty duly brought us crystal glasses and a cut-glass decanter of whisky, placing it on a small table next to my chair then leaving the room without a word.

"I'll leave you two as well, if you don't mind," said Marcelle, following her to the door.

"Of course, my dear." Her husband sat down on the chaise longue, then poured the drinks.

"Cheers." He raised his glass. "Now then, do you mind if I get a little confidential?"

"No, not at all," I answered, wondering what would come next.

"I looked up your history."

"My history?"

"Well, your naval history."

"Why?"

"Well, you mentioned the *Humbrol*, and she was built on the Mersey, in Birkenhead." I nodded. "Well, my grandfather had an interest in that shipyard."

"*Humbrol* was a well-found ship, but you can't protect a destroyer against torpedoes."

"Quite." He drained his glass. "Top-up?" I shook my head, whilst Reg poured himself a generous measure of scotch. "And from what I can see, you joined the Navy young?"

"You really have been looking me up."

"Yes, midshipman, seventeen," he said. "And what did your father think of that?"

"He didn't. Died at Jutland, some months before I was born."

"I'm sorry, stupid of me. But your mother?"

"She supported me, throughout school and at Dartmouth."

"And after that, oil pipeline trouble-shooter extraordinaire?"

"Not quite extraordinaire, but yes."

"And now you work for the Granville Institute?"

"You ask a lot of questions, Reg."

"I'm sorry, are you sure you wouldn't like a top-up?"

"No, really."

"To repeat myself, Jack," he said, pouring himself another drink and then speaking in a more aggressive tone, "I don't understand why Michael, my son, seems to relate to you, a virtual stranger, better than he does to me."

"Why would you think that?"

"Things he says, gut feelings." I thought for a moment. How much should I say of what Mrs Magister had said, or of what Michael had said?

'That's the worst thing, it's me who must look after them.'

"Sometimes we don't open up to the people closest to us," was all that finally came out.

"I suppose so," Reg replied. "And there's not much I can use from my childhood to guide me."

"Didn't get on with your parents?"

"No, got on very well with my father as far as it went, but I was sent away to school. That was what the family always did. It was Marcelle who wanted day schools for our children, and it worked well for the girls."

"Well, Michael needs you now."

192

"He doesn't seem to, but anyway, I'll leave you to talk with him. Oh, and would you like anything else, a coffee, perhaps?"

"Yes, if it's no trouble."

"Betty."

"Yes, Mr Le Conte." Betty appeared in what seemed like a split second, almost by magic.

"Could you please make Mr Sangster a coffee?"

"In here, Mr Le Conte?"

"No, the kitchen, please. And Jack," he said as soon as she had left, looking me straight in the eye as he did so, "you will tell me everything, won't you? Michael's my son after all."

*

Sipping coffee, I sat opposite Michael, wondering, amongst many other things, whether to tell him that I knew of the MOD house. Michael stared back, regarding me intently and unsmiling across the kitchen table.

"Now, Michael," I said, "you are due at school after Easter. I spoke with the headmaster today, and we will all make sure everything is okay. You will go, won't you?"

"Of course," he replied, still unsmiling. "It won't matter anyway." I wasn't sure what to make of this last comment.

"So, no bones broken from the other night then?" I eventually asked.

"No."

"And feeling well, you know, inside?"

"Yeah, Doctor Merridew said I was okay when he saw me again today." He gave his signature distracted stare for a moment. "Not sure that's what he really thinks, though."

"Why do you say that?"

"Oh," said Michael, looking away. "Grown-ups don't always mean what they say."

"I think that goes for most people, Michael," I said. "Now, look, we still need to talk about a few things. It'll feel like a bit of an interrogation, but it's my job, okay?"

"Yes, Mr Sangster, but you said last night you'd like to see the Face Stone."

"Mmmm." I nodded. "It's a nice evening, so why not? Let's take a walk down to the Face Stone."

"Yeah," he said slowly, looking to one side, the now-recognisable sign that he was feeling uncomfortable. "I'll get torches as well, just in case we need them on the way back."

"Alright, Michael. Better check with your mum and dad that it's okay we go out."

*

Leaving through the back door from the scullery, we walked across a rear lawn and on past some rhododendron bushes, to the back gate I had run through with Reg Le Conte two nights before.

We then entered Stapledon Wood and started slowly down the path, the last rays of sunshine filtering through the trees making for a warm and pleasant ambience, quite different to the nightmarish landscape I remembered from the last time I had followed this track.

"I saw on your school report you fought a boy, put him in hospital."

"Yes, he wanted me to stop drawing a picture, but I had to finish. I had to."

"Why?"

"It was in my head and I didn't want to lose it."

We walked on in silence.

"I spoke with your old headmistress, Mrs Magister, today," I said after a time, watching for a reaction. There was none. "What do you think of her?"

"She likes me," he replied flatly.

"Do you like her?"

"Dunno," he muttered.

"Do you learn much from her?"

"She gave me a ticket for the big library in Liverpool, that was good."

"And you went there sometimes when you cut school?" He nodded. "Lots of books about myths and legends, I suppose." He nodded again. "Did she talk about the woods ever, say the trees, or even, the, er... the toadstools?"

"Sometimes."

Walking on, we came to a rotting post beside the path (presumably the remains of the signpost Cyril had described), above which stood a large oak tree, clearly coming towards the end of its lifetime judging by the sparse foliage on its grey and twisted branches. I noticed a ragged rope hanging from one of the higher limbs.

"Was this the tree where you hung the dead crows, Michael?"

"One of them, yes."

"You like birds, don't you? Those tea cards you collected."

"Not these birds, had to shoot them."

"Why would you do a thing like that?"

"Had to hang them there, to warn off the others."

"Other birds?"

"And warn off the King. He said he would take my family if I got in his way. Sent crows to watch me, watch Mum and Dad, the girls. Loads of them."

"Michael, I have a friend at Chester Zoo, a vet. He says there are a lot more crows around than usual this year, so it's quite natural you should see loads of them."

"These were sent to watch me."

"Why," I then asked, deciding to go along with things, "rather than sending crows, would this King not just kill you if he's so powerful?" Michael said nothing and kept walking. "No, Michael, you must answer me," I said, standing in front of him and blocking the path. "If all this were really true, you would be able tell me why."

"But Mr Sangster," said Michael without any trace of emotion, "when I said I would stop him the King did try to kill me, on Sunday night."

"What?"

"He tried but he couldn't. Only managed to send me to sleep."

"Why couldn't the King kill you?"

"I don't really understand why. He says that like him I'm chosen to be a part of things and that he needs people like me to help him pass between his world and ours. And I'm protected by the juice of the…" The boy stopped himself, clearly about to say something he hadn't meant to. "He could kill the rest of my family, though," Michael then added, looking at me intensely. "Could easily kill you if he liked."

"That's, er… very interesting," I said, supressing a shiver at the matter-of-fact way Michael spoke about all this. "Sounds like this King of yours is bound by rules, just like the rest of us."

"He's bound by the moon, Mr Sangster, by the moon."

We walked on again in silence, the path every now and then negotiating its way over piles of moss-covered stones that appeared to have been hewn from dips in the ground (and which explained why I'd had such difficulty walking there in the dark).

"I went to that old quarry today, Michael," I said as we clambered across one such cluster of rocks.

"What?" he yelled, his voice both louder and more animated than I'd heard before.

"The place you talked about, on the other side of the hill, I thought it sounded interesting. Got in through your gap in the fence."

"And what did you see, Mr Sangster?"

"It's quite a place, all that machinery. And falcons, I saw your falcons."

"Did you see anything else, though?" he asked, voice even higher and wavering slightly. "Or hear anything."

"There was a gas burst that came up from the pond water. Gave me quite a start."

"Yeah, it does that sometimes. But was there, er, anything else?"

"Not really," I said, deciding not to mention the dead crow or Michael's lair. "Mind you, I only had a few minutes to spare, so I couldn't look around properly."

"Oh," the boy replied, going back to his monotone as we crossed the main path through the wood, which I could see now was actually quite a broad straight track covered with red sand ("This track would bring you to that quarry eventually, Mr Sangster"). We then continued down the hill, passing a small stone-bordered pool fed by a gurgling pipe ("That's the spring I sometimes drink from, Mr Sangster").

A few minutes later we stood side by side, regarding the front of the Face Stone, and I tried to imagine (with some difficulty) the young Professor Horniman, frolicking with his student friends on a summer's night over forty years before. Michael stared blankly, giving no hint to his thoughts.

"Looks like a door, doesn't it?" I eventually said, pointing at the stone recess directly above us.

"Yes, a door."

"This peaty soil's a bit damp, though." I lifted my foot out of a patch of mud and sodden leaves at the base of the stone.

"It's water from that spring, I think. Anyway, it's always damp here."

"Yes," I said, looking at the pattern left by the tread of my shoe. "But I don't see any other footprints."

"The King's, you mean?" I nodded. "He only comes here in spirit, Mr Sangster. He can't take physical form. Not yet."

Yet another convenient answer, I thought to myself. Did this boy never trip up?

"Show me where you usually sit when you come here, Michael."

"Over in that clearing, where you and Dad found me the other night." We walked to the birch-lined dell, with its fairy ring of unseasonably prolific agarics. I could still see the stone, but only just.

"It's not the best view."

"It'll be easier here… I mean, more comfortable."

"These fly agarics, did you ever try to eat one, Michael?"

"You shouldn't eat them. They're poisonous. Like it says on that tea card I lent to you." He didn't outright deny it, though, so I bent down and picked up one of the biggest toadstools then sniffed it, the sickly stench making my eyes smart.

"Pleasant enough," I said. "Must be alright to eat."

"No," shouted Michael, reaching towards me and grabbing at the fungus.

"Ah, ah, ahhh," I teased, holding it high and opening my mouth as if to take a bite.

"No." He jumped at me to take the agaric and we crashed together, my left leg twisting at the impact. I cursed my knee as it gave way in a spasm of pain, then felt myself tripping and choking as the toadstool rammed into my mouth. I gasped for breath, swallowed, then fell to the ground, my vision becoming blurred only seconds later. I saw Michael look down at me, then take an agaric himself and run his tongue slowly over its cap, his voice sounding slow and deep. He spoke to me as if in a bad dream, words like 'only' and 'feel' stretched out to 'ooooonly' and 'feeeeel'.

"It's the only thing for the pain," his voice droned in my ear. "I lick a little of the juice almost every day now. Can't you feel it soothing you?"

"I… I… can, I can," I answered, my vision coming back into focus, my skin tingling all over. I felt alive, superhuman, as if I could achieve anything. Looking up at the darkening sky, the trees, bracken, grass and Michael, everything seemed connected. "I want more, I want more," I muttered, and crawled across the ground to pick another agaric.

"Noooo…" came Michael's delirious reply. "You mustn't. Too much makes you think you can fly. Just stay down now and wait, he'll be here soon."

"Who?"

"The King Under the Hill, of course, he comes every day now. He's trying to get home, to get into the Face Stone door. But he can't."

"Why can't he?" I asked, finding the conversation perfectly normal in my drugged state.

"Because only his spirit walks for now. He has to wait until the time is right to actually use his own body."

"When will the time be right?"

"While the moon is covered, and on the right date. Then, just for a few minutes, he can walk the Earth, he can enter the door. It's the season, you see."

"The season?"

"Yes, he sleeps deeply for most of the year, but now, in the time between what he calls, er... Candlemas and Beltane, that's when he is most easily woken, when he is strongest."

"Where does he sleep?"

"In caves, near the old quarry. He was sealed in the rocks there by ancient men, thousands of years ago. They gave everything up to do it, burying themselves alive to make sure he didn't escape."

"But if the King's so powerful, why would rocks hold him?"

"He's bound by rules, so he cannot pass through rock, in body or spirit."

"So they sacrificed themselves?"

"Yes, the King can always be controlled through human sacrifice, for a short time at least," Michael said, continuing to lick the cap of the toadstool. "And those ancients must have thought the King was safe forever, but about seventy years ago, the King says that men became greedy, dug too deep, disturbed his prison with their tunnelling and explosions."

"So, he has been out for a long while?"

"No, he's been wakeful since then but still unable to get out. It was only about six weeks ago that explosives opened up the entrance to his cave. Now he will try to get home, but he mustn't, he mustn't."

"Why mustn't he?" I asked, my head now throbbing, my sight once again beginning to blur.

"The End of Days. He says the time is now right, and if he can get back under the hill, he can call others like him and reclaim the world."

"Why just him, why here?"

"He is one of many, dwelling in the secret places of the Earth, waiting until the time is right."

"Why reclaim the world?"

"He says we don't deserve the Earth."

"Who are we?"

"The human race. Everybody."

"When, Michael, when does this happen?"

"Tomorrow. I only have a day left to stop him, and I can't let you get in the way."

"But how can he reclaim the world from billions of us, with our weapons and armies?"

"He just can. I don't know, I... listen..."

I heard the sound of rustling in the undergrowth, that I would have said was wind had the evening not been still. Then, out of the corner of my eye, I glimpsed something dark, just a shadow perhaps, flashing past a gap in the trees. Then I heard more rustling and saw another dark flash between trees, then another, moving towards the Face Stone, where a moment later I made out the figure of a man, menacingly outlined against the rock.

"He comes," said Michael, backing away from me. "I'm sorry, Mr Sangster, I liked you, but goodbye."

I felt my head throb even more and lay down flat, only semi-conscious now and fading fast. I felt a sensation like searing heat against my skin and saw the figure was now standing over me, lifting something in its hand, a club, perhaps, ready to strike but holding back. The throbbing in my temples then grew louder, and I looked at the trees to see the moon shining through the leaves, which all at once began to move from their branches and grow, becoming beating wings, so that a thousand birds now flocked around the figure, filling the sky with blackness and noise. Still the figure, arm raised high, club in hand, didn't strike, seemingly frozen, for a minute or a lifetime, before my eyesight blurred again and I began to retch, eventually vomiting. My last memory before passing out was Michael shouting something out loud, throwing himself forward and shielding my face with one hand whilst pointing towards the Face Stone with the other.

*

"Mr Sangster, Jack, are you recovered?" asked Marcelle Le Conte. "You were in a bad way when Reg found you."

"Yes, thank you, apart from my headache. I think it was good that I was sick as well. Got most of the fungus out of my system."

"What possessed you to eat some, Jack?" asked Reg.

"I, er… just had it close by my face to smell the scent, then tripped. Swallowed it by accident."

"Did you really?" he replied, with a baffled look.

"And you say Michael has been eating the fungus for some time?" said Marcelle.

"Not eating, licking. But yes, says it makes him calm."

"That would be useful," she said ruefully. "But not at the expense of his health, or his mind. You say he has been experiencing hallucinations?"

"I checked with an expert earlier today, and that is quite usual. As long as he stops, Michael won't hallucinate any longer, so I'm content to close the case now, subject to Michael being monitored closely for a while. I'll prepare my report over the weekend and as long as the authorities agree, Michael can attend school after Easter."

"Thank you, Jack, you don't know how much—"

"Mr Sangster?" interrupted a voice from behind me.

"Yes." I turned to see a young man carrying a brown leather bag appear at the kitchen door.

"Doctor Merridew, I've just been seeing to the boy."

"Is he alright?"

"Um… yes, but let's have a look at you. Don't stand up." With that, the doctor gave me a brief check-up, stethoscope, blood pressure, eyesight and balance. "All seems well, Mr Sangster."

"Would you advise me to drive home to Chester?"

"Yes, as long as that knee's alright."

"You strapped it up well," I said, patting my leg.

"Then drive home, but try and see your GP tomorrow. A more thorough check-up would be wise, given the amount of fungus you ingested."

"Thank you."

"Mr Sangster, Mrs Le Conte," the doctor then said slowly, almost nervously, "may I speak candidly?"

"Of course," answered Michael's mother.

"Since I last saw Michael, I would say he's declined. He's certainly anaemic, and it may be due to these toadstools he's been licking. I would say he has a mild addiction, and although I've never heard of toadstools causing anaemia before, I'm not an expert on fungal toxicology so maybe it is the reason. But," he said, looking very hard at Mrs Le Conte, "with the symptoms I see I wouldn't rule out some underlying cause that needs immediate diagnosis and treatment."

"Oh my goodness," she gasped. "You don't mean leukaemia?"

"Let's not get ahead of ourselves, but I'd like you to bring him into the hospital for some tests. I don't want to delay, but with tomorrow being a bank holiday, we'll have to wait until Saturday."

"Just say when," Marcelle said.

"Afternoons are less busy, especially on Easter Saturday. Someone from the hospital will call you to confirm the appointment time." Mrs Le Conte covered her face with her hands, then quickly removed them as Michael's father entered the room.

"Are you quite well, Jack, has the doc seen to you?" asked Reg Le Conte.

"Well, as can be expected, thank you."

"Would you like to stay with us tonight? We can make you up a spare bed."

"Thanks, but no, the doctor's given me the okay." Doctor Merridew nodded. "I must be getting on home now." I shook my head. "How foolish of me to have managed to swallow some of that agaric, put you to all this trouble. Michael was very helpful, though, coming back to call for help."

"I'm glad you're alright, Mr Sangster." The Le Contes, the doctor and I all turned to see Michael standing by the kitchen door.

"You should be in bed," said Marcelle.

"Yes, Mother, I'll be off in a minute. Just wanted to say goodbye to Mr Sangster."

I looked meaningfully at the boy and he at me. I couldn't remember much of what had happened at the Face Stone and knew I should give no hint of the doctor's diagnosis or the planned tests. What I said next seemed almost banal.

"Now, Michael, enjoy the holidays and don't be late for school on your first day back."

"I won't, Mr Sangster."

As I heard myself speak and Michael answer, it was as if the original reasons for me being assigned to this case, Michael's truancy from school and the financial irregularities at the Manor Free, now felt peripheral. Something else, far more important had taken over, something still not resolved, and it wasn't the forthcoming meeting the following day with Wilkins, nor was it Michael's health, although the latter was concerning.

No, it was what the boy seemed convinced he had to do, something so important that nothing and nobody would stop him.

*

I drove slowly home that night, more than once wondering, despite the doctor's advice, if I shouldn't have stayed with the Le Contes, the effect of the agaric still occasionally bringing on dizzy moments. Nevertheless, I eventually made it home intact and called Sarah. I enquired about her sister's family and made her laugh when I described the lunch with Professor Horniman (especially when I mentioned the 'Younger Filly' comment) and also related my conversation with Mrs Magister. I consciously decided to avoid talking about the evening's drama (no reason to worry her at that distance, and anyway, I was safe now). Saying goodnight, I went to the kitchen and drank two pint glasses of water (the agaric had, amongst other things, given me a raging thirst), walked up the stairs, undressed and went to bed.

After a few hours of fitful sleep, I awoke with a start and sat bolt upright (the residual effects of the fungus, I assumed), my ex-wife's last words for some reason coming again to the forefront of my mind.

'Another world all around us. Things you wouldn't dream of. Outside of science and reason.'

I shivered, then wrapped myself in the bedclothes and slept, this time a deep sleep, a dreaming sleep.

And in my dream, my lucid dream, where I was fully aware that it was a dream, I was now sitting on the end of the bed, regarding our dressing table. It was a three-mirror piece, and in the moonlight shining through the bedroom window (the moon was almost full), the shadow against the wall from the central mirror, along with its two curved side mirrors, took on the appearance of a torso, sloping shoulders curving up to a head. As I watched, unable to move, as is so often the way of it in dreams, the shadow gradually took shape, until a fully formed figure, whom I quickly recognised to be the King Under the Hill, stood before me. I felt fear, the kind only experienced in nightmares, but, still unable to move, simply stared at him and he at me. Then the King spoke, perhaps out loud, perhaps in my head.

"You have the body of one of my watchers. Bury it, before the Paschal Moon."

"Do you mean the crow?"

"And you have a friend."

"Who is this friend?"

"He saved you, by the stone. I cannot pass through a chosen one."

"What do you want?"

"The boy will not stop me," boomed the King, his voice resonating in so deep a register that I seemed to feel my guts vibrate. "The time has come. Now, or if the boy prevails, then in the time of your children, or their children."

"Who are you?" I heard myself intone.

"I am a child of the rock, but you are just a child of the tree bark."

"That's what you are," I answered, this riddle-ridden conversation seeming to make perfect sense in my dream. "Not who you are."

"You need not ask. I am your conscience, a part of all things and I am the end of days. I will take back what is mine. I and my fellows. The time has come."

"Which time has come?"

"The time to stop the rape and ruin of the Earth, and now the heavens." He moved forward, looming over me, now only inches away. "Why, even before the Lughnasa, men plan to reach out and walk upon the moon, my moon."

"A sign of our resolve and ingenuity."

"A sign of your hubris and blasphemy."

"You cannot fight all of mankind."

"Oh," he laughed, "you may think yourselves safe, with your engines of war and your reason. And you may think yourselves invulnerable, but the humblest things can slay a man, can kill all men. My work will be simple."

"What do you mean, the humblest things?"

"You will know. You will know. You will know…" His voice faded, as did his image, and I awoke, fully, feeling my pyjamas soaked with sweat. I switched the light on, walked unsteadily to the washbasin, rubbed cold water across my face, looked at myself in the mirror then stuck out a rather green-looking tongue. The poison clearly hadn't subsided. I glanced over my shoulder at the right side of the bed, where Sarah would normally have been lying, and resolved to join my wife in York as soon as I could. I would spend tomorrow closing off the case, then drive up and surprise her.

GOOD FRIDAY
9AM

"Open wide and say ah."

I made the noise as requested, sticking out my tongue whilst the doctor pushed a tiny mirror on a stick into my mouth.

"That's it, Mr Sangster," he said, withdrawing the mirror. "Blood pressure and all your other vital signs seem fine. I'm no expert on this particular kind of fungus, but I'd say there's no harm done."

"The redness on my hands and face?"

"Yes, looks like sunburn, but likely just a mild reaction to the fungus."

"So I don't need to do anything else, take any medicine?"

"I could prescribe an anti-histamine, but honestly, I'd say just take aspirin when you feel the need."

"And my knee?"

"Should be fine but keep it strapped up and no more running for a couple of weeks. But, as I say, in general you're fine."

"Thank you, Doctor Omodiagbe, I'm pleased about that. I took quite a turn last night."

"You know," he said, taking off his stethoscope and sitting back in his chair, "when I was a boy, in the countryside close to my hometown, they would often imbibe fungi, use it as a kind of recreational drug. And in religious rituals too, to communicate with the jungle spirits."

"What did they believe in?"

"A lot of hocus-pocus, of course, but no matter how crazy they went, once the hallucinogenic effect had gone, things were fine. I remember they would just sleep it off, and I suggest you do the same. It doesn't last."

"Where was your hometown?"

"Nigeria, south-east, by the Cross River, you know it?"

"Near the Cameroon border?"

"That's right, a place where Christianity and Western education in general struggle to gain a foothold, where old rituals and ways still prevail." He then stood up and held out his hand. "Now, if there's nothing else I'll close up and say goodbye. You were lucky to catch me in on Good Friday, I'm due at church in half an hour." He laughed. "Mind you, I'm paid double for bank-holiday consultations."

"Thank you anyway, Doctor. And you've no idea how good it is to hear there's no lasting damage."

10:30AM

"My head still ached when I arrived home from the surgery.

After a hot bath, a cup of tea and the prescribed aspirin, I went to the study, settled at my desk and started to write my report on the Michael Le Conte case. The gist was that Michael, a clever, talented but emotionally fragile boy, could become an excellent and well-adjusted pupil with diligent pastoral care. I noted his possible addiction to the fungus and also that he would be subject to tests for a possible blood cancer or other disorders that could cause pernicious anaemia. There was his violence towards other pupils, which could not be ignored, although based on what he told me, I suspected a boy like Michael would never fight if his other troubles could be resolved.

So, subject to his health permitting and school attendance, my recommendation was close monitoring by the school staff and the local truant officer until the end of the summer term, with an appraisal after that to decide on what, if any, follow-up was needed.

I then came to the difficult matter of Mrs Magister, who, whilst perhaps meaning well, had acted negligently, both in her encouragement of Michael imbibing the agarics and failing to report the boy's problems. And all this because she wanted to prove a point to her peers. I dialled reluctantly.

"Hello, Mrs Magister?"

"Yes."

"Sangster here, calling as agreed."

"Oh yes," came the slightly hesitant voice over the phone.

"I should tell you there was an incident last night with Michael…" I explained what had happened by the Face Stone (at least some of it) and told her that I thought the matter with Michael truanting, subject to careful monitoring and his cooperation at school next term, was closed. I also explained the boy's potential health problems.

"Well," she said when I finished, "I suppose it's a happy ending of sorts, but, Mr Sangster, where does this leave me?"

"I've been thinking about that."

"And?"

"I think you should stop any teaching, including private tutoring. Focus on your research if that's what you want."

"So you won't report me?"

"I can't whitewash it all, I'm afraid, but providing you formally tell the education department you will no longer teach children in any capacity, then I'm sure you'll be able to answer questions that might arise as a result of what I do say."

"That's more than I could have expected, so thank you."

"Don't thank me. What you did was wrong, but I do believe in your work, so I can't see any good coming of having you prohibited from research. In fact, I will introduce you to a friend of mine at Liverpool University who specialises in fungi." As I spoke, I wondered whether Janie's lab tests would throw up anything new and resolved to call her later in the day. "You never know," I then said, "perhaps there is something in the agarics for this, what did you call it, hyper…"

"Hyperkinetic reaction disorder, Mr Sangster. The agarics alleviate it, I'm sure."

"Yes, although hearing voices is not exactly a desirable side effect."

"Pardon?"

"Michael. The agaric made him convinced there was a malevolent wood spirit out to get us all."

"Oh no, quite the opposite. Michael was talking about hearing things long before that. He said someone or, more accurately, something, would speak to him, when he was out playing, in that old quarry over the hill, I think. I suggested he eat the fungi to stop it happening, not just to sooth his anxiety. Let me see now, hold on…"

"But you showed me your diaries."

"From the point where he told me about the agarics, yes, but not from when I first started taking detailed notes." I heard her shuffling papers. "Now, let me see, ah yes, here we are. On the twelfth of September 1968, I wrote: 'Subject hears voice talking to him, claims someone is imprisoned underground. Convinced only he can hear this voice but that it is entirely real. Subject shows hyperkinetic reaction, yes, but no symptoms of schizophrenia or similar disorder.'"

"September, you say, hearing voices?"

"Some doctors would have drugged him, locked him up even, so now, Mr Sangster, perhaps you can better understand one reason why I didn't report as I should have."

*

As soon as I hung up, now with a sense of intense disquiet on hearing that the agarics might not have been the original source of Michael's delusions, I began to type again. But writing that morning was difficult, the noise of the typewriter banging in my ears, my temples throbbing from the previous day's agaric poisoning (and perhaps from the disturbing dream that it brought).

I cursed myself. What a very stupid thing to do, ingesting a potentially deadly dose of fungus whilst on a case and in charge of an unstable child (I even wondered for a moment whether I had subconsciously wanted the accident with the agaric to happen). And now I was getting carried away by something an hysterical child psychologist had told me, something that could easily be attributed to a boy's vivid imagination and wide reading.

For all that, I managed to complete the report and within two hours was putting the finished pages aside to give to Miss Stephens for copy typing at the office. That was it, I thought, the strange case of Michael Le Conte now closed, but I couldn't relax, the idea of Johnson coming to the meeting with Wilkins making me tense. Still, if all went well, perhaps I could go for that beer with Sam Youd (although the thought of beer actually made me gag that morning).

I took another aspirin, returned to my desk and leafed through my diary, intending to plan the following week's schedule now that the doctor had signed me off. It was one of those diaries that showed high days and holidays, as well as phases of the moon, battles and other historical dates, even solar and lunar eclipses. I remembered the article in *The Sun* and checked the diary, which noted that not only were we due for a lunar eclipse but a rare total eclipse at that, with the moon appearing huge, being close to perigee (its nearest point to the Earth, as the calendar explained). Perhaps, if the night sky was clear, I could watch it with Sam from a pub we sometimes frequented that was perched high up on the city walls. Yes, I thought, whilst dialling what I hoped would be my last call of the day, this could be a relaxing evening despite the meeting at the Manor Free.

"Hello, Harry," I said, to the sound of baby cries in the background. "Yes, fine, thanks, can you get Sarah please?" I then related my encounter with the agarics, but not my dream, which I wanted to tell her about in person.

"Yes, Sarah, I'm alright now... just a slightly delicate head... no, I'm fine to drive... yes, I miss you... yes, I'll go to bed for a bit... bye, miss you as well."

Putting the phone down I walked up the stairs, my limbs feeling leaden. Undressing then climbing into bed, I soon fell into a deep and (mercifully, after the previous night's experiences) dreamless sleep.

2 PM

"At about two o'clock I awoke again, feeling much better, just as Doctor Omodiagbe had predicted and, after dressing, went downstairs and put the kettle on. Just as I was taking a first mouthful of tea, the phone in the hall rang. Picking up the receiver, I heard the distinctive husky tones of Janie Dent.

"Jack, I'm fully dressed now. Hope that doesn't disappoint?"

"No, no," I spluttered, my mouth spraying tea across the desk.

"And I have a surprise for you."

"Really?" I said, hearing my voice turn to a croak.

"The lab report from that agaric, Jack, it makes interesting reading."

"Hang on," I said, wiping wet tea from my elbow. "Right, fire away."

"Well, firstly I made a mistake. You can have spring growth with agarics, but it's rare anywhere and almost unheard of in England."

"But it could happen, right?"

"Exactly, especially with the mild weather we've had recently. But listen, with the vernal mushrooms, the strength of the active ingredients is usually about ten-fold greater than in the autumnal growths."

"Vernal mushrooms?"

"Spring, sweetie, but listen, and here's the good bit. Your agaric was supercharged. Massive concentrations of everything, including a far higher than normal secretion of bufotenine on the cap. You would merely need to lick this agaric to get a high, and if you ate it, well…" She paused for breath, clearly excited by the findings. "They normally take a while to absorb into the bloodstream," she continued breathlessly. "But with this baby, why, Jack, it would knock you for six in seconds. It's—"

"Hang on another minute, bufotenine?"

"Yes, it's most commonly known as toad poison."

"What?"

"You know, the glistening whitey-coloured stuff you get on a toad's back?"

"Er, no, but you said supercharged. How supercharged?"

"Well, with the bufotenine levels and the other extreme concentrations, I'd say an order of magnitude about a hundred times the median levels we see in regular agarics."

"Could it cause anaemia?"

"You asked me that before, didn't you? Well, it might make you look temporarily off-colour, especially if you were going to vomit, but anaemia, no."

"Thank you very much, Janie. Now then, if you've got a few more minutes I'd like to introduce you to…" I told her about Mrs Magister and the potential benefits of agarics.

"Sounds like an old battle-axe, sweetie."

"No, she's really rather elegant. Anyway, you'd do worse than get in touch."

"Alright, sweetie, wouldn't usually, but just for you."

3:30PM

"Shall we go in?" I said to Director Johnson and Janice Hart as we stood outside the headmaster's house at the Manor Free. Both nodded and I knocked on the door, which was opened only a moment later by Miss Lyons, holding what she subsequently referred to as her 'pike' (which looked to me like a long broom handle with a triangular pennant attached to hooks on the top) and dressed in a guide leader's uniform, topped out with a battered hat that was large enough to accommodate her beehive and looked as if it might previously have belonged to a Canadian Mountie.

"Ah, Mr Sangster." She regarded my companions with wide eyes. "And oh, Mrs Hart as well, how very nice to see you."

"Good afternoon, Miss Lyons," said Janice.

"And you are?"

"Ambrose Johnson, Director of Education, pleased to meet you."

"Likewise, Eunice Lyons, school secretary, but I'm afraid you've caught me on my way out. Patrol leaders' get-together." She brandished the pike. "Let me show you in before I leave."

We followed her, Johnson inadvertently getting hit on the forehead with Miss Lyons' pike in the process ("Terribly sorry, my pike's rather long for indoors"), to the sitting room.

"The headmaster's inside, so I'll say goodbye now," Miss Lyons then said, turning and almost hitting Johnson again before striding off down the hall. We entered the room and saw Wilkins standing with his back to us, head down and apparently contemplating the hearthrug. Johnson put his hands on his hips and spoke.

"Hello, Tommy."

"Ambrose," cried Wilkins, turning round and pointing at the director.

"You two know each other?"

"Up at Oxford together, Sangster, weren't we, Tommy?"

"Oh, er... yes," stammered Wilkins. "Followed different paths afterwards, of course."

"Aye, we did that," said Johnson. "Me the army, you the church, eh?"

"But you both ended up in education," said Janice. "In your own different ways."

"May I offer you some refreshment, Ambrose?"

"No thanks, Tommy, we won't keep you long."

"Then let us at least sit down. Mrs Hart, Mr Sangster, Ambrose." He gestured to several armchairs circled around the fireplace. "I hope this room's not too hot for you, it's just that I always keep a fire until May Day. Feel the cold, you see."

"No, no," Johnson muttered, Janice and I also shaking our heads. "Now then, Tommy, we're not here to discuss the Le Conte boy."

"Are we not, Ambrose?" Wilkins asked, showing no real surprise.

"No, we are here to discuss a serious discrepancy in the school's finances. Mrs Hart, will you explain, please?"

Janice then took out a folder from her briefcase and removed the accounts and the bank withdrawal slips she had shown to me in the snug at the Bell, before reading out loud the various suspect items and passing the documents to Wilkins.

"Twenty-seven thousand pounds no less, Tommy," said Johnson, as Wilkins scrutinised the papers through his pince-nez. "Do you have any explanation, receipts for goods and services, that sort of thing?"

Wilkins stared blankly at Johnson without speaking for almost a minute, before eventually replying. "I have been expecting this moment for some time, Ambrose, and I do not have any excuse or other explanation," he said, standing up and pacing in his usual manner when anxious. "I shall return the money and resign."

"Mrs Hart, Mr Sangster," said Johnson, standing up, "would you mind waiting for me in the drive? I'd like to talk to the headmaster alone."

We duly left the room, and once outside the front door, I was about to suggest we sit in my car when Janice put her fingers to her lips. She then jerked her head towards the side of the house, where the end of Miss Lyons' pike staff could be seen protruding from behind the wall.

"She's listening in at the sitting-room window," whispered Janice, tiptoeing up behind the pike staff. "Miss Lyons, we thought you'd left," she then said loudly, at which the secretary jumped backwards, dropping her pike and knocking over Wilkins' many-geared bike, which was leaning against the wall.

"Oh, you gave me quite a shock," she exclaimed, lifting up the machine and balancing it carefully back against the side of the house. "I was just, er—"

"It's alright," I told her. "We've left Johnson and Wilkins together. I suspect they're working something out."

"Oh, I do hope so, Mrs Hart, because the headmaster really is a wonderful man. He's spent over twenty-five years as head of the school."

"That's no excuse for embezzlement," I said. "And the conditions in that boarding house are a disgrace. Boys are falling ill."

"I know, I know, and I tried to persuade him out of it." She sniffed and pulled out a handkerchief from one of the many pockets on her blouse. "But you see, last year the governors refused to let him live in this house on grace and favour when he retires. He would have been homeless and penniless in a few years." She then began to cry. "After all that he's done for the school. He lives for the Manor Free, Mr Sangster, and now I suppose he'll go to jail."

"Well, I'm not sure it will go that far, but let's wait and see." As I spoke, the front door opened, and out walked Johnson and Wilkins.

"I can tell you all," said Johnson. "That the headmaster and I have come to an arrangement. Will you tell them, Tommy?"

"Certainly, Ambrose." He pointed upwards with one finger, as he so often did when making a pronouncement. "I have agreed to complete the work on the boarding house. The whole of the twenty-seven-thousand-pound grant will be spent on first-class renovations, top to bottom."

"And not a penny to be unaccounted for?"

"Not a penny, Ambrose," Wilkins replied. "And, if I may make so bold," he then said, looking straight at the director, "I propose to rename the boarding house. It will no longer be Bolshaw House, but the 'Ambrose Johnson Residential Centre'. What do you think of that?"

"Oh, no need for that, but if you really want to, who am I to naysay, um…" Johnson's voice faded to a mumble, but I could tell by the look in his eyes he was pleased.

"Then that's settled," said Wilkins. "So if there's nothing else I'll bid you all a very happy Easter." Just then a car horn hooted, and I looked around to see the Harts' lime-green Austin parked by the gate.

"That'll be Geoffrey, I must be going now," said Janice. "So I'll wish you all a happy Easter as well. Oh, and Jack, it's been exciting." I nodded and smiled.

"You couldn't possibly, er, give me a lift to the Guide Hut, could you?" asked Miss Lyons.

"Yes, of course."

I watched them both walk up the drive, and after a brief explanation through the open driver's door (presumably to Geoffrey), get into the car and drive off, Miss Lyons' pike sticking out of the rear window as they went.

"Once again, Easter tidings to you both," said Wilkins.

"Oh, and Reverend Wilkins, may I just ask you a couple more questions?"

"I've answered all Director Johnson's questions already, isn't that correct, Ambrose?" Johnson nodded.

"No, these are just general things. A Paschal Moon, do you know what it is?"

"An Easter moon, a full moon, Mr Sangster, and a term that might have been used well before the Christian era. Named for the Passover festival.

"And Lughnasa, have you heard of that?"

"Why yes, Lughnasa is a pagan harvest festival, first day of August, I believe. Why do you ask?"

"Oh, I heard someone use the words recently, that's all, but thank you."

Wilkins then shut the door, leaving me alone with Johnson.

*

"You set me up, Johnson."

"I beg your pardon."

"This was never about the Le Conte boy, was it?"

"Alright, Sangster," said Johnson. "Let me confess."

Johnson, it seemed, had his eye on the Manor Free for some time but was unable to penetrate the secretive school. Knowing Wilkins from his university days was a hinderance as well, with Wilkins using this relationship to help obfuscate his way out of any scrutiny. Johnson had then seized the opportunity presented when Wilkins called him about Michael Le Conte. The headmaster had somehow heard of the Granville Institute and of me ("I think it might have been that case with the greyhound, got around that story did Sangster"), and was desperate to avoid any publicity over the boy's absence, both to protect the school's good reputation and to avoid close inspection from government officials like Mrs Hart. Wilkins' direct plea to Johnson for help, along with my independence and reputation for sleuthing, had seemed to Johnson the perfect mix.

"You don't think we'd have made you drop all your casework for a simple truanting problem at a posh school, do you, Sangster?"

"I was rather honoured when you asked me," I said, feeling quite deflated and remembering my initial reservations about wasting precious resources on a privileged boy at an elitist school, with the tables turning when Johnson seemed keen to abandon the case whilst I, due to my growing fascination with Michael's situation, felt compelled to continue. "And what about that argument we had in your office? You wanted me to drop the case."

"I admit I was in two minds, but that was a bit of an act. Worried I might have gone too far when you marched out."

"I thought you were dead set against carrying on."

"Wondered if I was wasting resources because of personal feelings about Wilkins, if you must know. Two minds, as I say."

"Hmph," I grunted. More fool me to have imagined I had been the one manipulating Johnson. I even regretting giving him my sherbet lemons.

"Anyway, Sangster," he said, as we walked up the drive to our cars, "I've got Wilkins where I want him now. He's agreed to all sorts, not just the boarding house works."

"But he'll get away with a criminal act?"

"Would you rather he be taken off in a Black Maria or spend his time making amends. At the end of the day the Granville's supposed to be all about benefiting the children, isn't it?"

"Well, perhaps."

"And from today, Wilkins is accountable to me, has had his wings clipped. Transparency, that's the word for the Manor Free from now on."

"I would have appreciated some transparency, Johnson."

"Would it suffice if I gave you my absolute assurance that Wilkins proved to me he still has the money?"

"I suppose so, but next time, I expect you to be open with me from the start."

"Understood, Sangster, but we did get a result with this case, didn't we?"

"Yes, the money will go where it should do," I sighed. "In fact, I had half-thought to ask you myself to be lenient with Wilkins providing he returned the money."

"Well then."

"And the Le Conte boy is safe," I added, wishing I felt as sure as I sounded.

"Well then," Johnson repeated, opening his car door. "Happy Easter, Sangster."

"And to you."

"By the way, Sangster?"

"Yes?"

"I'm feeling a little peckish after all the shenanigans with Wilkins. You haven't got any more of those sherbet lemons, have you?"

7PM

I did meet Sam Youd that evening, but we saw no eclipse, as it turned out the moon would only be obscured in the early hours of the following morning. The idea of meeting at a pub on the city walls abandoned, we convened at our favourite Jolly Miller of Dee Tavern, a very ancient half-timbered building above a barber's shop on Eastgate Row ('the best ale in Chester', Sam always maintained).

Sam somewhat dampened my feelings of recovery as soon as I walked through the saloon bar door ("You do look peaky, Jack") but was wholeheartedly approving of my plan to drive to York ("Worth the trip just to blow the dust out of the baffles of that E-Type of yours").

Conversation flowed easily, although I chose not to mention the Le Conte case or the Manor Free embezzlement, feeling both to be confidential. Sam was having trouble with a giraffe ("George, tallest giraffe in the world, and he's got toothache"), and I related my feelings of anxiety about neglecting Sarah. Sam's quiet advice, sound as ever, boiled down to putting Sarah first, then the Granville.

"You got a second chance, mate, not many of us do."

"You didn't need one with your wife."

"Okay, Sandra's a girl in a million, I know that, but nevertheless…"

He then broke off, sniffed the air and pointed under the table, touching my knapsack (I was aware he had been glancing at it all evening). "Jack, that thing stinks. What on Earth have you got inside it?"

"Remember those crows we saw by the cathedral?" I said, the relaxing effect of the evening disappearing at the realisation it was now time to show Sam the bird.

"Yes," said Sam slowly.

"Well, what do you think this is?" I placed the sack on the table and opened the top flap to expose the crow carcass, head lying sideways at the top so that its eye stared out at us. Sam, flinching only slightly at the sight (hardened by his vet training, I guessed), picked up two beer mats then peered inside. After manipulating the bird with the mats for a few moments, using the cardboard discs almost like forceps, he pulled back and looked at me.

"Killed by raptors?" he asked.

"By what?"

"Birds of prey, you can see the talon marks."

"Oh, yes, falcons."

"Shut the bag, Jack."

"Okay," I answered, buckling up the flap and placing the sack back on the floor.

"How long have you been carrying that thing around?"

"Er... since yesterday."

"Jack," he said, placing his hand on my shoulder, "I think you need to take your bag and go home."

"I will, Sam, but first, tell me what kind of bird it is. Please?" He looked away, placing his hand over his eyes for a second, before leaning back and speaking again.

"I think you've been overdoing it, mate, I really do."

"What is it?" I said, almost shouting this time. He looked at me and then held his arms up to signify submission.

"Alright." He put his arms down. "Not sure where you got it, but that's the carcass of a hooded crow, and a big one."

"Thanks, I'll bury it now."

"Now?"

"In the garden, when I get home."

"Of course, and I think it's time we were both getting home."

*

I thrust the spade in the ground so that it stood, unsupported, and wiped the last of the soil off my hands. That's it, I thought, the thing's buried, then walked to my back door and entered the kitchen, the disposal of the bird giving me a sense of relaxation, despite the feelings of tension with Sam in the pub (he clearly thought I was being irrational, but how could I tell him the truth?).

Physically, I also felt good, fully recovered from the agaric poisoning and the general stress of the Le Conte case. I called Sarah's sister again, but the phone was answered by a babysitter (Sarah, Rachel and Harry had apparently gone out for dinner), and so decided to turn in. By eleven I had settled down into bed and ten minutes later was fast asleep.

BLACK SATURDAY
4AM

B ut my slumber was short-lived, with a ring on the doorbell waking me abruptly, at four o'clock according to my alarm clock. Who could it possibly be? I pulled on my dressing gown and walked downstairs, opening the door to a uniformed policeman.

"Mr Sangster, Mr Jack Sangster?"

"Yes, is my wife safe?"

"Yes, sir, as far as I know," answered the officer.

"Then what?"

"It's something else, we've been contacted by the West Wirral force," he said, reading from a notebook. "They are with a family called Le Conte and believe you may be able to help with the case of a missing child, Michael Le Conte."

"I've been working on a case with this family, yes, and the boy was missing for a time a couple of days ago, but he turned up and the whole matter was formally closed today. What's the matter?"

"I don't know, sir, but this is about an incident that occurred tonight. If you wouldn't mind getting dressed, I'll drive you there immediately."

"Don't worry, Officer, I know my way. I'll drive myself, just as soon as I can pull some clothes on."

"I should really escort you there, sir, I—"

"No, I'll drive myself, I insist."

"Very well, sir, but hurry, please. The situation seems to be urgent."

*

I quickly dressed, then telephoned the Le Conte's house.

"Oh, Mr Sangster," said Marcelle, "thank goodness you've called. We found Michael's bed empty. He's gone."

"Did you look by the Face Stone?"

"Of course, and the police are combing the wider area, but we wondered if you had any ideas. Michael confided in you a lot this week."

"Er, I'm not sure," I said, trying to wake myself up.

"Inspector Cooper would like to speak to you, hold on and I'll pass him over."

As she spoke, and despite her obvious distress, it occurred to me again that the Le Contes' privileged connections meant that the police would come running, day, night or bank holiday. The kind of children the Granville Institute usually dealt with, if they went missing from their troubled households or care homes, would have received a visit from a uniformed officer and perhaps a social worker at best, and repeat offenders were often ignored completely. For all that, I felt a knot tighten in my stomach at the thought of Michael's disappearance. I desperately wanted to find him.

"Sangster?" said the inspector.

"Yes."

"You've got to know this boy better than most, so we'd like you here as soon as possible. But no heroics, come straight, alright?"

"No heroics, of course."

"Any ideas spring to mind?"

"I'll try to think," I said, still feeling slightly drowsy and finding it hard to concentrate. "I'm coming in my car now."

*

I wound the car window down, letting the night air wake me as I drove, and went over the week's events in my mind, especially the drugged conversation with Michael in the woods. The old quarry, the total lunar eclipse, the King Under the Hill and Michael's conviction that something terrible would happen if the King ever managed to enter the door in the Face Stone. I heard Michael's voice in my head.

'He's trying to get home, to get in the door on the Face Stone. While the moon is covered, and on the right date. Then, just for a few minutes he can openly walk the Earth, he can enter the door. It's the season, you see. He sleeps deeply most of the year, in caves near the old quarry.'

The old quarry, surely that must be where Michael had gone.

'Ruled by the moon', I then heard Michael and Professor Horniman's voices say in unison. Perhaps the time of the eclipse must be the key, I thought, remembering the front page I had ripped from the newspaper on the chair by Mavis Stephens' desk.

Was it still in my jacket?

I pulled over and reached into the pocket, feeling the folded sheet inside. Opening it out, I saw a diagram showing the path of the eclipse and timings in different places as it passed. This moon, the article said, would also be a 'blood moon', coloured red due to the effect of the Earth's passing penumbral shadow, and totality for the Wirral would happen shortly before dawn, at eleven minutes past five. I felt in my pocket again and took out the sheet of cyphers I'd taken from the makeshift table in the abandoned MOD building. The text was still gibberish, but the circles and lines were reminiscent of the diagrams in the newspaper article. Michael had been trying to calculate something to do with the eclipse, and there was no doubt in my mind now that the time of the eclipse was the key.

I also noticed a smaller paper fall to the floor when I unfolded the notes sheet and, picking it up, recognised the list given to me by the Jacksons. I had completely forgotten about that list and, looking now, the truth suddenly became clear.

'We thought it the responsible thing to call you,' Fred had said, and reading the list I understood why.

How could I have been so blind?

Besides a leaden-headed lump hammer and a hacksaw (for cutting and then closing off the ends of copper pipes, I assumed), plus a 'Bialaddin Paraffin Lamp', along with one gallon of paraffin (as I had seen in Michael's lair) and a heavy-duty padlock (for the cellar in the boarding house, I guessed), there were hundreds of pounds of sugar and weedkiller on the list, yards of wide-gauge copper piping, ten boxes of cook's matches and fifty boxes of Zip firelighters, altogether enough to cause a massive explosion. And if Michael was intending to let off a bomb of that size in the quarry, with its pockets of methane, who could say what would happen?

The car clock showed four twenty, and I realised there was very little time before the eclipse. Should I alert the Le Contes and the police or go straight to the quarry?

'No heroics,' Inspector Cooper had told me.

I pulled my ordnance map from the glove compartment and saw that the quarry was shown as much nearer by road than the Le Contes' house. Regardless of Cooper's warning, I would go to the quarry first and, if I passed a phone box on the way, would call the Le Contes.

I carried on through the night, passing two call boxes, both of which were out of order, and with few other cars on the road, I was bumping up the quarry lane in less than fifteen minutes. I began to wonder if I should have gone to the house first, despite losing time. I would be looking for Michael alone, I said to myself as I pulled my coat on, took a torch from the glove compartment and left the car. The sky was clear, with stars out but nevertheless dark, the full moon now reduced to a rouged arc by the Earth's growing umbra. I glanced at my watch. Four forty-five. Totality was less than half an hour away.

"Michael," I shouted, as I pushed through the gap in the railings then thrust through the undergrowth, shining my torch on bushes and rusting machinery and continuing to call his name. Other than my shouting, there was complete silence as I walked and, bar the torchlight, almost total darkness as the moon continued to wane, until I came to the pond and the horseshoe of towering cliffs beyond it, which glowed red from what looked like fires in the sky, burning at different heights (in the rocks next to the scaffolding, I guessed).

"Michael, it's me," I called across the water. "Sangster. Let me know where you are."

Still there was silence, but then I saw another fire appear, this time reflecting in the water by the far end of the horizontal willow tree.

"Michael, I know you're there, come down."

I climbed up onto the trunk and began to walk, balancing with arms outstretched, stepping slowly along the tree, looking up as I went to see another fire appear, then another. I came to the end of the trunk, which lay by the foot of the cliff next to one of the scaffolds, at the top of which yet another fire sprung to life.

I lowered myself slowly down to the ground, my bandaged knee still throbbing from the previous night, then placed the torch gently on top of the tree trunk (I would need both hands to climb up the scaffolding after Michael). Looking at the moon, which was now almost fully covered, I shouted up to the place where the last fire had appeared.

"We need to leave, come down."

Then I saw Michael, silhouetted by the fire at the top of the ladder. He turned to me.

"Mr Sangster, go back. Get away from there, you must."

"Come down now. I'll wait."

"No, I have the last fire to light," he shouted, then began to step across the fifty feet or so of walkway to the next platform. I watched as the flimsy structure buckled under his weight, and more than once winced as the slats almost collapsed. But somehow Michael managed to cross, and once more I saw his silhouette as the last fire was lit.

"Come down, Michael," I yelled, looking at my watch. Five eleven. Totality.

"It's finished now, I'm coming down," he called back and started to climb down the ladder, just as the night was shattered by an explosion, then more, one after the other, followed by a rumbling I soon realised was the sound of the cliffs beginning to collapse. I heard the metal of the scaffolding begin to groan as it fell, while the explosions continued, closer and closer to where I stood and to Michael, still descending the ladder.

Then the last charge blew, causing the scaffolding above me, with Michael clinging on half-way up, to shear slowly away from the cliffs.

"Look out," he shouted, and I stepped backwards, to see Michael's lead-headed lump hammer fall and embed itself with a dull thud into the ground next to me. As the scaffold toppled through clouds of dust, I looked up in vain for Michael then turned and jumped into the water, just managing to crawl under the willow trunk before the metal crashed down upon it. The rumbling from the cliffs carried on, and I kept wading, coming to the rusting and mostly submerged cab of the old crane, as the surface of the pond began to bubble.

Gas!

I climbed inside and crouched down as the water around me seemed to boil, before a column of fire at least as high as the cliffs shot up from the surface with a roar. It brought the whole quarry into brilliant relief for a moment before subsiding as quickly as it had appeared. Coughing up half-swallowed stagnant water, I stayed in the cab, neck-deep, until the rumbling, which carried on for a good minute, stopped.

Crawling out of the pond, I lay gasping on the ground, as the broken rocks and mangled scaffolding continued to make a grating sound as they settled. The fires still burned in places, on the ground and on the surface of the water, making the cliffs faintly visible, and also illuminating a pile of debris in front of me, marking the place where the last of the ladders had stood, and where Michael had been when the bombs exploded. I leaned against the now-charred willow tree, which had been split in two by the gas explosion, then pulled myself up and grasped the torch, which miraculously still lay on the trunk where I'd left it. Then, tasting blood from a trickle falling from my forehead, I walked to the base of the cliffs, shining the beam on the rubble and, with little hope in my heart, began to call Michael's name. I climbed onto the pile and started scrabbling at the stones, breaking nails and scraping skin in a frantic and futile attempt at digging, before banging at the rocks in rage and falling back to the ground, where I lay on my back and cried out.

After a time I sat up again, wiping blood out of my eyes and wondering when the emergency services would arrive. It was then that I heard it, a scratching sound from behind the rubble, faint but unmistakable.

Jumping up, I ran towards the noise, clambering over the fallen stones and twisted metal.

"Michael, is that you?"

More scratching, then a voice.

"Yes," came a weak reply. "I can't move."

I began to dig, pulling stones aside, the scratching continuing all the while. Then I saw it, the source of the scratching, a metal plate deeply buried and, protruding from underneath it, the unmistakable sight of two feet.

"Michael, hold on," I cried, pulling at the plate as hard as I could, but to no avail. I looked around and saw a broken girder, wedged between the rocks. Prising it out, I slotted the metal bar under the plate and pushing down with all my body weight, then felt movement.

"When this lifts a bit higher, try and slide out."

I kept pushing, the plate slowly rising as I did so, until I could see Michael's head and body.

"Now, slide out this way."

He began to move and after a few seconds was almost free from the plate, before collapsing and sliding back underneath it. I leaned down and grabbed his hand, then yanked hard, the girder slipping from my grasp and the plate falling down again with a dull thud, but not before I had pulled the boy clear.

"Come on," I said, throwing him across my shoulder. "It's not safe here, we need to get into the open." Limping over the rocks, I came to the water's edge and set Michael on the ground, before taking off my coat and laying it under his head.

"You came for me," he whispered, face bloodied but, as far as I could see, otherwise outwardly unharmed, although who knew what internal injuries the boy had sustained.

"You're alive, Michael, I thought you were—"

"No, I was protected."

"By the King, the toadstools?"

"No, the metal. When the ladder fell it went down slowly to the ground, and I was underneath that steel plate when the rocks fell and that gas jet went up."

"Thank heavens, lad, thank heavens," I said, even in the half-light and with his injuries sensing a profound change in the boy's mien. A change for the better, despite him clearly being very weak.

"Does anything hurt?" I asked.

"I banged my head, my stomach hurts a little and my ankle's twisted where I fell." I saw his eyes begin to close.

"Alright, help will be here soon," I said, knowing I hadn't had time to tell anyone where I was going but hopeful the explosions would have been noticed. "But until it comes, you must stay awake, so we need to keep talking. Tell me how you made those bombs?"

"Sugar and weedkiller poured into copper piping. Then you hammer the ends closed, light a fire underneath and wait."

"How many did you make?"

"Ten, and they were big ones. I set them all round the cliffs." His head fell to one side and I gently slapped his face.

"Michael, wake up. Now tell me, how did you manage to get hold of all that material?"

"Bought it from the Canteen, a little at a time. Those Jacksons will sell you anything."

"Money?"

"Took it from Mum's cash box. I let her catch me stealing from her purse and that stopped her thinking about the cash box, which had far more money in it."

"And where on Earth did you keep all the stuff?"

"I locked it in the cellar of the school boarding house," he whispered, and I remembered the shiny padlock on one of the storeroom doors.

"Weren't you worried someone would see you moving it?"

"There's a path through the orchard at the back of the Canteen that goes right up behind the boarding house…" His voice faded and his head lolled again, so I slapped him once more.

"And how did you get the stuff to this quarry, Michael?" His head stilled lolled, and I slapped again. "Tell me."

"Bit by bit," he said, eyes opening. "When nobody was looking. There's a back door to the cellar that's always open."

"In the dark?"

"Yeah, and I could store it here in an old air-raid shelter, there's one—"

"I know, Michael."

"You went to the old house?"

"Yes, I saw all your notes and your drawings." His eyes began to roll again. "You didn't, er… do that picture of the lady in the fishnet stockings on the wall, did you?"

"No," he said with a watery smile. "She was already there."

"And you moved the stuff from the shelter to the cliffs?"

"Yeah, tonight I brought the last of it and lit the fires. Took me much longer than I thought. The bombs only just went off in time."

I looked around as blue lights flashed through the trees and then back to see Michael's eyes close again. I shook him.

"You didn't lick any more of those toadstools tonight then, Michael?"

"No."

"The ambulance men will need to know that. You wouldn't lie to me, would you?"

"No, I've done what I had to do," he answered, as the sound of police sirens rang out through the night. "The King can't get into the Face Stone now, so I don't need to talk to him anymore." He looked up at the moon, which was now waxing into the thinnest of blood-red crescents.

"See, Mr Sangster, the eclipse has passed."

PASCHA

2PM

"Shall I ask for more hot water, darling, top up the pot?" Sarah asked me, as we sat in a tearoom overlooking a square in the centre of York.

"No, I think I'll burst if I drink any more tea."

"Your stomach's settled after that dreadful business with the mushrooms?"

"Toadstools, darling."

"Who's a picky Jack," she said, rolling her eyes. "But the cut on your forehead, it's still looking quite nasty."

"It's fine, and my stomach's fine. I'm just glad to be here with you, it's been a difficult week."

"Bit of an understatement, darling." She placed her hand on mine. "When that police inspector called yesterday and said you were in hospital I didn't know what to think."

"Yeah, Cooper doesn't always have the best bedside manner."

"Mmmm," she said, sipping her tea. "And I'm glad you're here too." She sipped again. "I think Rachel's miffed that she doesn't have me to herself, mind you, but to be honest, I was already running out of things to say to her and Harry before you arrived. I mean, nappies and baby food aren't the most stimulating subjects for the old grey matter."

"Doesn't make you broody then?"

"Er… no, not at all," she replied, reddening a little.

"Sorry, shouldn't have said that."

"It's okay, darling. Anyway," she continued, "how are you feeling about everything that's happened, now that you've slept on it for a night?"

"Well, the boy is safe, that's the main thing. Not sure if I mentioned it, but I called Michael's parents yesterday evening, and they told me his hospital tests came back negative. He's alright. No long-term injuries and, more importantly, no leukaemia."

"What happens to him now?"

"Out of my hands, out of the Institute's hands."

"Come on, Jack, you must have an idea?"

"Well, as I understand it, he's likely to face probation for the explosions, and he'll be monitored at a clinic to make sure he doesn't revert to licking those toadstools. Mrs Hart will then have regular meetings with him at the school, so case closed." I sipped my tea. "All the same, I can't help feeling uncomfortable."

"Uncomfortable, why?"

"Well, okay, the boy was self-medicating on fungal drugs and hallucinating, and he was also a known liar, but his story was so consistent. Everything seemed to make sense, even if it was crazy." She nodded and sipped more of her tea.

"Go on, darling, tell me."

"I mean, he even memorised the pagan names for the seasons, like Ostara. You and I had to look it all up, but Michael, a twelve-year-old, knew as much as your Professor Horniman. How?"

"A remarkably resourceful young man, as you've said yourself, many times. A little unstable but resourceful. He must have looked it up somewhere as well."

"And knowing about those skeletons found buried alive at the turn of the century. I mean, Wilkins said the only book that mentions them was a one-off."

"But that book was in Michael's school library, Jack, even if it was under lock and key. He must have seen it and memorised the incident, perhaps subconsciously."

"How can you be so sure, Sarah?"

"Don't you remember that case study I told you about? Teenage girl thinking she was a reincarnated serving wench?"

"What would I do without you?" I said, leaning across the table and kissing her cheek. "Of course, we have our rational explanation."

"But" she said, moving forwards, then stroking my arm in her customary manner when pretending to be conspiratorial, "imagine if it were true, Jack."

"Which part?"

"Well, if I were a chained Satan, sleeping god, green man, earth spirit or whatever, well, what better time to reclaim my kingdom than a total eclipse of the moon falling on Good Friday, the most miserable day of the Christian year. And on the thirteenth of the month as well."

"Unlucky for some, as bingo callers say."

"Yes, darling, but it's as if everything came together this weekend to create the perfect moment for the End of Days. I remember being taught that there was a lunar eclipse when Jesus died, during Passover."

"What, on Good Friday?"

"Same."

"Yes, but that's all hearsay, finding facts to fit myths, isn't it?"

"Maybe, Jack, but these eclipses clearly meant something to people years ago. You know, bad omens, harbingers of doom." She feigned a very serious expression and lowered her voice. "Perhaps the world of today, messed up as it most certainly is, really does deserve the final judgement. Ooooh."

"Yes, Sarah, and the Last Trump's going to blow any minute, hopefully before we have to pay our bill here," I answered in a similar tone. "But come on, the End of Days, in 1969? I mean, the world's better now than during the war. Why not, say, choose 1940 for the End of Days?"

"We have atom bombs now."

"Funny, Michael said that to me as well, but I got the feeling he didn't think the King under the Hill would bring about the End of Days through nuclear war." I sipped my tea, wondering what Michael did think the danger was. "So," I eventually said, "to put the Le Conte case to bed, if we apply Occam's Razor to all this, we just get a troubled but privileged boy, resourceful but a compulsive liar, taking drugs, cutting school like a thousand such boys before him, and fooling all the adults to boot."

"But you cared about him, darling, enough to risk life and limb in that quarry."

"Yes, he wasn't really in control of himself, and even if it was the effects of the drug, Michael was convinced he had to stop a catastrophe no matter what the personal cost to himself."

"Well, it's finished now, darling."

"I suppose so," I said. "Mind you, just to be on the safe side I did check the tidal almanac for the next lunar eclipse over the Wirral on a Good Friday."

"And?"

"It won't be until well into the twenty-first century. Neither of us will be around to see it."

"I'm thinking of that encyclopaedia, Jack."

"Sorry?"

"All those dots on the map, I mean, there should be a Good Friday eclipse over one of those sooner than that. Perhaps another sleeping king will bring about the End of Days."

"You're beginning to sound like Michael Le Conte." I laughed.

"Don't be ridiculous," she replied quickly. "But there's something else bothering you, isn't there?" I said nothing and she pressed on. "Please, I know that look, Jack. You're not convinced about any of this, are you?"

I then related my dream to her, and the intense sensation of terror that accompanied it.

"I must still have had the poison in my system. Doctor Dent did say that these particular toadstools had a massively high concentration

236

of toxins. And you know that when I do dream, it tends to include things on my mind."

"We all do that."

"And this last week, I've been thinking about the Le Conte case pretty well non-stop."

"Well, there you are. Now, darling, best to put it all out of your mind. You're quite good at switching off."

"Yes, you're right, Sarah," I said, her words soothing me up to a point. "All the same," I added, "it's those words in my head, that 'the humblest things can slay a man, kill all men', which somehow still trouble me. They didn't come from anything Michael or anyone else said to me, so what could the meaning possibly be, if anything?"

"The 'humblest things', you say. Hmmm…" She scratched her head theatrically, and in a way that I knew meant she already had an answer. "Let me see… yes, that's it, *The War of the Worlds*."

"*The War of the Worlds?*"

"HG Wells. At the end of the book the Martians all get killed by Earthly germs because they have no immunity."

"Immunity to what? I don't recall the book."

"You know, to viruses like bubonic plague, measles or, er… even flu or the common cold." She raised her eyebrows. "So perhaps you did read it and don't remember, like that girl with her past life. You see, old HG puts it like this, just as you heard in your dream. 'Slain, after all man's devices had failed, by the humblest things that God, in his wisdom, has put upon this Earth.'"

BELTANE
6PM

I adjusted my jacket and put on my peaked service cap, then stood in front of the wardrobe mirror. Still fits, I thought, the sight of myself in naval uniform bringing, as it always did, conflicting thoughts. Tonight, I would address a gathering of cadets at the Manor Free school, youngsters who dreamed about the glories of battle. What should I tell them?

"Can you get it?" Sarah shouted from the bathroom, as someone knocked on the bedroom door.

"Alright."

I opened the door to see the barmaid standing outside.

"There's a gentleman in the bar, says he's here to see you, Mr Sangster."

"Oh yes?"

"A Sir John Granville."

"Oh God."

"Mr Sangster, are you alright?"

"Oh yes, just, er… wasn't expecting that. Tell him I'll be down directly, please." Closing the door, I shouted to Sarah, "It's Granville, he's here."

"What?" she called back, the sound of a hairdryer making conversation difficult. I went into the bathroom to find her bending over the bath so walked over to the power socket by the sink and unplugged the appliance.

"What?" she said again, standing up, hair straggling around her shoulders. "My bra's all wet now."

"Never mind your bra, it's Granville, he's here, in the bar."

"At this pub, at the Bell?"

"Yes."

"Is he staying here?"

"No idea."

"Better go and see what he wants then." She bent over the bath again. "And plug me back in, would you?"

*

"Now then, my dear," I heard Sir John's reverberating tones ring out as I entered the saloon bar, "what would suit that lovely complexion of yours is a nice Carolina sea-island cotton blouse. Delicate white."

"Carolina, delicate white," said the barmaid, adjusting her hair as she spoke. "Do you think so?"

"Oh yes, I know a thing or two about textiles, lass. In fact, I…" He took his gaze away from the barmaid and looked at me. "Ah, Sangster, all in uniform, good to see you."

"Good to see you too, Sir John, and this is a very unexpected pleasure. Are you staying here as well?"

"No, we're at the Adelphi, in Liverpool. Business there tomorrow but heard you were up on your hind legs at the school this evening, so here I am."

"Oh," I said, wondering how he found out about my presentation.

"Brought the memsahib over as well. Thought to myself, what could be better than to hear one of the Institute's best chaps give a talk on, er… what is it?"

"Naval history, twentieth century."

"Great stuff."

"And Lady Evadne, she's here now?"

"In the car outside."

"On her own?"

"Oh no, we have a chauffeur now. Lost my license a month ago. That bloody Barbara Castle with her breathalyser." I nodded my agreement.

"You'll be wanting another drink then, sir?" asked the barmaid loudly, clearly put out that Sir John had now entirely turned his attention to me.

"Two large Bells, please, my dear," he answered without looking at her, then pulled out one of his enormous Winston Churchill cigars. "And would you have a light behind there, please?" The barmaid obliged with a match. "Thank you, my dear, and no ice or water in the scotch, alright, Sangster?"

"Oh, yes, no ice is fine."

"Do you have ten more minutes to talk?" he asked, puffing at the cigar.

I looked at my watch. "Er, I do, but we need to be getting on to the school fairly soon."

"Then I'll be brief, Sangster, and I know meeting on spec like this is a bit awkward, but it's the first time we've been able to chat face to face since you joined. Just the two of us, that is. How are you liking the job?"

"Enjoying it, Sir John."

"Let's drop the formalities, call me John. And it's Jack, isn't it?"

"Yes, John," I said. "And it's actually been a wonderful year so far if I'm honest. And thrown up a few surprises, changed my point of view on quite a few things."

"I've been watching you."

"Sounds ominous."

"No, all good, Jack. My instincts about you were right." He coughed as he said this, perhaps because of his cigar. "That time when I bumped into you by chance at the Occidental."

I remembered the 'chance' meeting, after a lunch with Janie Dent (who'd been researching fungal diseases in African oil fields). Sir John had almost offered me a job with his philanthropic institute on the spot.

"Now then," he continued, "the Institute's spreading its wings, and if you're up for it, I think we can achieve great things together. Great things." I noticed, as I had on occasions before, Sir John's façade of buffoonery diminish as he warmed to his subject. When this happened, I was always intrigued to find out more of what motivated his philanthropy. Was it the mere dabbling of a bored millionaire or had some event in the past driven him to try and help troubled children? Whatever it was, now didn't seem the time to ask, so I listened to Sir John's vision of the future rather than the past.

"That school near Truro that you helped plan during January, that's to be the first of my academies for gifted children. Full scholarships, the best in teaching, the finest facilities. We'll scout as many schools in the country as we can for candidate pupils. I'm hiring a full-time team to do this."

"Impressive."

"I do hope so," he said, flourishing his cigar high in the air, so that ash flicked over the bar, much to the displeasure of the watching barmaid. "Anyway, Jack, you must be wondering how all this will be paid for."

"Certainly doesn't sound cheap," I answered, considering the financial implications of full scholarships, the finest facilities and staff, and search teams working around the country. All this seemed beyond the modest budget of the Granville Institute.

"Well, this is hush-hush, Jack, but I've sold the textile mills. Stock exchange announcement next Wednesday. It'll bring me a sizeable war chest, and I'll be diverting a good wedge of it to the schools programme, as well us upping the numbers of special investigators. Education Department are very keen we do more with them in that line, and," he said, raising his glass, "in no small part down to your efforts on this last case."

"And what exactly would my role be?"

"I really don't know yet, but I do know…" He paused for a moment then looked me in the eye. "That I want, no, I need you to be a part of it all. But," he said in a lowered voice, "I will be expecting a lot of you, though. Perhaps sending you on assignments that mean being away for days, even weeks."

"Yes, si… er, John." I stumbled in my words, sympathising with children (and even adults like Cyril Blacoe) who couldn't seem to help calling me sir despite me asking them not to.

"But I do have a concern."

"Do you?"

"How shall I put it, Jack? Your wife is still of, er… child-bearing age?"

"Well, yes, but I—"

"I mean," he said, interrupting in the nearest tone I could imagine to his showing embarrassment. "Patter of tiny feet and all that, needing husband by home and hearth."

"Oh, I see. Er… please don't repeat this to anyone, but Sarah's known for a long time she cannot conceive. That's one reason I wanted to join with you and help other kids."

"Thought I'd put me foot in it there, Jack, sorry," boomed Sir John.

"Just don't mention what I said to anyone else, please."

"Mum's the word," he replied, in a voice that echoed around the bar. "Or perhaps not, ha. Er… oops. Foot in mouth again."

"Anyway," I sighed, "Sarah's pretty busy with her studies and lecturing, so I think she'd be okay with me travelling."

"Excellent," he said, flourishing his cigar in the air, even higher than the last time and with more ash flying across the bar. "And I must meet the two of you for dinner one evening. No time this trip, but I'll bring the memsahib up again, next time I'm visiting your neck of the woods. I met your wife at that… at that… er, where was it?"

"Christmas drinks at the Grosvenor."

"Ah yes, beautiful, a dead ringer for Hedy Lamarr. So, you definitely think she'll come round to the idea of you travelling on assignment?"

"I hope so."

"Wonderful," he thundered, so that the barmaid, who was now cleaning glasses with her back to us, started and turned around. "Let me have your answer in a month."

7:30PM

S arah and I were standing outside the school assembly hall, trying to decide which door to use, when Miss Lyons appeared, resplendent in an ankle-length burgundy taffeta dress that Sarah later described as 'something like the New Look, from about 1947, darling'.

"This is my wife, Sarah. Sarah, this is Miss Lyons, the school secretary."

"Ah, yes, Mrs Sangster, nice to finally meet you."

"Hello again Miss, Lyons."

"You've met?"

"Well, I feel as if we have," answered Miss Lyons. "Your wife and I have been speaking on the telephone quite a lot recently."

"Oh, that's nice," I muttered, now quite bewildered.

"Did you manage to get everyone?" Sarah asked.

"Er, yes, yes, I believe everyone I called is here, and, um… Mavis Stephens confirmed the others," the secretary then said, holding her hand to her forehead, clearly distracted and in a state of agitation. "But I'm still recovering from the shock of it all, I—"

"Is everything alright, Miss Lyons?" I interrupted.

"It's the Sods, Mr Sangster," she said quietly, leaning towards us. "They've struck again."

"I'm sorry?" said Sarah.

"They put turf on the headmaster's chimney," the secretary whispered. "Smoked him out, they did."

"I'm sure they did," I whispered back. "But that was sixty-eight years ago, wasn't it?"

"No," she said, wiping away a tear. "They did it again, just last night. Reverend Wilkins was in there for, oh, I don't know how long before those brave firemen could get him to come out."

"Is he quite well?"

"In the main, thank you, but the headmaster nevertheless inhaled a lot of smoke. He's not speaking as clearly as usual."

"I'll try to make allowances," I said in what I hoped was an understanding tone. "Now then, we'll find our seats and see you at the reception later, perhaps?"

With that Miss Lyons, whose heels were even higher than usual, tottered away.

"What on Earth was all that about?" Sarah asked.

"Earth's the right word. Practical joke from around the turn of the century, I think. A group of boys put a sod of earth on the headmaster's chimneypot to block the smoke from escaping, and it sounds like some of the present Manor Free boys thought it would be a laugh to do it again."

"Oh," she said, looking bewildered. "Anyway, it's coming up to the time. Better go in, hadn't we?"

*

"They're all looking at us, Jack," whispered Sarah as we sat in the front row of the school assembly hall.

"No," I whispered back, "they're looking at you."

"Who would look at me?" She blushed. "I don't deserve to be on your arm."

"Of course you do," I said, having noticed men's eyes (boys and adults alike) following Sarah since she entered the room (we were some of the last to arrive, the 'get-together' with cadets and their adult trainers having started several hours before). And I was used to staring, people always surprised to see a glamorous woman of thirty on the arm of a grey-haired fifty-something man, although I did wonder for a moment if there wasn't more staring than usual tonight. "Anyway, no need to feel self-conscious, Sarah. Now, does my uniform look alright? Does it fit? Medals on straight? Did I give Dawlish my transparencies?"

"Yes, Jack, don't fluster," she said evenly, apparently forgetting her initial embarrassment. "You've practised for days. It's going to be fine."

"You don't have to stand up in front of two thousand people, mostly bored schoolboys," I said, although the size of the crowd didn't particularly bother me. No, it was the number of adults present that I knew personally, and that I had only known since the start of the Le Conte case, that was really disconcerting. Why were they all here?

"You'll love it, darling."

"Someone's invited Professor Horniman."

"It was the least I could do when I heard they forgot to wake him up after your lunch."

"It was you then?" She nodded, and I tried to control a laugh. "What time was it they found him again?"

"Six o'clock the following morning, when the cleaners arrived."

"Ah, and look, there's Mrs Magister and her husband." Sarah's eyes followed mine to the unlikely-looking couple, walking to their seats along a row on the far side of the hall. Mrs Magister, even taller than she'd appeared when we had met, and dressed in her trademark black, strode purposefully with a diminutive man in tow (I imagined him to be on an invisible dog leash).

"Oh, she's just as you described, darling. And who is that waving to you?"

"Inspector Cooper," I said, seeing the thin form of the detective looking over at us from an adjacent row of seats. "Amazed he's turned up, I thought he didn't like me. And look, next to him are Johnson and his wife, then Mavis Stephens, and even Mrs Hart and her husband, see."

"There's Sir John and Lady Evadne," said Sarah. "And isn't that your awful Doctor Dent sitting next to him on the other side?"

"It is, and that's Sam and Sandra further along. What are they doing here?"

"Oh, must have heard you were talking tonight, these things get around, you know, darling."

"No, I don't know, darling," I answered, looking across the hall at all these familiar faces and sensing some sort of conspiracy. "What exactly was it you were speaking to Miss Lyons about, I want to—"

"Shhhh, Jack, it's about to begin."

"But I was going to show you the Le Contes. Sitting near the back, whole family's here, even their gardener and housekeeper."

"Later, darling," she said, her voice suddenly drowned out by a deafening blast from the brass section of the school orchestra.

*

"Ahem, good evening, ladies and gentlemen," wheezed Wilkins, looking quite the academic peacock in his silk-hooded gown with scarlet and black robes, topped off by a similarly coloured tasselled mortar board. "And thank you to Mr Williams and the orchestra, for that, er… rousing fanfare." At this the conductor stood up to take a bow, several trumpeters mistaking his rising as a cue to start playing again, before being waved down by Wilkins.

"And, ahem, I bid you all," he coughed, as the trumpet noises gradually subsided, "welcome to the final session of the 1969 Combined Cadet Force annual get-together." Wilkins then tapped the microphone and sipped from a glass of water. "A little quieter, please, Mr Dawlish. I may have a frog in my throat, but I can assure our gathering it's really not much more than a tadpole." He looked around, presumably expecting some laughter, but he got only a whine from the loudspeakers either side of the stage so tapped his microphone again.

"Thank you, Mr Dawlish. Now then, before I invite our guest speaker, I feel I must…" He proceeded to read out a long list of the achievements of the Manor Free school's cadet force, without mentioning any of the other schools' forces, a fact not lost on many of the visiting teachers in the audience (many of whom I saw frowning or shaking their heads as Wilkins croaked on, so that I cursed him in my mind for creating a bad atmosphere just before my talk).

"Ahem," he coughed again after completing his list. "Well, our guest speaker tonight is JG Sangster, Commander RN, who will enlighten us on the fascinating subject of, er…" He lifted his pince-nez glasses and squinted at a slip of paper. "Er… Royal Navy capital ships between 1906 and the present day. Our speaker joined the Navy as a midshipman in 1932 and rose to the rank of Commander, seeing action in the Battle of the Atlantic and the forest, so…"

"The Far East," I saw Dawlish mouth to Wilkins as he squinted through his spectacles.

"Sorry, my mistake, my mistake. Not the forest at all, but the Far East, ladies and gentlemen. So, without further ado, please put your hands together for Commander Jack Sangster."

"Go on, Jack," said Sarah, giving me a gentle push as the hall echoed with applause. "And don't forget your crib cards. I'll hold your hat."

I went to the stage, shook Wilkins' hand, noticing immediately that he still smelled of smoke, then turned to the audience and gulped. Two thousand people crammed into the hall were watching me.

"Mr Dawlish, is your slide projector ready?" rasped Wilkins. Dawlish gave a thumbs-up. "Then dim the lights and show the first slide. Commander Sangster, you have the floor."

I gulped again as the image of a line of World War One battleships shone onto a screen behind me. Then I glanced down at my first crib card and spoke.

"'There's something wrong with our bloody ships today.' These were the words of Vice-Admiral Beatty at the battle of Jutland in 1916 as he watched ship after ship explode in front of him. What he didn't say was that with each explosion, over a thousand men, many of them no older than twenty-one, had likely lost their lives."

I explained a little about the battle (both sides claimed victory), then proceeded to explain the evolution of the battleship afterwards and that by 1945, these floating behemoths had been overtaken by aircraft carriers and submarines as the most important ships in the Navy, and that our nuclear submarines now had the power to destroy entire cities.

"So, as you have seen, today's Royal Navy, and other navies like it, have the power to end everything." I finished with slides of an undersea Polaris missile launch then a mushroom cloud, which led to some umming and ahing amongst the audience.

"Now, I know my talk is all that stands between you all and the drinks reception, so I'll be brief and just close with this thought, if I may. The days of glorious naval engagements between battleships are long gone, and this is the world we now live in, the nuclear age." The audience went quiet, then Wilkins walked to the microphone, leant backwards and whispered to me out of its range, then began to slowly clap. The audience clapped slowly with him.

"Thank you, Mr Sangster, for that most illuminating talk. Are there any questions from the floor?"

A blond sea cadet at the front raised his hand.

"Yes?"

"Was your own ship sunk, sir?"

"Yes, I'm afraid so," I said, taken aback. The boy had clearly done his homework, presumably after reading the programme at home and seeing my biography.

"How did you let it get sunk, sir?"

"I didn't 'let' it get sunk. And 'it' had a name. HMS *Humbrol*, a destroyer. We were torpedoed by a Japanese submarine off the coast of Burma, August the sixth 1945. That's the same day the atomic bomb was dropped on Hiroshima for those who are interested." I felt my voice crack a little, my heart racing at the memory. "No warning, two broadsides, *Humbrol* went down in ten minutes. We lost over eighty souls that day, probably the last ship to be sunk in the war."

"Shouldn't the captain go down with his ship, sir?"

"No, I was… I was…" I stammered, as the boy kept talking.

"Doesn't that make you a coward, sir?"

"I was last off that ship. Last off her, I tell you, I—"

"Thank you for your questions, young man," said Wilkins, coming to the rescue. "Time's up. Now then, everyone, another round of applause for Commander Sangster, after which I believe we have a splendid reception waiting for us in the refectory."

The audience gave another short handclap and then, almost as one, stood up and headed for the doors.

*

"Could have done without that kid," I said to Sarah as we entered the school's refectory, which was thronging with people, the deafening sound of small talk making it hard to be heard.

"Don't worry, darling," she shouted over the noise. "Overall I think your talk went quite well."

"Hmmm, did it? Anyway, they're serving on those tables by the wall. Let me get you a drink." After queuing for a few minutes, I returned with two glasses of wine, to find Sarah with Sam and Sandra Youd.

"Excellent talk, Jack," said Sam.

"Yes, Jack," Sandra added. "You came over very well, and the uniform still fits you perfectly."

"Thanks, I wondered about that when I was changing this evening."

"Now, darling," said Sarah, "you go and mingle. I'll be very happy here with Sam and Sandra. Go on." I took her cue, negotiating my way through the crowd (feeling people's eyes upon me as I passed) and over to Sir John, a head taller than most and easy to find in any gathering.

"Hello again, Sangster," he yelled, clapping me on the shoulder.

"Sir John, Lady Evadne."

"My husband has told me a lot about you," said the memsahib, smiling sweetly.

"Not all bad, I hope."

"Oh, no, John says it's remarkable how you saved that boy at Easter. And Doctor Dent here is even more complimentary."

"Hello, sweetie," came a husky voice, its owner, who stepped out from behind the two Granvilles, wearing a low-cut blouse and, as I had once heard a very short minidress described, the merest hint of a skirt. "How I do love a man in uniform."

"Janie, fancy seeing you here."

"Oh, I wouldn't have missed it for the world."

"That's right, Sangster," said Sir John. "Neither Evadne or I would have missed it either, and we simply couldn't have come without inviting Janie."

"I didn't know you were friends."

"Friends," bellowed Sir John. "Known Janie since she was a slip of a thing. Who do you think it was that put me on to you in the first place?"

"Oh," I said, slapping my forehead. "Of course, that lunch last December at the club, Sir John. I thought meeting you was a coincidence, but it sounds like I was set up."

"Not so much set up, sweetie," said Janie. "Just given a little nudge in the right direction."

"Humph."

"Anyway, Sangster," said Sir John, "glad I came tonight, been talking with that Reverend Bentley-Winkings chappie. Says the school needs help with funding a new physics lab. Told him I'd ask you to look into it."

"Did you?"

"I did," he replied, before shooing me away with his arm. "But for now you're neglecting that lovely wife of yours. We'll come over and say hello later."

I negotiated my way back to Sarah and was about to ask Sam to come and help me with some more drinks, when a series of ear-splitting clangs rang out. I looked around to see Wilkins, holding a brass bell and hammer and standing on an improvised stage in the centre of the room.

"Ladies and gentlemen, pray silence," he said, croaking more than ever as he raised his voice to be heard. "For a few words from that well-known captain of industry and philanthropist, Sir John Granville." At that, Sir John, with some difficulty judging by the groans, raised his considerable bulk onto the dais and, holding his hands in the air, addressed the room.

"Now those of you who've met me will know I don't mince words, and this evening, those words are simple. Not two weeks ago, a brave man saved a boy's life at the risk of his own, and that man is here tonight. Ladies and gentlemen, Jack Sangster."

Sarah, Sam and Sandra then stepped back, along with others close by, leaving me standing in the centre of a circle as the room erupted into thunderous applause.

"Now then," Sir John continued, "let's have a few words, Jack."

I saw the Le Contes (all except Michael) standing by the dais, furiously clapping, along with Director Johnson, Miss Stephens, Janice Hart and Mrs Magister. Even Professor Horniman, permanently established by the drinks stall, took time to set his glass down and clap. Then Inspector Cooper called over to me.

"Good job, Sangster," the detective shouted out for all to hear. "If it hadn't been for you, we'd have been too late for that lad." I nodded to him and, lost for words looked wildly around, until I saw Sarah mouthing 'say something'.

"I was just lucky to be in the right place at the right time," I managed to declare. "And I don't really know what else to say, except that I had help from so many of you."

"For…" sang Sir John, drawing the word out and raising his arms to conduct the crowd, "he's a jolly good fellow, he's a…" And so it went on, the song finally ending on three hip-hip hoorays, after which, and to my great relief, the room quickly went back to small talk.

"Alright, Sarah, I've done my bit. Let's go now."

"Yes, darling, you've been through enough." We said our goodbyes to the Youds, then left by a side door.

"Inspector Cooper came and spoke to me while you were talking to Sir John," said Sarah once we were out in the corridor.

"I was quite touched when he shouted out to me just now, I—"

"No, Jack," she interrupted. "It's those two boys, they've been found. It'll be in tomorrow morning's papers."

"Alive?"

"Bodies washed up on the marshes."

"No foul play or anything?"

"He didn't think so," she said, wiping a tear from her eye. "Just drowned by that treacherous tide, like the girl in the poem."

"They don't all come home, Sarah."

"No, they don't all come home," she echoed. "But you made sure Michael did."

*

"There are the Le Contes," I said, seeing Reg waving to me from further along the corridor. "If we go over to them let's not mention those boys, they'll read of it soon enough. You okay for an introduction?"

"Yes," she sniffed, and we walked along to meet the family.

"This is Reg and Marcelle Le Conte, Sarah, and these two young ladies are Claudia and Flavia. The chap with the medals here is Cyril Blacoe, served on *Victorious* with me, and this is his wife Betty, whose family have worked with the Le Contes for generations."

"Hello to you all," said Sarah. "But where's Michael, I'm intrigued to meet him."

"Oh, he's here tonight," Reg replied. "Just went out, to the bathroom, I think."

"Actually, Sarah, I need the loo myself. Can I leave you here for a minute?"

"Of course, darling."

*

I looked in vain for a bathroom but did see the steps up to the Skyway and remembered the toilet I'd inadvertently strayed into, past the door that led to the old buildings. A few moments later I was in the stone corridor, which, despite the late hour, was still lit, albeit dimly. I then heard raised voices and a thud, after which a figure appeared from the toilet door, hobbling, hand held up against his face. I recognised the blond sea cadet that had heckled me.

"Are you alright, lad?" I asked him.

"Just fell against the wall, sir," he answered, voice muffled and face close enough for me to now see a blue bruise across his tearstained eye, along with a reddening weal sprinkled with blood droplets on his opposite cheek, a missing front tooth and what looked like a cut where he had bitten his tongue. "I'm fine, sir. I won't tell anyone, I won't."

"Are you sure you are alright? You should go and see the matron with that."

"I won't tell anyone," he mumbled, peering over my shoulder with a look of pure terror before running off, hand still held against his face. I looked after him and then turned back to see Michael standing in front of me, eyes wide and glaring. I remembered Paul Rylance's enigmatic comment: 'If anyone said anything Le Conte would just give them a look. Then they wouldn't say anything again.'

It was now easy to see why, I thought, feeling dread myself at the sight of the boy's eyes, which (and it was hard to rationalise this at the time or afterwards) appeared to be lit up with malice, shining brighter than seemed natural against the half-light of the stone corridor.

"You're not a coward, Mr Sangster."

"You… you…" I stammered. "You did that, didn't you? I should report it."

"I followed him to the bogs."

"On my account?"

"You're not a coward."

"Yes, thank you, but if he tells anyone, or I tell anyone, well, you're on probation now. You know what will happen."

"He won't tell anyone," Michael intoned, eyes still piercing mine as he spoke.

"No, I don't suppose he will," I said, moving towards the door of the 'bogs'. "And I suppose, given the consequences for you, neither will I, but don't go beating people up on my account again." I stared back at him, wondering for a moment just what kind of an adult this boy might become if left to his own devices and if I was wrong to say I'd keep quiet. Should I let him know there might be consequences? "Or anyone else's account for that matter, Michael, otherwise I will certainly tell the authorities, alright?" was the best I could think of in the moment. I imagined many different responses in my head during the days and weeks that followed.

"Alright, Mr Sangster."

"Now I must get on, my wife is waiting," I said in what I hoped was as cold a tone as possible, disinclined to talk further. "She's with your family actually, and you should go and join them as well."

"No, wait," he said, grabbing my arm. "I need to tell you something first, something bad."

"Yes, Michael," I said, my heart sinking at the word 'bad'. What now with this boy?

"I led you there, to him."

"What?"

"That night at the Face Stone. I knew… I knew…" Michael faltered and looked to the ground.

"What did you know?"

"It was the day before the eclipse, and I thought if I brought him someone, I could control the King, at least for a day, until the eclipse was over."

"Control him, how, surely…" Then I halted, blood running cold as the truth slowly dawned on me. "You mean…?"

"Yes, you were to be my sacrifice."

"Why me?"

"I needed someone quickly."

"Yes, but you could have persuaded anyone, one of the boys at school. Perhaps even," God forbid, I thought, "a family member. Why me?"

"It just seemed right," he said, eyes now watering. "You see, grown-ups are better for sacrifice than kids, and you were a stranger so meant nothing to me."

"Nothing?"

"Nothing to me," Michael repeated. "I'm sorry, but I couldn't see a way to persuade Cyril to come and the only other man around was my dad, and I love my dad." He shook his head. "And I needed someone who would really want to come. It's what the King expects."

"Want to come, eh?" I said, my mind now racing.

"Yes, when you first came to the house, that night when you found me, I knew."

"You knew?"

"I crept down the back stairs and listened to you in the kitchen, talking to my parents and the doctor. I knew then you would be back and wanting to ask more questions, find things out, so I decided to try and make you ask to see the Face Stone and the King."

"And why," I asked in a whisper, "was I spared?"

"For one thing, you ate that agaric. It can protect you from him."

"And the other thing?"

"Because in the end I couldn't let him do it," he answered. "I stood in the way and his spirit couldn't pass through me to strike you."

So, I had been nothing to Michael but a sacrificial lamb, duped into thinking I'd gained his trust. And (in the mind of Michael at least) I'd been saved by a twelve-year-old boy, the very child I thought I was protecting. I wondered what Reg Le Conte, who imagined I had a closer rapport than he did with his own son, might have thought about Michael's real motives for seeming to let me into his confidence. Perhaps Reg would have been pleased?

We stood in silence for over a minute before Michael spoke again, his lower lip now quivering. "I led you to him to die," he said, beginning to cry out loud. "And then you came for me at the quarry, pulled me out from under those stones." He threw himself against me, arms clinging, head buried in my chest. "Would you have still come for me, if you'd known what I'd done?"

"Yes, I would have, Michael," I shouted, shaking him by the shoulders. "You believed you had no other choice, so you did the right thing."

"Yes, in the end I suppose I did. He wanted to end everything."

"How?" I shouted again. "You said you didn't think it was atom bombs."

"I… I don't know," Michael stammered. "Just something else."

"And d'you think those bombs of yours have really stopped this End of Days?" I asked more gently, removing my hands from the boy's shoulders.

"The King's sealed in the caves for now, and I don't hear his voice anymore."

"You've been hearing his voice for a long time, haven't you?" I said, remembering Mrs Magister saying Michael had told of the voices long before he tried licking the agarics.

"Doctor at the hospital told my mum and dad it was the methane gas in the rocks. Makes you hear things that aren't there, he said."

"Do you feel safe now?"

"Well, the King's awfully strong, and he'll try and get out again," Michael answered, gritting his teeth. "Next time there's a moon eclipse on the right night in spring."

Then he rubbed his eyes and (for the first time since I met him, I suddenly realised) smiled, the smile, as far as I could tell in the dim light of that corridor, of any carefree twelve-year-old. And it was hard to see properly, but Michael's cheeks also seemed to have gained a rosy hue so that despite his beating of the blond sea cadet and the admission that he had literally planned to have me killed, I couldn't stop myself feeling some warmth towards the boy.

"But that was a big rock-slide, Mr Sangster, and my dad says the council's going to fill that quarry in now," he added. "So yes, we're safe, at least for a very long time."

"All's good then, isn't it?" I said. "If you truly believe we're safe." He nodded, still wiping his eyes. "And I've got something here I need to give back to you, Michael."

I opened my wallet and brought out the two tea cards Michael had given to me at our first meeting, the agaric and the crow. He took them silently, and I thought of the two drowned boys and Sarah's words.

'They don't all come home, but you made sure Michael did.'

"Now," I said to him, "if you'll just wait here for a minute while I use the loo, we'll go back together and find your parents."

10:30PM

I was lying on the bed in our room at the Bell, sipping a glass of scotch and chewing the remains of a roast beef sandwich.

"How d'you think it all went?" I called to my wife over the sound of running water.

"Oh, marvellous, darling, I was so proud," she shouted.

"No, Sarah, I meant how did my talk go," I shouted back, realising we were at cross-purposes, our conversation since we left the school having mostly been about the public accolade from Sir John. "Did I sound too flustered when that little so-and-so of a sea cadet started asking about my ship?"

"It didn't distress you too much, talking about the sinking?"

"I didn't like thinking about it, but no, unless I looked upset. Did I?"

"Not at all." Even through the bathroom door I sensed Sarah was telling me what she thought I wanted to hear. "And by the way, what did the headmaster whisper to you at the end?"

"He just said, 'Couldn't you have mentioned any ships that didn't sink?' I think he expected something more jingoistic, Britannia rules the waves and all that."

I didn't tell her Wilkins also said he hid the money from the boarding house grant in a bag under the sitting-room floorboards and had to retrieve the cash before escaping from the smoke, knowing if the money was lost (or found by the fire brigade, for that matter), his embezzlement would be exposed.

'They shouted at me to come out, but those firemen would have soaked it all, Sangster, soaked it all, I tell you,' he had wheezed in my ear.

"I wanted to show them the other side of things, Sarah," I then called back, whilst smiling to myself at the thought of the smoke-swathed headmaster scrabbling under his floorboards. "Was I right to?"

"You're a war hero who became a pacifist, darling," said Sarah, coming out of the bathroom in her nightdress. "That's one reason I married you. And you're so well informed."

"But that's what I'm always saying about you, Sarah."

"No, seriously. It's impressive but makes me feel quite inadequate as well."

"What, you, with all your degrees, inadequate?"

"They're just academic. No experience, no real-life knowledge. But you, with everything you've done, that you do now, the people you have known, the men, the women and me." She looked down and touched her stomach, eyes tearful. "Barren," she whispered. "Surely I'm not enough for you?"

"Sarah," I said, gulping my scotch and feeling my throat tighten. "I have something I need to say. Something important, something that I was saving for the right moment."

"I knew it," she replied, eyes now watering heavily. "Come on, Jack, just tell me straight," she implored. "Please?"

"Sarah," I laughed, standing up and putting my arms around hers, feeling her body go rigid, "you've really got it wrong."

"Have I?"

"Yes, what I wanted to say was that I've been offered a sort of promotion, and it'll involve an awful lot of travel. More assignments like this last case, but I'll be away more than I'm home, a lot more."

"Away?"

"I'm afraid so."

"I can't do with living like that," she said, sitting on the bed and putting her head in her hands.

"But I've felt alive in these last weeks, Sarah. I can't go back."

"I know," she sobbed through her fingers, then pulled her hands back. "I could cut down my lecturing hours, come with you sometimes?"

"I'd like that."

"Oh, Jack," she sighed. "I've felt alive as well."

"I know."

"And I can do the Open University anywhere."

"Anywhere there's a TV," I said. "But Sarah, what was all that about just now?"

"Oh, I don't know. It's just that sometimes, I look at you and think, why me?"

"Sarah," I said, pulling her close to me, "there's barely a day goes by that I don't look at you and think the same thing."

4AM

L ater that night, I was woken by the chiming of a nearby church
clock. Looking at Sarah, black ringlets spilling across the pillow as
she breathed gently beside me, I wondered whether I was wrong
not to have told her about my conversation with Michael outside the
'bogs'. And if I had, would she still have thought the Le Conte boy
worth saving?

Then, as only seemed to happen when I was half-awake, Eileen's
last words came involuntarily into my head, clouding out any other
thoughts: 'Another world all around us. Things you wouldn't dream of.
Outside of science and reason. Open your eyes, Jack.'

Pale light from a streetlamp was shining through a gap between
the curtains, illuminating the silhouette of a dressing table, the mirror
arrangement of which was similar to our own dressing table at home,
with a central glass and two side pieces sloping away like shoulders.
I sat up, recalling my agaric-fuelled dream, half-expecting the King
Under the Hill to appear at any moment.

But the dressing table remained just a dressing table.

I kissed Sarah on the neck, then lay down and went back to sleep.

ALSO BY THE AUTHOR
ANGEL'S BLADE

A profound secret that echoes down the centuries is uncovered by a uniquely talented girl, who in doing so jeopardises her own life and that of the only person who can protect her...

In the spring of 1970 a beautiful and precocious pupil goes missing from a residential school for gifted children in Cornwall. Jack Sangster, with his reputation for sleuthing, is assigned to help police find her.

At first nonplussed by the girl having apparently disappeared into thin air, Sangster gradually gains the understanding of local people, legends and landscapes needed to unravel mysteries far, far deeper than could have been imagined, so that despite initial scepticism, he wonders...

Could events from two thousand years ago in this remote corner of Europe really have repercussions that might rock the very foundations of western society?

Governments on both sides of the iron curtain, and even hallowed religious institutions, certainly seem to think so, and with the powers that be using the girl's disappearance as an excuse to close the school, pressure mounts from all sides.

It will take all of Sangster's nerve, skill, and determination, as well as a generous measure of luck, to discover the truth before it's too late...

JEHOVAH'S WIND

Unwillingly thrown into the search for a missing teenager, Sangster must try to thwart an obsessive man from exploiting captured Nazi technology and even his own son to achieve a twisted ambition...

It is summer 1970, and Jack Sangster has been sent to investigate the disappearance of a local boy at a remote Dartmoor hotel.

Already suspicious that the government is taking a far greater interest than the case merits, Sangster senses that not everything is what it seems in this wild and illusory part of England, a feeling compounded when he comes under intense scrutiny from his boss as well as authorities at the very highest level.

And as the case unfolds, despite emotional distractions and frequently encountered red herrings, Sangster eventually realises shocking events that at first seem potentially epoch shifting more likely ensue from the tragic imaginings of a man driven to madness by grief and disease.

Nevertheless, with more than one life at stake, and a connection to his own wartime past making Sangster doubt rational explanations, it becomes a desperate race against time to do the right thing in the face of a discovery that could literally 'change everything'.